Dark Of Light

Third Edition

Stone Riley

A Post-Modern
Historical Romance Novel
of the
Ancient Mysteries

Paperback Format

Copyright And
Publication Details

Title: Dark Of Light
Subtitle: A Post-Modern Historical Romance Novel of the Ancient
            Mysteries
Edition: Third Edition
Publisher: Spirit Hill Studio
Author: Stone Riley
Format: Paperback
ISBN: 978-0-9852618-7-0

This is a work of fiction. Some characters are based on actual persons, such as the old geezer in Episode Three. Everybody knows novelists do that, of course, but we usually print a lie here saying we don't.

Published by the author through his own Spirit Hill Studio as a Lulu Enterprises trade paperback 2015. Manufactured by Lulu Enterprises, Inc., Morrisville, NC 27506. http://www.lulu.com

This is the third edition of this book. The first edition was published by the author in 2006 in paperback and several electronic formats.

The author's website is www/stoneriley.com. You can buy this paperback book or obtain it in other formats there.

The author is a multidisciplinary artist active in the Pagan movement and social justice causes and living west of Boston, U.S.A. His politics: Peace through justice.

Book and cover design by Stone Riley. Cover painting: "Shrine Of Ishtar Beneath Jerusalem's City Wall" by Stone Riley and Zoe Salmon, acrylic on canvas 48 x 24 inches.

Dedication And Advisory

To my Goddesses and Gods,
in love, respect, thanks and praise,
this work is hereby dedicated.

Hey Honey,
you know it's you I'm talking to.
You make the work possible.

Without you it would be something else
and a damn sight worse.

Of course sometimes we do kind of
wrestle for the paint brush,
but that's cool.

So thanks.
I love you very much.

The Structure of the Hexagrams

1. General Considerations

The foregoing supplies most of what is necessary for an understanding of the hexagrams. Here, however, there follows a summary regarding their structure.

The I Ching or Book of Changes
(Wilhelm / Baines version)

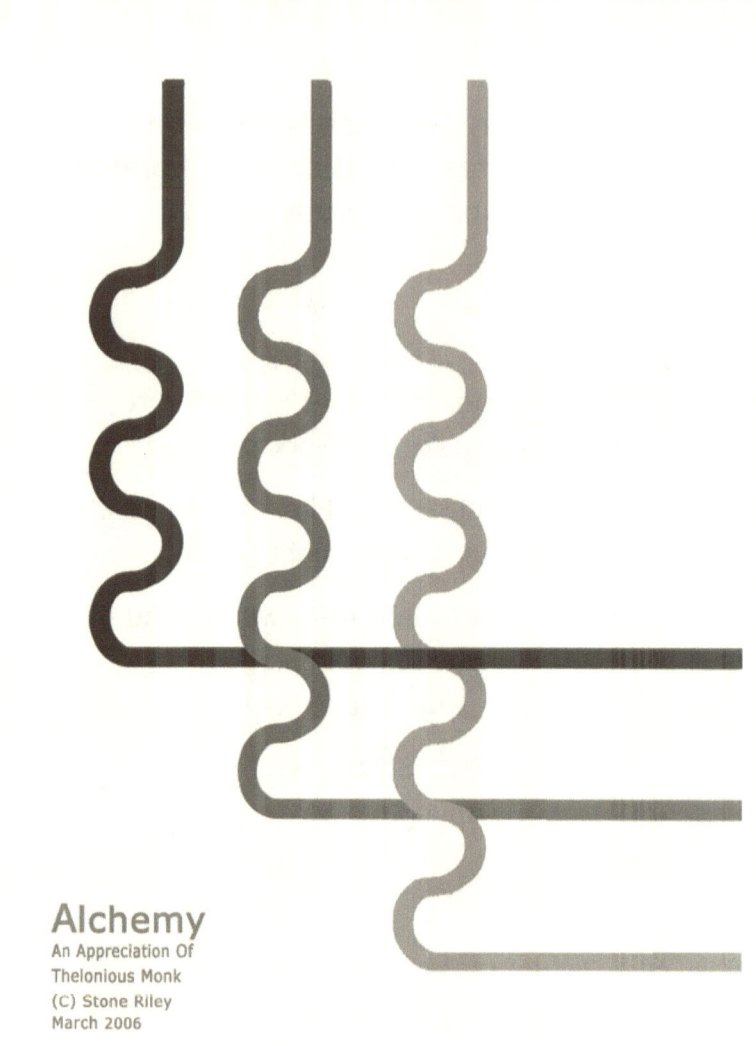

Alchemy
An Appreciation Of
Thelonious Monk
(C) Stone Riley
March 2006

Alchemy: An Appreciation Of Thelonious Monk
Digital print by Stone Riley
Original size: 11 x 8.5 inches
Originally published by the artist in a portfolio of
digital prints titled "Black And White".

Dark Of Light
Table Of Contents

1: Episode Point One:
Precis

Kindly Note:

1.) The facts presented in this book are historically, geographically and linguistically incorrect in far too many ways to list or even count, sometimes deliberately. Sorry.

2.) "The Guildhall Book Of Holy Sketches" (as I call it here) was apparently, on the other hand, a real document, though rare enough that not one copy nor even scrap of it has recognizably survived to us from Greek antiquity, and secret enough among its users that no written mention of it has yet been firmly identified in the Greek philosophers we do possess, not even Aristotle. It was, if our historians' guesses are correct, a scroll, a sculptors' and painters' and poets' and actors' pattern book full of standardized small drawings of incidents from lives of deities, heroes and such, to show each character's characteristic visage, physique, poses, costumes, associated places, plants and animals, their hangers on, appurtenances, equipage and et cetera, and as well their activities together in the rich fabric of the standard tales of Greek literature, folklore and religion. I have the Guildhall Book Of Holy Sketches doing duty here as a wealthy couple's pillow book.

2b.) In his book "Meteorology" Aristotle tells us that forces in thunder and lightening make mushrooms rise on the earth.

3.) The "f . . k" word is printed in this book a lot. In case this liberty offends you, gentle reader, please let me explain the usage before you venture farther on. Let me first assure you that, unlike some other current writers of historical romance, I have only offered you one scene of horrible sexual brutality, and that only happens through a kind of terrible accident of human circumstance for which the perpetrator in the scene can even be pitied, and he is heartily sorry afterwards, and this experience even helps impel him forward in the quest for true love, a quest which is, of course, fulfilled in a later graphically described and highly detailed sexual encounter. And for another thing: I've used the word always within context solely for plot and character development and with redeeming social importance too. I have certainly not intended to excite your prurient interests, not even if you have some, not even if that's why you bought the book. For example, as you will see, one of the literary motifs of significant social import which are herein very cleverly interwoven is the universal tension between most of us and society's stuffed shirt stuck up mannered sophisticates. For example, there is one exchange where a very well bred lady has an opportunity to verbally instruct a coarse fellow who has previously, in a situation of vulnerable trust, taken shocking advantages. You may be sure she utilizes the wretch's own kind of "colorful" speech in a commendable effort to communicate effectively. True, the word does sometimes appear here with its expletive or "naughty" sense, but only when a character is naughty or expleting. And I have most often used it simply as a straight-forward item of thought and speech with its common meaning, where it's simply meant to indicate that one or more common people are contemplating, speaking of or doing the kind of things you and I both have in mind right now. I would have felt stupid, frankly, if I had told you that a backwoods woman confides to a cobbler's son about an eventful evening when, among other significant plot and character developments, she "had int......rse" with a certain man of the boy's acquaintance. She f . . ked the guy, for the gods' sakes. People f . . k a lot

and everybody knows it. I'm going to try to show you how
we actually do it, and what we do it for. As you will see, for
the most part, in my sympathies, the common folk finish on
top so I have used this ordinary Earthy item of our language
largely as a token or celebration of commonplace abiding
truths. Indeed, it is a central philosophical thesis of this book
that finally, taken all in all, on the average, we humans f . . k
for holy love.

4.) But here in this book which purports to more or less depict
an actual pivotal event on which the fates of famous republics,
mighty empires, and great civilizations actually turned, you
might look dubiously upon the very prominent place allotted
in our story to simple downright f . . king. Well, if that bothers
you then just re-read the title page. This is an historical
romance novel. And anyway, that was an age when politics
were very personal. And anyway, human war is so brutal and
unending what but sex could be its cause? And besides; there
is some actual evidence to support my rather tenuous conjecture
that King Phillip II of Macedon, being a deeply and profoundly
religious man, was very hot for priestesses.

5.) Greeks of the time described herein had an effective
harmless herbal contraceptive medicine, a plant of the carrot
family now believed extinct, which was cultivated in a small
area of the North African coast and widely distributed across
the Mediterranean region. Women who could obtain it and
afford it took the herbal powder in small regular doses, or
stopped doing so, to reliably plan their pregnancies. Physicians
viewed it as an aid to happy family life. And they had this
medicine for many generations by the time of our story. This
actual true fact is not mentioned elsewhere in this book (other
than this paragraph) but it was most definitely considered
throughout when imagining relationships between men and
women, the social status of women, the economics of sex, its
use as recreation, technical and theoretical developments in the
art of love, etc. My imagining of these results is based on

what I saw happen with my own eyes when The Pill became available in my society, except: In this book many years have already passed with safe, effective and convenient contraception available to many women. I am especially guessing that this had a profound effect on religion, as understanding gained from the art of love was expanded to apply to spiritual arts in general.

6.) There is a common belief in many societies that female orgasm aids conception. (Not that it is necessary, but an aid.) Modern science must tend to agree if speaking statistically (pleasure >< trust >< frequency . . . etc.) and that might be expressed in biological evolution. So maybe this traditional belief is true. Detailed research (e.g. the hormonal sequence of female orgasm) would be interesting. In any case, if this belief were firmly held in a society it would affect relationships between men and women and all the rest as per note 5 above. And this is mentioned elsewhere in our story.

7.) Today surprisingly little is firmly understood by our historians about the ancient Greek religion. Except for a few brief passages in a few of their essays and letters, the Greeks did not write personal testaments about their faith. Even though we have a vast quantity of their literature, almost all the religious information in it consists of simplified standardized symbolic stories. Imagine if you tried to reconstruct the heart and spirit of Christianity (the guidance and consolation it can offer in this world and the psychic connections with divine realms that it can provide) just from the stories of the life of Christ, even with his sermons omitted. The old Greeks very seldom tried to write out clearly the experienced essence of their faith because that would have tended to undermine the way they kept it. They kept their faith in the form of "mysteries" somewhat like the unassuming mystery of Santa Claus that we keep for small children in our society today: a kind of universal collusion in an artistic fiction for the sake of certain ideals and hopes that we believe are needed. And yet the old Greek stories (unlike ours today of Santa) are jam-packed with numinous psychological metaphors, et cetera, so as to be very powerful even for quite mature persons in the generations since. So their stories are useful to us. Together with the large quantities of their sculpture, architecture, and suchlike other relics that we also possess, plus the general understanding of Greek antiquity amassed by researchers in many fields of study, these powerful stories have made it possible for some of our deepest thinkers to produce a few written works of mystical experience that are surely very close to the ones that we may wish the Greeks themselves had left. In this pious little fable that is now in your hands (my flawed and modest contribution to that body of serious scholarship and art that is so full of treasure) I have largely relied on several modern authors including: William Shakespeare, Robert Graves, Carl Kerenyi and Barbara G. Walker. Thanks.

8.) A few of my readers might be curious about the ancient Greek metaphysic science (which I have summarized herein as "Musical Electric Force harmonics"). I very heartily recommend for you a small blue book that is available in many stores. You'll know it when you see it.

9.) The spots marked "(lacuna)" in this manuscript are in fact real lacunae, places where some very interesting text was deleted irrecoverably from an early draft through a horrifying computer incident at 2:36 AM 1999 CE for which the author was entirely responsible, though not to be construed as legal liability for any pain and suffering caused the reader.

9b.) This is the third edition. The text has a boatload of small improvements clarifying points of plot and history that were obscure, obscuring others.

10.) In this book, Syracuse refers to Syracuse in Sicily rather than New York.

11.) Per the ancient customary silence, and per note 1 above, I herein preposterously deny Amanita, the cock's foot grass and all. I did not see a way for hallucinogenic drugs to be sacredly depicted in this novel, beyond a few curious hints, while seeking certain other truths as well. My apologies to Wasson, Hofmann, Ruck, Smith, and their singing Lady in the mountain forest. I beg their pardon.

12.) A note on prose style: I'm trying for a net effect that might be called "orchestral realism". That is, I am trying to induce your brain to think about as many things as possible simultaneously.

13.) Finally a note on syntax: I make long sentences. Speaking as a poet and information engineer as well, I hope they're well constructed. I hope you like the rhythms, harmonies and dissonances. I hope, even though you'll often find the journey to the period is as long and winding as the voyage of Odysseus, that you will also find it to be eventful and never dull.

2: Episode One:
Bus of Fools

Suddenly, even as she spoke, Vicki realized what she was doing: the extremely stupid thing of shouting to be understood by a person of a foreign language. Here in this fellow's foreign country. "We are going to Eleusis! Is this the right bus!" How very rude. But the platform behind her, outside the open door, was certainly quite loud with the countless intermingling voices and automotive noises of a crowded city; that could be a reasonable excuse. At least they had politely waited at the back end of the queue. The map was in her hand and she was showing it to the driver, pointing at their destination; she had folded and creased it flat and tidy with their expected route on the front like Philip always had.

The man squinted hard not down into the map but up into her eyes, his eyes glinting bright beneath the bill of his official Athens transit driver's hat. Then he looked her up and down as she stood there waiting in the narrow entrance of his vehicle, he acting like she was applying at the Pearly Gates for Heaven sakes. And yes; then a consulting glance up to his saints; three figurines of the expensive hand painted sort, bountifully wreathed and heaped about with a cloud of floral decorations on a wide shelf above the windscreen, from there gazing down beneficently on his whole mobile congregation. She half expected him to next demand her passport.

Was he frowning at her boobs? He was. Vicki knew they must seem prominently on display; loose inside the dirty shirt but with the fabric quite pulled tight by the shoulder straps of her heavy pack; and too her whole chest was splashed with the shirt's bright snaky rainbow spiral pattern. And the red sweater must improve on the effect, she suddenly thought, as it was buttoned underneath like one of those bare breasted prehistoric bustiers on those statuettes from Crete; but still, they were not disproportionately large. And her bloke liked them. How could this one here dare stare at them to disapprove? The objectionable sod. If he were secretly Saint Peter, he really seemed to be a nasty incarnation.

But she was filthy. No denying that. Well, damn it, she was a hippie. Officially. She'd claimed the title on a photo postal card to Mum, first thing on arriving in the airport in London back on April first, and since then had grown to really like the newfound membership. Vicki straightened up and looked straight back at him. As she must! She was a goddess! This was her own Summer of Love, a holy honeymoon with life. Fucking underneath the stars. Fucking while the rain came down on their little square of yellow nylon sanctuary. Fucking lying, sitting, standing up, rolling on the grassy dewy ground, drunk or stoned or sober. At least once of each, at any rate. She'd even grown to like that word, speaking it right out loud whenever conversation might permit. Fuck; fuck; fuck; fuck; fuck; fuck; fuck; fuck; fuck; fuck! What would Mother say? What would Mother's friends say? And anyway, she felt a rather desperate sense that a bit of madness just might save her sanity, so why not nymphomania? As she sometimes said. And she'd left home as a virgin so to speak, officially at any rate. And the good old tower of Big Ben; that had been the photo on the postal card to Mum, looking just exactly thick and tall enough, at least privately to her, to be a suitable representation of the THING her mother, in a very private final chat, had accused her vehemently of going out to find. As though it were some treachery.

The driver frowned silently, looking up above her head at the huge pack that pressed the roof. He might want extra fare for it. She had the yellow tent and half their other stuff as well. Philip had struggled with the weight very manfully for all these weeks, with his poor wounded hip growing worse and worse until his quick lively step had grown quite halting, until she'd made him give it up just yesterday. Goddamn Viet Nam. That's what he'd shouted to the skies when she took it off his back.

She glanced around to see if there was room in here for them and all their mud stained gear. There was. The wide rear seat was empty. She must remember now to look after details like that. Taking on the larger load, she'd seemed to take the lead as well and Philip had seemed to rather sink into a sort of guilty torpor. Goddamn Viet Nam. And goddamn her loneliness too; goddamn the necessary sin that she regretted. But perhaps her man would lead her to a healing.

It seemed a long long time and many miles already since they'd found each other's eyes and flesh in that first night in London. It had been her first cheap hostel dormitory bed, a woman and man from opposite ends of the Earth, she Australian, he American, and certainly the first time that she had found herself settling down quite nude onto a cot quite deliberate of every sound and move, sitting by him, twining her legs among his legs then grasping his private part surprisingly hard while kissing him then nipping at his nose and ears and lips, herself starting in upon the sexual relations with a nude fellow who had been so patient of her reluctance, surrounded by other folks more or less equally engaged on other cots, and all of this in a dark large echoing perfumed chamber lit by a single lamp on a decorated shelf, a chamber also possessed of the great treasure of an open door through which a midnight glow and voices of all the Universe's vagabonds from every time and place seemed to ripple in with flickering shapes of colored energy. Looking back, it seemed to be the shadowed cave at a Gypsy camp in a certain large Spanish painting, a very holy scene. They'd gone to Spain to see the paintings. He'd been asking people "Where can I get a bath?" when they first met; those were his first words to her, with an air of amusing appropriate smiling desperation, and she couldn't help but tumble into love at once. To tell the truth, she'd never actually slept with a man before. Not slept. Well, strange situations do call for strange measures. On the second day he'd carried his cot to hers and cleverly tied the mattresses with bits of string so as to not slip apart. He was an actual West Texan cowboy of all unlikely things and used, he grinned, to handling things that buck.

Trying to force this awkward passage past this disapproving guard, she wedged the map into a sweater pocket and managed to pull out a handful of coins for the driver to choose. Europe on five dollars and fifteen cents a day apiece; that's what her man had calculated as they lay so happily in tender smoky incense scented darkness, darkness that was full of secret or merry laughter, mysterious cries and whisperings in unknown tongues. She had been worshiped A strong man with a brilliant smile, a far better man than this frowning one, had worshiped her. One who even had the sense to tot a budget up. There and then they had pooled their cash. But now of course the autumn winds had begun to blow. She was pregnant and he didn't know.

"Eleusis?" Vicki asked again, thrusting out the coins, and still got no reply.

Really giving up, really ready to seek some other means of transport or a different destination, Vicki turned about and shrugged down at Philip who stood outside the bus leaning heavily on the mechanical things of the doorway's edge, rubbing fiercely at his aching buttock. He had his foot up resting on the lowest step.

"It's no use." she said.

But Philip raised a hand for the driver's attention.

The man leaned down to see around her.

Philip touched the wounded medal which he always wore dangling from a pocket flap, always wore there dangling crooked on its soiled purplish ribbon even despite the hostility and derision that it sometimes drew from their fellow vagabonds. He started in to speak but had to stop and clear his throat, started in again with clear dignity but with a depth of sadness, his head held cocked like some proud rooster ought to do; "Please sir. Can we go to Eleusis?"

Vicki turned about again to look for the response. And she was amazed. The driver sat back in his seat then gazed up at her face with new respect. Respect for her? The man's eyes traveled slowly from her face up to the bulging pack above her head, down to rest a moment with no embarrassment at all upon her breasts, down to her thighs and legs that held a sturdy stance, down to her feet clad in their road worn muddy boots. And then he looked upon her belly. Was she showing? Already? Impossible. Could he know?

"Parakalo!" the driver cried, somehow full of joy. "Parakaaalo!" It was a deep melodious voice that rose along the word's stretching length into a shout. And he was grinning, waving her in, pointing back toward empty seats that waited. "Parakalo!" he cried as Vicki stepped on back and then he rose to lean down, bracing on a railing, and grabbed Phillip's arm and, with a calculated movement like a sailor, pulled him in.

"Elephesis!" cried the driver, turning to other passengers who were watching, earning smiles and laughs from them.

Some of the passengers applauded. Many smiled as this pair of courteous tramps, she and he both now embarrassed, made their difficult way to the last wide seat across the back. A young fellow even rose to help the very limping man. Then the kind young bloke even helped them with their stuff. The driver even watched to see them safely ensconced there, the big packs lain down in the aisle to make an ottoman for Phil, before he pulled the lever to slam the door and blew his horn quick seven times and they all trundled off.

3: Episode Two:
Flashback

Phillip Maselin, a sun burnt white man aged twenty-one, was sitting on a municipal bus riding through the streets of Athens, Greece in cool September 1971; or maybe not. Where are you when you think you sink into the kind of dream that really entirely seizes your mind and heart while you fall? It was the same dream again, of course, but it deceived him now at first like always. Not because it felt extremely real, not in the way that walking in the sunlight in a sane world does. It was a madness, dark and fearsome madness, just as he realized anew each time. It was some unexplained possession. But there was also something stern and courageous and demanding that led the way, something he could almost trust. That unnamed unseen something said quite unmistakably into his ear that some tremendous knowledge must be dreamed completely and cleanly and purely to its very end. So far he had not found the necessary guts.

He thought that he was groggy waking up. His head was pounding like the huge compression of a cannon firing endlessly nearby. That was the bouncing of the bus this time, for he had leaned his head back against the window when the sleep had irresistibly called his consciousness again into the past, and yet he was now waking to find a bulky bandage covering his right temple wrapped around onto his cheek, also covering that eye.

He realized a piercing stink was in his nostrils, realized that this amazing stink itself was pain. Involuntarily he gripped the edges of the cot and strained so that his head started up with his free eye open wide. It was a vial of smelling salts. A firm strong hand was on his chest urging him to lie back down again.

A black woman's face, quite dark complected, was bending close so that she filled his vision.

"Let's have a peek." she said. The bandage disappeared. The monstrous headache too. She had a gadget in her hand that shined a sharp light in his eyes. "Well this is really good;" she said; "you'll be alright. Nothing went inside. Afraid you're going back to duty though. They stitched you up real nice. When you get back to the world, just let your hair grow out long and the scar won't even show. Hey, sign up with the hippies huh? The dizziness should go away when we quit pumping you with happy juice."

This time was only three weeks in, so suddenly the joy of life awoke in him. He had been hit and yet he would be clean and whole. And neither would this unwanted circumstance rob him of the chance to prove his worth. The heavy awkward helmet that the army made him wear had saved his life. And yet this now began to seem to be the dream. It started out like this each time. Soon, he knew, he'd wish to be absolved by his own death. And beyond that would come even more. Tenderness and murder would become entangled, sex and horrid violence, and yet the joy to be alive awoke again. And with it came serenity flowing abundantly from his heart.

And with it came incredible beauty to the woman's face. Gazing on that still and radiant countenance, it was impossible to speak the wealth of its exotic loveliness. The skin was smooth as milk but dark with mystery, the soft lips amply broad for kissing, textured just like silk must be; the amber eyes were deep. He felt an urge as if impelled by all of Nature and, in this confused state, thought that in this intimate time and place the act would surely be accepted. He found the strength of will to reach one hand to her. She was bending close, doing something with the wound beside his head but he was drugged against the pain. This man's hand which he was moving fumbled almost of its own accord until it found a round full mother's breast. At once this seemed to him a joy past knowing. His fingers very gently squeezed as if his parched dry mouth could taste her milk.

In natural charity she left it there. She was busy, carefully washing.

And then he could not let her go. It was a strain to even keep from squeezing hard. Oh, he wanted that amazing thing between his lips, that object of desire. God help him, it was good to be alive.

God help him, he then found the strength and sense to joke. He shifted so to look into her face and let go of his desperate grasp to simply clumsily pet her. He smiled as well as possible and heaved a sigh and slurred out the stupid words which, with luck, might seem amusing: "You wanna fuck yet?"

The corners of her silken lips turned up. He had made her smile. It was a pride to give the woman pleasure.

She was smiling now very openly as if she had not smiled in quite a while. How many men, in this time and place, were man enough to give her that?

Letting the wounded soldier's hand have its clumsy gentle way, needing to go on with her proper business with the wound, she shook her head slowly and said with all sincerity; "No, but thank you." And so her voice was softly brushed into his memory.

Three long weeks into this universe of shit, and he was innocent still. He did not know if he had hurt someone or not. All that he had done was fire his rattling self-detonating gun machine out toward some movement in the forest. Then later on, when he saw them falling at a distance, it was still enough to say they were his willing mortal enemies. And when his comrades bought the farm, as the awful saying went, after the frenzy and confusion settled down, he'd simply shake his head and say "poor bastard" as if some kind of luck must always smile more amiably on him. That was the way of friendship here. He was hit one time already and survived, even without a scar that would really show when he finally reached the world of sanity.

But then to actually see close up a moving living body in a human posture suddenly torn apart by his own act – to see the gouting blood and flying lumps of flesh which he himself had certainly made, right before his eyes and little more than an arm's length away – that would bring a strange new state of consciousness. To clean the enemy's sticky blood and bits of meat first off his weapon then his hands and face; that was different. And when he'd bent to wash, he'd seen the dark water in his helmet cradled in his lap turn immediately black red. At first he'd simply wish that he would die to balance that particular act and all the other slaughters done by him or anyone; if his guilty death would be enough.

But then, a few months on, there would come another step into the blazing river. In a moment which felt like blazing holy inspiration, spirit had rebelled against the guilt and found sufficient explanation. Little comfort now that chance had never placed into his hands a tool to act by this new will that grew watered by his secret tears; for in his heart a choice indeed was made. He had reasoned clearly and quite madly that a fuller sacrifice was due the deathless Gods of War, they who stride across the battlefield. Some inoffensive offering surely was required to fill their righteous hunger. In a dark low subterranean bunker lit with lamps and filled with acrid herbal smoke, he had immediately stood like Coriolanus and preached this new doctrine at some ingenious length to his fellow warriors. They had hailed him as a great philosopher. They had sung a song of home. Then he gradually came to think that he at least was competent to be the sacrificial priest if not the innocent victim.

Little comfort that the lucky bullet came ripping through the forest and ripping through his butt to send him home before he sent himself to Hell or prison. Comfort that might be to some, but to this powerful man the judging of himself is his. He is the one who strives to know and thereby rightly govern himself.

So the dream lets him linger in the woman's smile for only long enough to know how holy is its joy. The hard dream now, on this bus in Athens, lets him just begin to remember the easy dream that came to a wounded soldier then. Shot with a hypodermic needle, he spreads his arms and finds that he can fly as though the air were flowing water. He finds the beautiful exotic woman has embraced him. She clings upon his bosom with her firm breasts pressed between, smiling proudly when he looks at them, gazing into his eyes, embracing with her strong arms and strong legs too woven around. And so they fly as rippling trout fly in a rippling stream, all bodies one. He feels the penetration of their union then, feels it even more physically than he would ever feel again, feels his tender swollen member pressing in and then growing really extremely large inside of her, inside of her unspoken pleasure, resting there unmoving, held tight in her warmth. The sensation is astonishingly real. Seeing that he feels this gift, she smiles again and kisses him. The taste of yellow honey flows from her tongue and a great enormity of joy opens all around as though a yellow flower has opened.

But then, of course, he knows what must come next. In that awful time and place he had turned away from what she taught. He had argued with her beauty. He had thought he could demand her gifts by right.

The yellow petals of the flower turn, even while they're opening, until they've turned into the yellow sunlight through the woven reeds of walls around, reflecting on the woven roof above and floor below. This grassy temple is the little whore-house by the river. It is a shady spot where breezes flow down from the hills.

His copious sweat is splashing on her. She is rather upside down with her buttocks on a thick hard cushion. She becomes a thin teenage girl, the dull sheen of too much hashish in her eyes, and tears dripping from their corners to the thin hard pillow. This pallet where she earns her livelihood is hard as well. Her skin is bronze in the dappling light with purple bruises here and there. His powerful fists grip her little titties like his life depends on holding on. The poor girl's thighs are lifted on his chest, pressed shut between his arms, her thin calves around his neck, so if his manhood misses of its proper mark it will at least find other female flesh. His loins are pounding at her bottom with a well experienced consistent rhythm while his fists jerk her body up to meet each blow then push her down again.

She is helplessly enwrapped in him and yet her hands are shoving at his shoulders. Her lips stretch open, showing teeth like gleaming pearls, so he stops and bends down to force a kiss onto her mouth. He thinks this is an act of tenderness.

Escaping from his kiss, the girl shuts her eyes and turns her face away and speaks; "Please G.I.; you hurt."

This is a fond retreat where customers can lounge at leisure in the yard outside. He hears the laughing voices of his friends. He thinks of gleaming beer cans in a tub of ice. He thinks of bathing in the rippling river and then dozing nude up on the shady bank. He does not wish to spoil this place with cruelty as some men do. He looks at her again, pulls out his dick and lets her loose.

She falls completely open. She is lying there below him with arms and legs all fallen wide, her hips raised up, her face still turned aside and eyes still shut, and with his old man still hard, encased in yellow rubber, now lying disappointed on his thigh, not even pointing at the red folds of this open cunt.

But now she's lying there without complaint. And he has paid his money. And he hears loud rough male grunts elsewhere in the house. And he has heard that at this house the whores in fact are legal slaves by some peculiar ancient local law. He thinks that certainly he has his rights. He is a foreign warrior come here to defend this place at his own dear expense. He is himself now stationed at this very section of their tense perimeter, defending this whorehouse from invaders. So of course he picks up the narrow girlish hips with his hands and shoves himself inside.

"Ah!" she cries, now shrill. "G.I.; you hurt!"

In physical reality he did not murder her. In physical reality the stress of war rose to a fuming boiling point that brought all of the incredible delusions to a new sharp brilliant focus in the center of his brain; so that he looked in all directions, found no weapon close enough to hand, merely imagined that he held a long broad gleaming silver knife that he had held somewhere before, descended slowly to pierce her throat in imitation of every woman's female parts, and then crouched above the girl with his fists pressed onto the pallet to left and right above her shoulders and the knife withdrawn and fallen by. In physical reality the poor girl's eyes were even shut so she was not compelled to watch the awful grimaces that passed across her patron's face. She only heard his labored breathing dimly through the haze of her own pain and medication, wondering fearfully what it meant. In truth he did no greater harm than any of his brothers who passed that way. If souls are judged somewhere perhaps she'd testify for him.

In truth he rose up from that bed of torture, found his weapons, clothes and armor, found his friends, found a savory lump of hashish as big as the end of his thumb, and let the hot smoke raft his brain away into oblivion.

But in a different truth he'd done the murder.

In that other truth, three years on, he rode now in a city bus in Athens, Greece, bound for Eleusis. In this reality he was an unschooled pilgriming priest who now and then led on a follower or two – one who'd chanced along the way to make the highest sacrifice of all that can be made, the death of innocence – for such archetypal roles are very real in the human heart. He was, in fact, a human being with great depth of mind and soul. To the Greeks one of his names was Heracles. In some other place, with other law, there might have been a proper priestly training for this sacrificing individual and better ideals and further riches too; but here and now he must struggle with enormous impoverishing guilt. In this other truth of spiritual things Phillip Maselin was cringing from the knowledge of the undone deed he knew that he had really done, pressed upon him now again by the insistent dream. But this time at least there was some progress.

Crimson blood was spouting from her newly opened cunt up into his amazed staring eyes and flooding down onto his hands upon the yellow floor. And yet he did not awake like always before. More than ever, this time he remembered how it happened. At first it was her words: "You hurt." He knew that much already. And he had often thought this was a clue to larger wisdom. Who was hurting? The poor girl's words were huge with ambiguity, speaking as they surely did of universal pain. But this time he found the strength to fit this clue into some lock and turn it like a key and see what door would open. There was only a moment of strength remaining but it was time enough to gain a bit of ground.

The door which opened was somehow behind him. The great yellow light was blasting out with sharp blades of red, accompanied by some perfume scent which could not be recognized. Explosives? The woman and man were floating together at some focal point of power but she was innocent and he was not and the weird trigonometry of that conjunction seemed to force their roles. Now the Gods of War arose behind him in all their blazing power. Impelled by them, his hands went down and did the work again which they now must seemingly do in slowly infinitely repeated rhythm. Then in the center of that troop of horrid deities, on which no human can truly gaze and keep a grip on mortal sanity, there arose an even larger darker power.

The power of this enormous shadow grew and moved around him. And yet this was not the oblivion which he hoped some deity would grant. And this one was surely the universal female whom he had betrayed. And this one, if it spoke, would be the voice which lured him on. He understood that this greater one was somehow all of death and life together, for him his past and future. All of it. For the Greeks one of her names is Fate. Where would she lead? But there was no time now for more. The vast full oceanic aura of this thing was in him as he woke, then gradually fading from his vainly grasping thoughts.

The bus was swaying to a stop, bouncing his head one more time on the window glass. The damn thing needed new suspension springs. He reached up one hand to feel the new bruise then shook his head hard and rubbed the heels of both hands hard into his aching eyes. Then scrubbed his dry palms on bearded cheeks that seemed to be his as well. He blinked and blinked but found no tears. This different world condensed slowly to a grainy focus.

A neatly dressed young man with plastic horn rim spectacles and a young woman even more dolled up were in the seats to left and right before him, turned around to see. Their legs were out in the aisle amid his useless outstretched limb and the heap of gear. They had been observing while he slept. They seemed fascinated by the show and yet he didn't mind because they looked okay with it.

Phillip Maselin realized the sweat was pouring down just like it always did, despite the remarkable new clarity and calm this time. He definitely must get one of those famous Turkish baths someplace some time beyond the fucking Blue Horizon. Had he flailed about? Vicki said he sometimes did. His cramped position was uncomfortable. His canteen was tied onto his pack someplace; clean water that he badly wanted. The bulky braided purple kerchief around his head was shoved down tight; it had made a bruise instead of padding one; he pulled it off. He grasped the seat back before him and heaved upright and leaned forward to fumble among the bundles and all the tangled legs. He wished old Pop was here somehow. He would have said, as Pop had one time said when coming conscious from a very brief encounter with a certain horse: I guess this must be Monday morning, but how come I don't remember Sunday night?

Vicki began to rub his neck. To no one in particular, Phillip croaked; "Water. Please."

The young man found it first. Apparently he understood some English. That was helpful. Anyway, the large plastic bottle was right there in plain sight and it was bright blue. Phillip now recalled; this one was the helpful guy who had helped him limp here from the front. The fella even opened it to hand it over.

And the fella spoke in English too. He smiled cautiously and said; "Hello pal. My name is Socrates; but I am still a student only."

Reclining back, Phillip managed one single terse tight laugh to show he liked the joke. Should he introduce himself as a philosopher? He writhed a bit to seek some comfort and finally only held two fingers up in the magic runic sign of peace that had started out in hope but now by 1971 had come to seem so ruefully pointless. He tried to smile, saying; "Peace unto thee brother! Call me Phil. Or Raving Lunatic. Or just Shithead. Whichever." That was a quote from someone he had known in Viet Nam; himself. He'd spoken that line numerous times to introduce himself to new recruits, to show his priestly self to them immediately.

Vicki could not ever stand to hear him talk like that. Coming close, she touched his brow to wipe away the sweat with fingertips. She used her sweater cuff. In her elaborate and beautiful Australian accent she whispered; "How ya doin Sweetie?" It was a phrase she'd learned from him – the question which he often asked when she awakened – but in her voice the clipped Yank contractions became a verse of song. And so he drew his lover even closer for a kiss that in this time and place between these two became extraordinarily tender. When that was done he put the bottle to his lips, tilted it up and poured it in and rinsed his dry mouth as well as possible and gulped it down. He thought of finding some clean bit of cloth or such with which to give his teeth a scrub.

But then the young man pointed to the woman who was with him and said, in thick but perfectly understandable English; "You listen to her. Okay? She is a medical student. Psychiatry."

Phillip swallowed once again involuntarily. He had managed to evade the U. S. Army shrinks. He said, "Huh?"

4: Episode Three: Special Beer

Vicki was thinking this: If this creature was the sort of woman whom she looked to be, she would dislike her very much. The small young woman was extremely neat. She looked quite conservative. She wore the kind of professional lady's puckered asshole suit that you only see downtown in Sydney or Canberra; grey skirt and jacket, really nice white lace trimmed blouse shut at the lacy collar by an onyx pin. She had been obviously uncomfortable to situate herself among a pile of dirty gear, and then embarrassed more to see somebody drop like a stone into sleep and start to writhe and mumble. The bloke – the sod with the bad luck to be muffing the little heap – he had been a help but how conceivably could poor Phillip be any of the sheila's business? But now the truth was out: a baby shrink! Yes, she looked the part. And, damn it, Phillip was interested. Damn, damn, damn. There was a pair of tits hanging off the front if it; ergo good old Phil is interested; you could always count on that. And now this insufferable bitch seemed to begin striving for a posh Limey accent with long vowels, and seeming to relish saying "mmm" through pursed lips.

And, despite this multitude of nasty provocations, Vicki was resolving to be fair.

The mammal thing was speaking to Phillip, saying; "Mmm . . . my name is Diotoma. Mmm . . . from ancient literature. Mmm . . . do you know this name?" She gestured vaguely with each sentence, twirled manicured fingers in the air in evident impatience with the world.

Vicki briefly blew a modest little raspberry, just a little "Pllllt." This was preposterous; Baby Professor was handing out exams in ancient literature. She forced herself to stop but then, thinking on it more, could not stop her head from wagging as her favorite little charming exclamation from adolescence came popping out; "Damn, damn, double damn; stuff it in and call me Ma'am!" The strangers glanced her direction for a puzzled moment first but then apparently concluded that they might continue to ignore her.

And good old Phil was sitting there raptly studying the bitch with the olive complected oval classic Mediterranean face. And the dark brows arching over gleaming eyes which reminded Vicki of that portrait of the dancer in El Prado, the one with the stupefying unbelievable provocative stare. And the manicure and clean hair. And the elastically suspended boobs. And the armpits which undoubtedly must be scented with a reasonably good cologne. And the nose that had not awoken yesterday with two enormous swollen zits each of which, even appearing alone, would have dwarfed Mount Etna. And good old Phil was saying to this dolly; "Diotoma? Okay, well, maybe; I'm not sure." He still seemed groggy from the sleep and from The Dream. He was now vainly trying to push back his beautiful long and loose but, she must admit it, rather dirty hair. He scratched his bearded chin. He seemed to be honestly searching for a scrap of memory in that fascinating way of his. He was proud to be a self-educated learned man.

The woman rather shrugged; "If you are going to Elephesis, I thought you may know."

Vicki chose to interrupt by leaning forward, reaching out a fingertip with which to nearly poke the woman's finely delineated aquiline nose. "Psychiatry?" she asked. "Now what is that about?"

This was not intended as the boorish fart it was; it was actually intended as a calculated provocation, a test of her own. Vicki had watched headshrinkers and, even worse, had heard them privately discuss their work. Waiting for her final year of nursing college, being strong and sturdy and badly needing funds, she had committed the regrettable mistake of accepting temporary employment at a loony bin. She had found herself dropped into a pit of active evil where cruelty measured out rewards for innocence, where she herself was certainly without the means of bringing in one straw of good. Three weeks of that were quite enough, thank you very much. So now, here, might this prissy girl dare to suggest that her books held better therapy than real erotic love?

The vaguely worded and offensive interruption had left Diotoma struggling to reply so Vicki pressed the advantage. She tossed off a rather haughty laugh and continued; "There's a song: Anything is a phallic symbol if it's longer that it's wide. Have you heard it?"

Diotoma tossed a laugh herself. She was quick witted. "I have. Yes. Ha. Longer than it is wide. Anything." She gestured an oblong object with her hands. "Yes. And if it is square it is . . . mmm . . . vagina. Yes . . . how shall I say? Good satire! Good song! The idiot Sigmund Freud!" But then she seemed to be sincerely pleading: "Believe me; I do not do that. I follow Doctor Carl Jung. Listen please. I wish well for you. This occurrence now is very interesting; you being here and Socrates at once, you see. Perhaps coincidence. There are no foreign tourists to Elephesis in these years. Very much unusual. Both of you . . . mmm . . . appear to be intelligent. Are you going to there? Really?"

"Oh yes!" cried Phillip. "I've read about it. I've got Professor Mylonas' book." He put on a grin. "I've been packing it around since Munich and it weighs ten kilograms."

Socrates laughed at that flattering if gross exaggeration, really laughing simply at the effort of this foreigner to cast a friendly line across the language barrier, and also feeling glad to have a chance to break the women's tension. And young Socrates spoke up quite enthusiastically: "Doctor Mylonas! Yes! What luck! Do you hope to meet her? You must take my telephone number. It is only a dormitory." There he shrugged. "I and my sweetheart are staying in the country for this week-end – we have no privacy you see, but my sister's brother has a farm – but you should call in the city Tuesday night. But you must visit the Sacred Precinct as soon as possible! You must! The photos in the book are not enough. I go there for my studies often, you see. I help the digging. She lets me stick back together some of the bits and pieces, and drawing sketches. I find things in the library. The doctor has inspired me to devote my life to archaeology and history and mythology combined, as she has done."

Diotoma beamed at him with clear affection. Even though it was the slightest possible touch of fingertips upon his knee, her touch was done with a strength of tenderness. To Vicki this – and the next words Diotoma spoke to Socrates before two strangers on a bus – explained the evident discrepancy in their ages, only a year or so at any rate. Diotoma said to him; "My dear friend, your signature is in the book in several places, on several of the drawings." She was obviously, to some extent at least, a loving mother to this good precocious boy.

And Socrates shrugged with a most becoming show of modest pride. "Oh, very little." he replied. He mimed the act of signing with a very tiny flourish of the pen. "One can scarcely read it."

And Vicki felt her coldness toward the woman melting into admiration. Here was a woman with a man in a way that she had never seen before. Was there any possibility of at least some part of such a role in the relationship between herself and Phil?

So on the moment's urging, in this sense of admiration, Vicki quite sincerely sought advice from Diotoma. Interrupting the tender silent look between the two, Vicki asked; "So, what do you think? About us going to Eleusis?"

But then the bus lurched to a stop and Diotoma nearly slid out of her seat so she must squirm to pull the tight skirt back down over her knees. She then gazed out through a window and, although she did not hesitate to speak, her voice seemed deep with regret. "I am afraid . . . mmm . . . I am very sure of this. He will be rejected."

Phillip had been leaning forward smiling. Now he instantly jerked back as though he had been physically struck and Vicki's eyes leapt to his profile. What a thing to say; Vicki thought; such arrogance. So typical. Such a blow to hope. And Phillip instinctively chose silence as the best reply. He set his jaw into the stern defiance of the sick. This was such a startling contrast to the quick and subtle motions which she knew and loved, it brought a stab of pain. And so Vicki reached to touch his face, firmly turned his face toward her with fingertips on his chin among the wiry curly beard, but could not think of words. She loved him; that was all. And so she only smiled into his eyes.

And God bless him, he leaned on her. But then he fairly well collapsed. He reached an arm behind her waist and leaned to press the unseen scar beside his head hard into her breast. His free hand went to cup beside her other breast as well. Tears started to Vicki's eyes and nearly fell. She embraced him, caressed his hair and felt some brilliant colored power flowing back and forth between them. She glared at Diotoma.

Socrates, either shocked or embarrassed or touched by all of this, swaying as the vehicle started off again, shook his head, removed his glasses, rubbed his eyes. He spoke something to his girlfriend in Greek, something that she did not like, in a tone definitely of reproof for what she'd said. Then he spoke to Vicki; "Okay; all right. You are serious. You are no tourists. This circumstance, I think, has meaning. But listen to her. She is studying psychiatry, Jung's psychiatry. She knows."

So Diotoma continued, now again staring away from them toward the world outside; "Perhaps I know; perhaps not. Perhaps I know many things." And she looked to Vicki. "He was in Viet Nam apparently. This is correct? The medal he is wearing?"

Vicki answered with a very bitter tone; "He was wounded. He did some things. I don't understand it but that's why he has to go."

"Yes!" Diotoma said, suddenly angry and sharp herself. "We have Viet Nam soldiers in Hellas too. I have seen their treatment in hospital. We are your allies there. Only one battalion but you don't know even that, do you? Do you? War is terrible and that one is very bad. But also Elephesis is a terrible place. Perhaps he should not go; I mean perhaps not yet."

"No!" Socrates really shouted. "It is beautiful!"

Diotoma reached to touch her fellow's knee again, now with a reassuring hand. "I do not mean the ruins. The ruins are very beautiful. The hill. The well. The rock. The view. I speak . . . mmm . . . metaphorically. This is a metaphor for what is going in his head. It can be very hard to go into the temple, to the Hall of Mysteries. They will not let him even to the Sacred Precinct, this way he is. Other gods posses him. The way you are, my sweetheart, of course you do not see these difficulties. You are there. Remember, the walls are high for reasons. You understand? I speak of the wandering soul arriving to the temple. There is no key for outside of the gate. It must open from within to those who are prepared. Mmm . . . how should I say in English? It is very dark before the light."

Phillip came up to answer that. Clutching at Vicki's shoulder with one hand and the other grasping the edge of the hard seat, he managed to pull himself up in an instant nearly straight. He shook his head so that the long hair flew about. "No." he said quite loud. "You are wrong. It is very bright before the dark. And I do know. I have been inside the temple. And now I've got a key. I'm going back."

But Diotoma answered too; "My poor friend, you are mistaken. You have been inside a different temple. You have been perhaps inside of one that stands beside a river, yes? That one is inside the city wall before the start."

Phillip's stern jaw dropped. He gasped. "Before the start? That was before the start?"

But now Vicki had truly had enough. Not only for her dear man's sake but also for herself. Whatever this mysterious trip might turn into, she was here. Truly, she had come here on some business of her own. Far away from here, some time beside this time, a crime was done. She had procured and undergone abortion. At least she'd found the best conditions. At least it was a proper sterile clinic, a very sympathetic nurse, an old physician with a shaky hand. It was reasonably early. It was necessary. There was a voluntary donation toward reproductive education for the poor and she had emptied out her purse, reserving only taxi fare. She had murdered her own baby on a Thursday afternoon; that's how it was construed at law. The nurse had kindly offered the suggestion that she ought to dine on soup and bread. At least there had been rain. And that was in a land where she could only ever be a maiden, wife, widow or whore; even if these choices made of countless women raving grieving ghosts while they yet breathed. She had run away into the wide world seeking some sufficient answer for it, refusing to believe forgiveness must be bought for innocent transgressions, seeking something else instead.

And then they found each other. At last, finally, after that vast oceanic commotion in that first beautiful blessed narrow bed, resting there, lying on him, his tender softened manhood, to her immense unspeakable delight, still marvelously carefully held inside; there this man had, quite reluctantly, only at her urging, taken her fingers and placed them here then here upon his scars. And he had said he walked a path of healing. Some magic doctor of the Texan Indians, apparently from what he said, had pointed onward east the very day of his arrival home from war. And she had told herself that she would follow. His road was surely hers. He seemed to be well on the way. And, by every god that ever was, this man had worshiped her. Despite her felony – even though she had quite deliberately, that afternoon in casual conversation, in his presence, confessed it to two friendly unknown women, a lesbian couple they were – despite that awful fact she had quite unmistakably felt herself blossom with astonishing Divinity in this man's hands and in his sight in that dark place. And this strong man was he whom luck or destiny or fate had chosen to beget her second child.

But now the thing was clearly out of hand. Where were they going? And the man, it now appeared, was sicker than she'd known, shaky on his seeming sturdy legs, now like some mountaineer suddenly fallen to the far end of a dangling rope. He was no longer to be trusted as their scout. So she was thrust into the lead and she must lead by marker stones that she could find. She must find the way by what she felt to be her proper goal. The faith must simply be that her path was his.

But yet she was afraid of seeming selfish. She could not say exactly what she meant, could not speak her need that might conceivably be separate nor demand her right of leadership.

Vicki sat up straight. She took Phillip's hand and pressed it into her secretly pregnant lap and now put her arm around his shoulders. She said to them; "Look here you freaks. I have not read the book. And I am definitely not a shrink. But I am a nurse. You understand; I have graduated already. From Folkstone College of Nursing in Brisbane, Australia. I have worked with the sick. And there is one thing I certainly do know." All three were staring at her quite attentively, poor

Phillip most of all. "When a person is trying to find healing, you must simply not tell them where they cannot go."

Diotoma was impressed. "Mmm . . ." she said; "mmm . . . yes. Even, even there are surprising outcomes. There are always special cases. One does not know. Mmm."

But Socrates, for some reason, got his teeth around the bit. He said; "Wait one moment now. Wait. The ancient authorities are very exact, very exact. This is testified by best authorities. There was a cleaning ritual required. Very certainly required. Especially for those who had taken human life." But on that spot he stopped. He suddenly saw how very serious this thing was he had just then said, how far it seemed to be beyond his ken. And then he realized the even greater mystery of where his thought was leading. His gestures rather froze: an open palm held in the air, a slight tilt of the head. He was now wondering how to say it or if the next thing should not be said at all. Perhaps he'd lost sight of the conversation's meaning for this wounded man before him and gone astray on theory. But he was an honest scholar and it was the truth – with beauty in the thing somewhere which should not be lost nor tarnished – so he looked in Phillip's face, careful of the reaction. And then he suddenly held up a finger and, though rather struggling with the foreign twists of tongue, he managed to hurry through the words with their intended emphasis quite firm: "Especially for those who have taken innocent human life. Innocent human life."

For a long moment Phillip, rather slumping as he was, stared straight back at Socrates. But then Philip very slowly nodded. He said; "Yes. I read that in the book. I just picked it up in the store and opened it and that's what it said. Page one-oh-two up near the corner. See? I decided to go right there. That's the main reason why. It was what you call in English: divination. An old witch showed me how to do it."

"Oh!" Diotoma said, as though she finally understood. "You have just been called. And now you have simply got it . . . mmm . . . wrong way about. Arse to frontwards. Yes?

That is the phrase? You do not want the Sacred Precinct yet!"

Phillip shook his head in disagreement.

"Listen to me, sir, please. Will you listen? Yes? Elephesis was designed in steps. You understand? The ancient priestesses and priests were very smart, not such as the idiot Sigmund Freud, whom we now struggle with. No, they were expert. They made smaller steps. Yes, you do need the Sacred Precinct, yes, and the Hall of Mysteries. But there are steps before. First you go to be instructed so there will be abandoning of guilts, the cleaning. Proper instruction, see, by people speaking language you understand. Then the long walk, then the Sacred Precinct and then the Great Mystery is revealed. But first of all, before all that, you need the celebration. Understand? You need the party with the grand parade and songs and dancing on the beach. First of all, that!"

"Yes!" cried Socrates. "This will solve the question." He clapped his hands and stamped a foot just like a college student gone on holiday should do. And he shouted as loudly as he could; "We all need beer!"

There was some startled laughter elsewhere on the bus.

"Beer?" asked Vicki. "Not soup and bread?"

"Yes;" Socrates answered; "the special sacred beer. Oh well, you do not know? May I explain? Every year, you see, year and year and year, the whole city Athens got up and walked the grand parade to Elephesis. Statues being carried home, everything. The mystai, the, oh, the new initiates, they went along in front – followed a tall priestess with a big basket on her head and a little boy who was a priest and king, the mystai kind of following their own different journey – and only these mystai and old initiates too would go into the Sacred Precinct at the end. But the whole Athens people come along behind and for them it is a great party every year. This time of year, the autumn. And they had big jugs of special barley beer from which to drink."

Vicki could not help but smile. Her hopes were up again. "Sacred beer?" She tried to find some joke as though it were a brand of beverage you could find among the offerings in a shop, but nothing came to mind. "Dancing?"

Socrates and Diotoma answered both at once; "Yes!"

The girl went on; "Sacred dancing. Hypnotic . . . mmm . . . psychotropic songs and dances on the beach when the sun gone down and spirits come up dancing on the waves of the sea and every stream and brook. And the stars and moon all dance with the spirits on the sea."

"What a trip!" cried Vicki; "Sounds like they had some LSD."

"Oh well;" said Socrates; "that is too coarse, too hard. Too uncontrolled. Too powerful itself. And they had not any need."

"Mass hallucination." put in Phillip. "Diotoma, I know you're wrong about me. There were special cases even then; the whole thing was sometimes done at once or with the order mixed around. There was some emperor for sure, at least. But they really were experts." He turned to Vicki; "They didn't need any kind of actual shit at all. There was a little something in the beer – probably catnip or chamomile or something, maybe hardly dope at all, just something to help mellow out the alcohol – but really they tailor made this mass hallucination trip. See? Tailor made it with the songs and dances year after year to get everybody really into this specific vision for everybody with the mermaids coming up and dancing in the moonlight on the surf. And they did it every year for . . . what?" He turned to Socrates. "How many years?"

"One thousand and eight hundred years at least."

"Oh, jeez!" Vicki was impressed. "Gollywhop me please! Stuff a whistle up me snoot and make me sneeze."

Good old Phil had given her a whole other side of this in explaining for these recent weeks. To hear him tell, for all these days and nights, it was some huge ordeal. Some torture trip like a ninety-nine day fast and then they nail you to a freaking cross. And then you drag the cross through town. And then they make you swim. That's why she hadn't read the book.

So now Vicki turned to the only woman present who seemed to know the scoop, so she might find out the truth about the other perfectly obvious and extremely interesting possibility about the stoned out party trip, and she asked Diotoma; "Was there fucking?"

A large giggle burst from Phillip's lips. But then he thought and said "Probably not. Wrong kind of trip. Mermaids can't, you know. Only temporary abstinence though, for sure, just for that particular thing. Abstinence; it probably helped for that specific thing." He looked to Socrates for confirmation but only got a blank look in return. Phillip shrugged.

"No?" Vicki asked, looking inquiringly at each of them.

But somehow neither Socrates nor Diotoma seemed to know what she was asking. She repeated the word, pronouncing quite distinctly, but they didn't seem to know it. Could that be true? Apparently it was. And Phillip now only sat there straining to hold in a grin.

She asked Phillip; "So there wasn't? Not even back in the shadows?"

He only answered; "My little chickadee, I love you very much."

And she replied; "Well, that's nice."

Surprisingly, he flashed a wink. He said; "Why don't you explain to our new good friends what fucking is?"

So then a whole panorama of possible pranks opened in her mind. What fun! What should she say? "Mmm . . ." Vicki said. "Well, you see . . ."

But then she glanced again at Phillip. And there was something different in his eyes: anger. He flashed the wink again: conspiracy. Against these two.

Her first thought had certainly been the simple kind of harmless trick which she had learned among their fellow tramps, the sort of hook and gaff that lent a lively dash of sauce to ordinary chat and finished up with grins all round and pretended cries of outraged pain. The target of the jest, discovering that they had been jerked about a bit, might clutch their chest and wail in agony or rise and pantomime a limp. But these two had really hurt her man and now he wished to take this chance to hurt them back. And he expected she could do it for him. Or else he felt that they were standing in his way and wanted her to somehow clear them off. Or else they'd simply made him mad. This was different. She had seen this in him now and then before and always thought it justified. But thinking on it now, Vicki found that her own anger had quite melted; these two wished them well. Did this arise from Phillip's weakness? But Phillip wanted help and he was trusting to her wit. And anyway, a little fun would do no harm; surely they could stand some sort of friendly jab.

What was the subject? Sex. She must pretend to explain the favorite American word for it. She spun it round. Conjugations? Just to hear the conservative girl speak the delicious dirty word a time or too unknowingly in peculiar forms and then to see the dawn arising, that might be a laugh. Fucketh? I fucketh thee? But that was a King James Bible joke and surely wouldn't work in Greece. Well, she had no Greek but did posses some college Latin. Fuckimus? Fuckiassimus? Fuckimaximinimus? Nothing seemed to have the gaff required. She could get personal. They were on a weekend holiday to someone's farm. Domestic animals? Perhaps. But there should be a lead in from religion, more or less, to fit the general conversation. A cleansing ritual? Ah!

Vicki said to Diotoma; "Water!"

"Yes?"

"I was asking if they bathed in the sea."

"Oh. Well. Perhaps. That would be sense, I think. That was proper other times."

"Wait;" spoke Socrates; "are you sure? Isn't this word something . . ."

"Yes, of course!" Vicki cried aloud, hoping that a little volume in her voice might be convincing. But the fellow only frowned; she must focus on the other one. "Fucking;" she told Diotoma; "it means cleansing of the soul like Socrates was saying, or, really, anytime you go out for some clean fresh air or anything like that, to get revitalized."

"Oh?" said Diotoma. "Clean air is like bathing in the sea. The sea of life. The waves like breathing. Mmm . . . yes. Interesting. But 'mermaids' he said; what is that word?"

"You two are going to the country for the weekend?"

"Yes!" Diotoma answered with some pleasure. "It is a nice place."

"Nice air?"

"Oh yes. Much better than the city."

"So you're going to get fucked. You're going for some fucking. You are going forth to fuckimus."

"Fuckimus?" the woman asked carefully with a little earnest doubt but still no real suspicion showing. She was puzzled mainly by the sudden appearance of Latin conjugation.

"Do you want to learn some English?"

"Surely."

"Just repeat after me: I'm going to the country for some fucks."

"I am going to the country for some fooks. Fucks."

"I shall fuck me darlin's fucker till it's jam."

"What? I shall fook me darling's fooker till it is a jam?"

"And when his fucker's jam, I shall find a handsome ram."

"What? And when . . ." But now the day was dawning. She was unsure a moment more, wondering what sort of jam could possibly be meant and then what sort of ram; but the poem's structure was so completely doggerel and her informant seemed so naughtily amused that two and two finally added up at least to three and she knew she was being cranked. A fear of stupidity fled across her face, a blush began, but then she realized that if she did not play along she would not hear the ending. To what obscenity, exactly, was the silly poem leading? And for the sake of almost scientific curiosity, she chose to toss her prudery into the game. ". . . his fooker has become jammed . . . yes? . . . jammed! . . . then I shall find . . ."

But Socrates held up his hands and cried in real alarm; "Now wait! Please wait here; wait!"

There then ensued a whispered little chat between the two in Greek. "Fook" was repeated several times and "jam". Socrates was quite in earnest, quite offended, but still Diotoma softly and reassuringly laughed until he got along to explaining "ram". His voice rose with gesticulations. Her blush returned quite full and warm. She glanced about furtively while yet he spoke until, at last, there was no more explaining to be done.

Diotoma looked at Vicki, saw that the vagabond was holding in a most mischievous but good hearted grin; encouragement without malice. So Diotoma could not help but grin as well; and yet she thrust one dainty finger right at Vicki's nose and shook it there and cried in admiration that she could not hide; "You are a nasty woman!"

And yet the prank led into argument.

Socrates, feeling obviously betrayed, nodded vigorously saying; "Both of you require the cleaning ritual; yes for sure. The ancient authorities were quite exact.

(lacuna)

was one thing she did love dearly. He conjured up the strength to show a grin and even made a small dry laugh. The others calmed a little, Socrates reluctantly.

Phillip asked Vicki; "Remember that freak in Avebury?"

Immediately the place came flooding back. Oh yes she did remember Avebury. Most assuredly. England. Green. A rare dry day in spring but very cool. Quite heavy dew. The giant interlinking circles in the land of giant standing stones that stretch away beyond the visible horizon, one and one and all. A tiny Mediaeval village in the middle. But which freak did he mean? The witches surely. A very English very peculiar couple. His white frizzy hair and baggy seedy tweed jacket with mismatching plaid shirt and tie; the old lady screeching out strange songs very badly in some form of Gaelic. This pair of old witches had shown around this little pack of young folks come in a bus from London, with dowsing rods and pendulums, guided them through some very interesting meditations you can do among the huge rough rocks that stand up from the sheep cropped grass. Time travel. Really. Ancient visions. Ancient conversations that have lingered in the Earth. Ancient beings who invite you in through strange doors to strange places that are familiar. And being human in this place. Both of them had come away very surprised and utterly convinced, at least of certain things, beyond all reasonable doubt. There is magic. And they had discovered something indescribable about time. Time is not real.

And then days later, many miles away over sandwiches and soda pop and smoke on some park bench in Paris, she had confided to Phillip that the funny old goat had made a pass. He had. Telling it, she had to giggle. It made Phillip fairly roar with laughter. New to all of that, not knowing what a proper hippie ought to do, feeling really buzzed out and highly spiritual, sitting lotus fashion behind one of the tall huge misshapen boulders in its deep vibrating shadow, she had kissed the geezer on the cheek and let him feel her up a little and a little more. She was a goddess for that moment then, discovering her divinity was not conferred only by one certain man. It seemed like such a lovely way to activate the magic. She did not tell Phillip these specifics. This had been a lovely summer.

"Remember that guy?" Phillip asked.

"What? The old witch?"

"No, no, no! The freak you argued with."

"Oh no!" she cried. "How dare you even mention it? A fool's errand! What a stupid thing for me to do."

"All afternoon."

"Arrgh!" Vicki cried. She waved her fists.

Phillip then took up the tale. "See," he explained, "this really stupid nit wit believed the Earth is hollow. Hollow. You know, the Earth is all empty inside with a whole other world in there. Dinosaurs. A jungle. Really. He went on and on about it, claimed he could even see it. We were doing these very serious weird spiritual meditations and he just kept piping up with this incredible shit that he could stick his hands down and feel everything inside."

Socrates and Diotoma were smiling gamely now but were not laughing. Tension still. The language barrier?

So Vicki tried; "He said Jesus Christ is down there. Moses. Preaching to the dinosaurs."

Still no laughs.

"You argued with him." Phillip mentioned. "You were the only one who did. All afternoon."

"Arrgh! I couldn't stand it! What a waste of effort!" But now she felt a danger that the story might be turning her into the butt. She tightened her arm round Phillip's back to make him stop and said; "Darling, that was a lovely day in any case."

He looked into her face and frowned. Just for a flash the frown turned ugly but then just as quickly disappeared.

A chill went up her back. She had seen this frightening flash of his toward other people sometimes and merely thought it was a weakness in his strength. And with his weakness greater now?

But at least the tension of the moment past was broken.

Diotoma asked her boyfriend for a summary in Greek, and then she laughed a tiny bit at last. She got Phillip's point. Shrugging broadly she said; "So pointless to argue these things. Dinosaurs? Christos? Atlantis? Legends may be myth, perhaps with meaning. Who can know?"

And then a rapping at the window and a muffled shout; "Hey hippies!"

"Holy shit!" cried Vicki. "It's the driver!"

The bus was stopped. Right up beside a grocery shop.

"How long have we been sitting here?" Phillip asked.

"Hey aneekhto! Aneeeekhto!" cried the driver on the outside of the window, hefting up a heavy wooden crate of large brown bottles that sure as anything did look like beer. He had another crate beside his feet. His official hat was pushed back on his head.

"May Demeter and Dionysos bless you!" Phillip shouted.

Diotoma clapped her hands and threw the fellow kisses.

Her boyfriend stuck his fingers in his mouth and started whistling very shrill.

Vicki bounced in her seat and then, thinking how to outdo Mistress Priss, rose, turned toward the driver, grinned, and vigorously waved her tits. The rainbow colored tee shirt quite came up and so she thrust out her belly at him too.

But suddenly all of them saw the problem. There was quite a serious difficulty.

Socrates, having quickly left off whistling, was now struggling to slide his window up. That's where the driver stood, straining with the heavy box. The spectacled young man began to curse. The damn thing sure was stuck. What would they do? The next seat in front was occupied by a broadly grinning very highly amused old frail gentleman bent above his cane, with a suitcase and a sailor's cap, and who, in any case, was not among their party. So Socrates began to struggle with the next window back, beside the wide rear seat, but could not manage it from there. Vicki was over on the other side of Phillip and afraid to hurt his leg by climbing. Phil was reaching for the window, trying to be a help, but in truth had found that he could scarcely move.

But Diotoma was a smaller woman. Laughing louder, she stood up in the aisle among the heap of gear and found a footing. She wagged a reproving finger at Vicki and called; "Hey! You nasty woman! Look at this!" She pulled the tight skirt so far up her black lace panties showed. She did a pelvic jerk. A fringe of curly hair was even visible against her inner thighs. Then, reaching out to grasp at Phillip's shirt, and yet constrained by the fitted jacket of her suit, hoping that the thrill was worth whatever injury his leg sustained, the small woman climbed right up into his face and over to the empty space where she then quickly and easily helped her boyfriend with the window.

Phillip had certainly kept his mouth and fingers to himself. He was a gentleman. And yet you may be sure he had not shut his eyes.

Vicki stamped her foot and shouted; "Oh you slut!"

The big brown bottles started coming in.

5: Episode Four:
Two Bicycle Mechanics, A Sumo Wrestler,
Five English Comedians,
A Congregational Minister,
An Arab And A Jew
All Walk Into A Cheese Shop With
Parrots On Their Heads

Peter, the driver, stood up and took a pace, paced the one step back, sat down in the sand again and leaned against his rock. He threw his hands high and wide into the air in an eloquent show of disgruntled resignation. "Pos pane ta praghmata? Thavmaseea!" He took another slug of beer.

They were sitting on a beach gazing out across the gentle surf and the wine dark waters of the Adriatic Sea toward the setting sun. To left and right were hilly headlands that curved in around to form a crescent bay with this low bit of strand tucked neatly in. Behind them a crescent moon and countless pinpricks of the brightest stars were just now starting to ascend above the land. Night certainly was falling here; it was that first long moment when you realize for sure it's growing dark. The magic that seemed to drench the time and place seemed like a thing that you could simply nearly touch, like something in your breath or on your face.

Peter made some other longer emphatic exclamation and repeated it with variations, waving a hand here and there in various directions. At the termination of his largely waving arm his hand repeatedly shaped a gesture which, beyond a doubt, was sexually obscene.

The old man – the frail old gentleman with the suitcase, cane and sailor's hat – more or less translated: "He's cussing the cocksucker army again, doing better for 'em too. Their papas sucked cocks, their uncles did, their grandpas; ya see, and many different ones."

Phillip nodded.

The old sailor wrinkled up his dark sun burnt face until it was transformed from its customary grin into what seemed intended to be a humorous sneer. The comic look certainly got a startling touch from the way his face had shrunk against the bone with age. Behind an open hand, in mock of secrecy, his finger pointed at the driver. "He's a Christian too."

Phillip smiled.

This tough old bird certainly was Greek but spoke his English with the mingled accents of the whole world's shores. The stretch and up-turn of a phrase would tug the ear with a hint of Brooklyn nearly and then the next word might nod somewhat eastward toward Bombay.

There were only Phillip and the two of them sitting there, reasonably comfortable among a pile of large speckled brownish rocks worn smooth and round in fleshly forms by the storms of ages, half buried in the sand. They had made a fire of driftwood trash but the breeze was growing cooler with approaching night. Vicki, Socrates and Diotoma had gone exploring. The other passengers apparently had gone away.

The bus had been struck by a large military truck which had burst their front left tire and somewhat stove in the frame. The bus now stood disabled, kind of kneeling down, up behind them by the road.

There had been a lot of gesturing and shouting. The confrontation had seemed really dicey for a while; Phillip, struggling to hang out the open window, had believed the drivers might well come to blows and the soldier had a holstered pistol at his belt. He seemed to reassure himself by resting a hand there.

But, faced with Peter's obstinate refusal to be a sheep and the screeching protests of three old lady passengers who all hobbled out to lend their bit of weight, the soldier had refrained from making an arrest. And these were the days when civilians sometimes disappeared into the military barracks, although the corpse at least would be released, some official explanation would be issued and the opposition papers would be allowed to print your name. The soldier finally only jotted down the bus identification number, climbed up to his truck cab and drove away.

There was a suburb of the city crowded in among the small steep hills behind where they sat, beyond the road, beyond the bus, below the climbing stars and moon; white square houses and little shops with orange tile roofs all of which, if you gazed on them in this changing light, seemed to ripple with their changing colors.

Before them the sunset was lovely, very brilliant, out there far across the waves that seemed to rise from the horizon to meet a human gaze.

They were theoretically awaiting reinforcements from the Transit Authority but it was Friday afternoon and well past five o'clock.

The aged seaman took a swig of beer, his bony hand showing surprising strength in the easy way he lifted the heavy bottle with a single finger looped around its neck. He then wrinkled up his thin face again, this time in the semblance of a secretive cunning leer, tapped Phillip on the knee of his outstretched gimpy leg and said; "Hey amigo, you got some smoke?"

"Well, sure." Phillip answered. He had given up cigarettes himself as a useless expense but on this trip he'd made a practice of keeping a couple packs for trade or comradeship. He tugged his heavy bag over and fished around inside of it.

He found one pack, a good German brand. He carefully tore the top and tossed the bit of paper in the fire, pulled up a butt and held it out.

The sailor frowned.

Phillip shrugged. Okay, he thought, might as well be generous. He turned the pack around to offer the whole thing, gestured with it. "They're yours." he said.

But the old man still frowned. "What you thinking?" the fellow asked.

"Huh?"

"Come on Chingo; what you got? Nobody's looking."

Phillip smiled and asked; "What are you saying?" Apparently this might be Miller Time.

"Eh? Well, all I'm saying, this remembers me the time I shipwrecked on the beach in India."

"Oh." Phillip laughed. Actually it sounded pretty good. He did feel beat from the whole long summer, his bum leg certainly had pissed him off, and a mellow high would help. And he might make a friend. Maybe. But still he hesitated just for fun. He slowly took another satisfying draught of beer then asked; "What was that like? Shipwrecked in India?"

"Good! Pretty damn good! My purse was full of silver!"

"Dancing girls?"

"Those were the days. They set me dancing too in Kali's temple." He briefly mimed a snaky wavy motion with his arms, arms which had no doubt been muscular in youth but now were thin and ropy with the unbuttoned cuffs of his baggy threadbare denim coat falling from them as they made their serpent movements in a surprising show of fluid grace. He said; "Gin and tonic. Big tall hookahs"

So, with another laugh, Phillip's preparation now began. He stashed the damn machine-made cigarettes, reached way in to the center of the bag and pulled out his well loved herbal kit, as he affectionately called it. It was, to the untutored eye, a pipe smoker's leather pouch of the ordinary sort that has a zipper pocket for the pipe and little tools, another for tobacco. And indeed it held an ordinary looking wooden pipe with ordinary looking tools. And indeed there was tobacco, but with a fair size lump of hashish wrapped air tight in silver foil buried in there too. His medicine had got him through some situations.

First he took another long and lingering gulp of beer. It fortified his strength. The leather kit was in his other hand, not yet unzipped. He waved it and the bottle in a vague imitation of the old man's Kali dance, mimed a comic version of an appropriately fierce look and asked; "You're not a cop?"

"Don't be stupid!" The old man swelled out his bony chest and struck it with his fist in a quick blow, declaring; "In six countries I am a hunted man!" But he shrugged and frowned. "Ah, long ago. All forgotten now. So long ago. Days come and come, and more and more. But strange days sometime though. Piracy."

"What? You a pirate? Bull."

"Ha! You don't believe? Old sonabitch like me, call me a liar?" He glanced to the coast that curved around, glanced back toward the town. He hooked a thumb in that direction. "Yes;" he said; "maybe this the place it was. Looked like this. Same country anyway; not too many bays like this one. We anchor right out there." He pointed toward the sea. "I was captain; me and my boys we come up here in the boat and rob the bank. Daytime even. Took off to Sicily. Killed some poor bastard local cops; by accident. Not in the plan, I swear. That's what pirates always done here in Hellas; come in a boat and rob the citizens. Real old kind of job." He shrugged again. "What the hell did I know? Real old kind of job; always like that in this country. Wanted money. Got off clean though, long ago. Big war, you know, long war, things turn upside down. You start to thinking somebody owes you."

"Jesus shit; is that the truth?"

"What's wrong, you don't trust me? Come on, shut up. What you got inside the little bag?"

"What's your name?" Phillip asked. He was speaking almost in some sort of charity. "Maybe I have heard of you."

"How is that your business?" the captain answered rather hard, suddenly proud again. "I am a man; all you need to know. What right you have to hear my name? Do what you're doing now."

"How 'bout the Christian?"

"He'll be okay. Hurry up. The sun's going down. The others will come back and want a share."

And so then, once begun, this young man's easy handling of his stuff began to feel exactly like the comforting familiar magic ritual it was. In fact this was his favorite old pipe from Viet Nam, a treasured and artistic souvenir, and it had often been a comrade worthy of his trust. The carved wood bowl had been deep brown but now was scuffed and chipped, the nose and chin of the little face on the front long gone and fallen to the Earth somewhere. He had carved and smoothed and dyed the face with boot wax himself, a private soldier's simple wartime rendering of a handsome African woman. His black friends in his troop had welcomed him for this possession even though they also envied him the treasure.

He fitted in the stem and blew it clear, packed in a pinch of the specially selected light tobacco, expertly shaved off a generous helping of the dope, another pinch exactly large enough on top to help it light and cook. He tamped each layer down as though he were an old time musket man, holding the special sharpened teak wood tamping stick ready in the crook of his little finger. No crumb was lost. He carefully and quickly closed and put away the kit. He sucked the trace of flavor from his fingertips. And all these gestures quite distinctly hinted at his own past sin and all the memories that might come flooding back at any moment.

So Phillip was already in a spirit state, holding and staring into the beautiful woman's face, thinking that he did not know her name, suddenly thinking that hers too must be the voice that lured him on, until the sailor's wizened steady hand held a flaming stick above the bowl. That little flame cast a moving shadow on the marred but radiant countenance.

The captain said; "You wish to speak to her."

Two words immediately rose from Phillip's heart and tumbled from his lips: "Thank you."

The little portrait sculpture somehow seemed to smile.

"Now smoke."

Obediently, he turned the face away out toward the world and put the stem between his lips. The flame descended. The herbal mixture flared.

(lacuna)

tones as always; "You fellows better finish before my wife gets here. She'll get her nose up about that stuff you're doing. I promise that. She's a real Christian."

It did strike Phillip as pretty odd that the fella now seemed to be speaking something understandable; maybe he'd known English all along or maybe he himself now understood Greek or else it was simply drug induced hallucination. Phillip damn sure did feel buzzed. But maybe – he quite naturally began to suspect – this was another dream. A new one. He squinted out across the water with suspicion, looking for some other hint.

The old skipper asked Peter; "Your wife? She bringing your dinner?"

"Of course. We're married. I telephoned. She'll take a taxi."

The captain handed the pipe to Peter. Peter acted some surprise. He looked into the woman's face. He sniffed the bowl. He drew a cautious mouthful, quickly puffed it out.

"Mmm . . . not bad." He shook his head, perhaps in wonder at this lapse of judgment, and passed it on.

It was Phillip's turn but he was only cradling the pipe in his hands, looking at it in his hands. He looked out to the glowing surf again, up at the crimson sunset shot with yellow rays. He felt the chill come through his jacket and felt a shiver so he said; "Everything seems so real."

"Yeah;" the skipper said; "you need this stuff. It wakes you up." Then he tapped Phillip's knee. "Look here."

The old man pulled a necklace out from his collar, a thick string with a big silver coin dangling from it. He held up the disk and somehow used this sparkling thing to flash the firelight into Phillip's eyes as though it were a magic mirror. He said; "I make you a bet. This will be my stake. Look at it eh."

There was a thread wrapped here and there across its gleaming face to hold it on the string, and grime caught in the snakelike coils of thread, even curly chest hairs from the man who wore it, but Phillip could somehow see it clearly by the still but radiant living presence that seemed to stand out from the gleaming surface. The coin bore a picture of some ancient regal female figure wreathed around with sheaves of grain and unknown lettering. It was bigger than a silver dollar and it shone. It was antique.

"Four thousand years;" the old man was saying; "four thousand years ago the royal smith stamp it with his bronze hammer with these holy magic signs. Four thousand years it lays in a chest of olive wood waiting in the buried treasury of Agamemnon King of Men. You can buy a house and land with this, my friend, wherever in this world you wish; or I shall finally buy a ship to sail the Burning River."

"Hot damn!"

"And I am offering this prize to you in a simple wager. Your wife shall bring you dinner. Eh? That is my side. I say when she returns here, she will bring your meal and so your marriage will be proved. Your side is that she will not and so you are not married. Eh?"

Phillip had to laugh. He fell into his native western drawl; "I ain't got nothing to bet like that."

"Ah!" the old man cried, holding up a finger. "That is the beauty. See? You must only promise, if you lose, that you will give to me the greatest treasure that you have. Whatever it may be. However small. What, don't you trust me?"

But yet the offer did not lure him in the least. Phillip sat back. He vaguely waved his arms again to indicate the old man's dancing girls. He said; "You want my wife but you can't have her. I won't give her up. Never."

"No. That is well said but no; I do not want your wife. What good would such a one be for me, whose time for that is past? She would kill me in my bed. And as well, she is not your greatest treasure."

"What? No. Whatever it is, I will not take your bet."

"You do not trust me?"

But Phillip nodded. "I do trust you. You'd keep the deal. I know that. It's only . . ."

"Yes?"

"Oooh . . . I see."

"What do you see?"

"I need instruction." This new dream. "This is my time for instruction." That dark power he had seen, that tremendous spirit which had risen from among the deities he knew – that bit of progress – it had unexpectedly brought him this next step. So then Phillip struggled to discover and drag out into the open whatever he had been thinking that had opened this revelation to his consciousness. The ghastly bet. "I'm going to find everything I need myself. No matter how long it takes. It may take a real long time, but if I can't find it for myself it won't be mine."

Peter laughed out loud. Peter asked the skipper; "How long it took you to say that? Many years and leagues of water, I am thinking."

The old skipper truly smiled. He smiled like a father would have done. In fact his old shrunken face, which looked as if it had been carved of dark hard olive wood left rough about the grizzled chin and cheeks, now seemed for a fleeting moment in the dancing light to take on the half forgotten countenance of Phillip's father.

The old sailor answered Peter; nearly in Old Pop's voice he said to Peter, "Smart kid, eh?" He tucked the heavy coin and its string back in around his neck. He patted Phillip's knee.

But now Phillip very seriously asked the captain; "What is my greatest treasure?"

"Huh? Why, of course, the three week's son and daughter in your wife's belly."

"What?"

"Yes, and I would have kept the bargain. I would have come and found you anywhere and fetched the boy at least away as soon as he was off the mother's teats, I would, and gave him to be raised among the horses like was done before. I would, for they are generous. If you had gambled such a life away, then it would not be proper for you to teach a boy like that one. Way too dangerous."

"What!" Phillip cried with the explanation sinking in. "No, it isn't true. She would have told me. She hasn't told me."

Peter shrugged. "Just three weeks."

"Three weeks?" Phillip asked. "Well, then, she wouldn't know herself. She might suspect it but that's all."

But Peter nodded like a sage. "She knows."

"She felt it when it happened." the captain said. "And she smiled at you. Remember? And then she felt the two take root inside of her like poppy flowers. She knows."

"Damn!" cried Phillip. "Damn women. She should have told me. Things would be different."

"They have their secrets." Peter said.

"Damn!" And then it took an ugly turn. Phillip really blurted out: "If they would just tell you things! But no, they've got to twist you around, don't they?"

The skipper was immediately reproachful. "What's that? What do you say?"

"Oh, it just makes me mad, that's all. Like when they put their arm around you and call you darling just to make you do what they want. It just pisses me off so bad. Is that love? A friend wouldn't do that."

"Ah, son," sighed Peter, "being married; it is not so easy. Friend or enemy; it is hard to tell sometimes. That is real love. That is holiness. That is the world of saints and gods."

"Fuck that shit. I have already had all the enemies I will ever want. Yes indeed!"

"So;" the old man said; "if she don't treat you right you will Goddamn hit the Goddamn road. Eh? Yes? You will?"

For a moment Phillip could not speak, struggling to examine himself for a truthful answer somewhere in between hard anger and soft desire. But then he realized. His wife was pregnant. He had just found out. His child. This child would be an amazing gift to him and to the world. How stupid could he possibly be?

"No;" he said; "I won't leave her. Not her. Not ever."

Phillip wiped a hand across his brow, discovered that the hand was trembling. Trembling? He now realized with deep surprise that in that moment just now past he had been enraged. Enraged. At her. Yes he had. But why?

"What's wrong with me?"

"Aaah!" the captain sighed.

Peter said; "Yes, smart kid."

"Look here;" the captain said, reaching out a reassuring hand to Phillip's knee again; "You have had all the enemies you need. Truly. More than enough for any man. And even, to you, they were innocent. What did they want except your death and what is that to a man of war? But you kill them anyhow. So maybe some time you kill again with no good reason. No wonder it is hard for you to love. Everything is riddles. You cannot trust; you cannot trust yourself because you are a murderer, a real criminal and no bullshit."

Phillip touched one hand to the scar beside his head, the other to his useless hip. There seemed no reason in the world to trust. He touched the medal hanging from his pocket flap. He'd gone to war in hope of doing something good but all he'd found was this.

"No!" the captain cried. "Not your wounds. These wounds are honest, even if they are a crook's, for you have borne them as you should. You know that. These wounds are strong. The hurt that has been done to you; that is not your pain. The hurt that you have done, even to your willing enemies, that is your pain. You say to yourself that it was all your doing and all for nothing and so you cannot trust yourself. You do not trust your judgment."

Phillip answered, "Oh. Yes. That's it."

"And you say this to yourself: So much more painful is the hurt that I have done to what was truly innocent and unoffending."

"Oh!"

"And yet I tell you that you are not guilty of the crime you think. The only innocence which you have murdered is your own and you are in your rights for that."

"No!"

"You did not kill the girl."

"No?"

"You did not even rape her by the law there then. You left her when she told you go. You did not rob her, for you paid."

"She was a starving little girl!"

"You were a soldier driven mad by war. That guilt of her slavery is not yours; you have not any right to claim it. Not this time. It belongs to others; others took you to her, she to you. For their stupid reasons, not for yours this time. You would have set her free if that were in your power. Yes? Yes, you would have set her free. And yet you blind yourself deliberately by claiming all of the guilt. Deliberately! You claim some great crime and you hope the greatness of it makes it holy."

Peter said to Phillip; "You did not do it."

"Then what is wrong with me?"

"You?" the old pirate answered. "In this life you have lived now? You have killed your enemies. That is all. But oh, that is enough. That was enough to make you even sacrifice the best things in yourself, to seek a balance." He paused. He spoke again; "And even then you knew enough to struggle with the judge who was yourself."

Peter was nodding sagely, speaking to the skipper; "This is not the king he was before. No; this one has learned. He can see Victory now for what she is, a thing to which a proper man must court with charity and justice. Not like before, I think. No more the old stupid joy in slaughter. No more the glory in the battle adventure. He has become a better man."

"Good thing;" the captain answered; "he was a sonabitch last time. His crimes are remembered, and the crimes of his first son even more." He took a moment for a thought. "But what did he know before? Perhaps he knew all this before but now he fits the puzzle different. Always been a thinker."

Peter said; "He has really turned philosopher."

Phillip tossed out a mocking laugh.

The captain reached to Phillip's crippled knee again but this time grasped it hard and shoved so that a hazy jab of pain came through his senses. "Shut up;" the captain said; "you have always turned in the direction of philosophy."

"Bull shit. What do I know?"

"You try to know yourself. If that is no good starting step into philosophy, then my name is not my name. Before, you never asked about yourself. You asked many things, but not about yourself."

"Damn;" said Phillip; "what a dream." He shook his head.

How on Earth could a dream tell you so much? On Earth? Where are you when you dream like this, he wondered. Where is this place? Those meditations with the witches, the whirl of faces for the summer, the beautiful kind clever woman who trusted him so much that she loved making love with him, the surprising blessing of the book about Eleusis and now actually beginning on a trip that might actually turn out to be the ultimate reality; apparently it was adding up pretty good. And if she was pregnant that would be even so much more. And twins! In any case, he had scarcely ever thought before about having kids before and now it seemed like a promise of a future of uncountable wealth. First the progress with the old dream and now this new one appears so unexpected. Maybe he had followed the old one to its end. Maybe it was well and truly done. Maybe. But still, no doubt this one too would start to fade away into obscurity real soon so that he must lose his grip on it as well. But maybe it did seem different. Maybe. All this did seem to be going on extremely long. And it did give him a remarkable feeling of some reality that was more real than any he had ever known.

The cooling breeze came rolling from the sea at that moment, as if on cue in harmony with his thoughts. It tickled at his beard and hair and teased his nostrils with the seeming reality of deep salty power.

Phillip gazed up into the sunset. Yellow and crimson, colors that repeated in his fantasies for some mysterious reason. And yes, he told himself, it looked as if the sun had hardly sunk an inch in all this time. He looked at their little fire and realized no one had added any fuel, except perhaps the crinkle of the tiny bits of paper he had tossed into the flames, and yet it burned as bright as ever. He found the pipe with its gentle smiling face again now cradled in his open hands and saw the herbs still glowing softly. It seemed as if they had been talking for an hour or nearly two. Any moment now he would suddenly find himself in darkness, or else this very helpful dream would either fade or start to stretch and change its shapes or place or characters so he would forget too much of it.

But then, Phillip thought, the old outlaw – the one who had outlived all the cops and turned at last into a real philosopher – he had just then mentioned his name. He had not actually said it or offered to but perhaps the mention was a hint that secrets were ready to be revealed. And with this thought Phillip realized at once that it might be a bit of knowledge that could help him hold onto awareness of these things they had discussed. It might key all this into some living myth beyond his fantasies.

So Phillip bent toward the old man and tried to whisper very confidentially; "What is your name?"

The old man nearly told. Phillip was watching very carefully and saw the name just starting to take shape on the thin supple lips. But no. Not yet. Not yet. So another thought suddenly struck: could this dream go on and on? Would he never wake from this? Was the magic now reality? Had he gone crazy for good and lost himself in this?

"Peter!" said the skipper.

"Yes?"

"We have cleared away some of the brush; maybe now we find a path up in the hills and then among the trees."

Phillip asked; "What do you mean?"

"Yes!" cried Peter. "We must decide what is next."

"Ah;" the skipper said; "we know the dances and the song are next. Yes? Here on the beach, and the humans come with bright torches all around so every man and woman and child dances as they must. And the water spirit maidens rise to dance the dance which answers all, and sing the song as well. The Moon and Stars come down."

"Yes!" said Peter. "Yes, all true. So very true. So then our proper question is: what dance shall be done by the king of men? What dance of his would be answered by the true answer?"

Phillip had rather struggled to keep up with their sudden quick obscure debate, dragging on along behind the wonder whether this was after all mere fantasy or must entirely be something else. But he had kept up well enough and now spoke: "I'll dance my memories."

The others stopped. They looked at him with some surprise.

"Well;" the skipper said; "smart kid."

Peter nodded, saying; "He has changed."

Phillip shook his head at their surprise. He almost smiled. He said; "It's simple. What else have I got? What else could I dance? What else do I need an answer for? What else would be answered by the true answer?"

The others grinned. He looked around at both of them. Was he right?

Both of them began to laugh, a

(lacuna)

will burst upon you. There is a long walk yet, up from the sea into farms among the hills that leads to dark forest; at the forest edge a gate will open. Only then you find the thicket with the big rock that has the little house inside of it, and only then the lightening storm will come."

"Oh. Alright. Whatever. Yes."

"And first of all you dance."

"Yes. I see."

The captain chuckled. "How do they say in your country? Mmm . . . you ain't seen nothing yet."

Another space of silence.

The pipe was in the captain's hands. He spoke to it again. This time he listened to it too. And then he put the stem to his lips and began to puff. Seven times he puffed, the cloud of smoke from his lips growing more voluminous each time, the herbs finally glowing up so bright they seemed to flame. He held the last puff in.

The captain somehow leaned so close that he could throw an arm round Phillip's shoulders and Phillip felt the magic power of the man pull him closer still till there was nothing in his vision but this wide-eyed face which seemed to be the skull of death and yet the great commanding and demanding force of life.

And in these eyes the vision opened.

It was some other place and he some man whom he had been before. He was in the battle, and a very different combat than he'd known. Soldiers came all rushing round to heave and shove at one another in the tumult of their rage, all in a cloud of blinding boiling dust that swirled around their every motion. The dust was caked upon his sweaty face, his vision narrowed by a missing eye.

Nearby bright metal of the soldiers' weapons flashed amid the countless screams of outraged pain and spouts of blood. A shadow glimmered so he turned his shield so that a glancing blow fell clanking on the golden armor of his leg and so he reached to jab his long and gleaming silver knife precisely through the glory seeker's throat. He was the captain of the captains and a dueling master too.

And here he stood upon the precious only road eastward to Athens from his distant home. Here he stood with the ranks of his own proud battalion crumbling to some sudden unexpected pressure evidently thrown across the center of the field which he had thought would be easily won. These Athenian militiamen were small but tough and mad as demons. Very quickly he must somehow find or rally up a solid block of men exactly here at once, or else the whole adventure could be lost; the fame and treasure, empire, everything. He counted up the means at his disposal; estimated they were lacking. And so she'd lured him to the end at last. So much for sending up smoking prayers to fickle Victory. Unless . . . where was his brigade of cavalry? Might they be returning now? Was it an hour past when he had sent them galloping off far out of sight to stop the enemy's reinforcements or was it more like two?

And then the face of ages spoke. The great gale of roiling smoke came flooding from the lips to blow his beard and hair as though he were entirely immersed in it, while the lips slowly shaped these words as though from potter's stretching clay: "I . . . am . . . Oodeeseeoos!" Philip Maselin inhaled it deep and gazed within.

One of the captains shouted "King, you better get us out of here!"

Another grabbed his shoulder with a hand whose stumps showed missing fingers; "Phillipus, friend; your horse is waiting over there and you cannot command the army from inside this dust; the center of the line is mine by rights so let me hold it if I can, to be my everlasting glory not your shame."

And yet he answered; "No; if I leave, the men will follow. Here's your orders: Call the rally here round me immediately and have them sing that hymn they know to Lady Luck. Where is my son with his six hundred horses?"

6: Episode Five:
Street Scene

An old lady had put a little boy in Vicki's hands. He was eight or nine, much too big for the rather short and stout and very earnest old woman to lift, and so she had stood up in the aisle, grasped Vicki's hand and opened it and pressed the boy's small hand in there and wrapped it shut. The child had stared up from one to the other of them with wide frightened eyes. Vicki had, of course, picked up the child and pressed him close. This was following the crash when she had jumped up in alarm and hurried forward for a better look. The bus was canting forward, sinking like a ship, she thought, and the driver had by then slammed open the door and leapt out and begun shouting violently in a confrontation with some adversary in the street. Up above the windshield glass, drawing her eye, two of his saints had tipped. No wonder he was angry.

This granny lady's two old granny friends had followed the driver out and she too seemed compelled to go. She had emphatically spoken something from the heart like "beega bugga boo" which Vicki perfectly understood to be a powerful blessing.

And Vicki then had spoken up, in her Australian English, first to the child and then to everyone; "Everything's okay." She had smiled and nodded while still hugging him close, catching all their eyes, speaking very calmly with increasing volume and large slow gestures of her free hand as she began to see it was having a good effect. "Don't be alarmed. No one has been hurt. Everyone please sit back down. Yes, please sit back down. There's no emergency."

So now, with all things seeming safe and sound again, the child had grown attached to her and she to him. And anyway, she could not see a graceful way to give him back because the three old grannies all looked alike and none of them had seemed inclined as yet to come forward with a claim.

They had found a small well lit cafe where she and the boy and the grannies and Diotoma and Socrates and perhaps a dozen other passengers had crowded in. It all felt like she was shoved along by friends with the child always tugging forward on her hand. Food and drink appeared; a plate of cheese and bread were placed before her with a glass of pomegranate flavored sparkling water. It was very good. Even the bottle's paper label with its sprig of leaves and red fleshy dimply fruit was very pretty. They soon grew merry.

The fact is, growing up, she had never had a little boy to play with. Her mother and her mother's friends, to tell the truth, had always been overly protective in their fear of men. So for the first time now she was learning that little boys can be delightful when they're good. This one had a tiny wooden flute on which he could puff up his cheeks and toot a really charming childish tune for her and it was fun to see how well he loved his toy. He walked about to serenade the smiling crowd who rubbed his head and touched his face with finger-tips. Vicki gathered up some nice remains from various plates to neatly tie into a yellow striped napkin for Phil and stashed the bundle in her red sweater's pocket.

And yet, of course, she worried. How was Phillip doing? His leg had limbered up a bit in walking to the beach. He had seemed all right but soon she must be getting back although she was uncertain of the way. But if she left she'd only have to find the beach and she had certainly seen the beautiful sunset out across the bay. And yet the street outside the small windows in the front was growing dark, the sunlight quickly disappearing. But wherever they had come, the beach was west and she had learned Polaris in their wanderings. Thinking on it, she knew the Moon should be visible tonight as well, a waning crescent rising in the east. So was the weather clear enough to let her do this simple bit of celestial navigation?

Vicki rose and went to stand out in the front door of the restaurant. It was too bright with artificial light to see. She ventured out the three steps more into the center of the narrow cobbled street.

Yes, the starry purple sky was clear except for wisps of high thin crimson cloud that looked like cuts into its fabric. There was the crescent Moon just up the sloping street, low and seeming close beyond the furthest rooftops, shining silver in her radiant glory above a distant line of shadow hills. Far beyond, perhaps, there seemed to be the distant glitter of a further sea. It took the woman's breath away; the beauty of this little human town with all of its inhabitants for all their generations, set among the glories of the Universe. There were the hills; somewhere over there, and over there as well, the all embracing sea. All of it like rippling circling supple yielding spheres touching spheres touching spheres. All like whispered breathing rising falling always each toward all. There was the radiant sky above, the cobblestones below, and all that humans know of mortal life between. There was some trick in it that made the eyes perceive each separate thing and yet see all together.

It was the distant line of hills that really seemed to beckon. No, it was one particular shadow of a hill, the furthest one that she could see standing rather far beyond the others on that distant shore. She let her fantasy be drawn there. Quite like some glittering bug, she buzzed out from the town across the farms in that direction, feeling now the wind of spirit power that flowed from there. Upwind she flew as though immersed in the great river of all that lives and dies and lives, along the winding narrow road between the fallow autumn barley fields that glowed with their fertility. Up she came to that final hill itself and alighted on a tree trunk at the edge of the huge grove that stood very tall on its slope. She looked among the giant trunks. There emerging from the hillside lay a large rounded rock quite like some lump of flesh. In the rock there was a little door as though there were some place inside where you could go, as though it were the magic house of some family of Earth beings from some real life fairy tale.

There was no need for more. Vicki shook her head to wake. Now she knew where she was going. Was that Eleusis? She didn't care. It might be just as easily some other point of interest on this country's haunted map. It might be the place where some primordial Titan woman brought the gods to birth, or the spot where some young slip of a girl mated with the mighty King of Hell and was transformed to immortality herself, or something of that sort. There were a lot of stories. She had sifted through them in a college book by Doctor Graves. That might be the one original rock where Heaven's lightening found the Earth. It might be almost anywhere but it was magic for her now. That distant wooded hill was the one spot in this land from which all life and death flowed out. Most certainly she would go and try to look inside the door. And step inside?

What could it be, four or five miles perhaps? An easy hike if this fine weather held.

If Phillip wished to follow her, if he could walk tonight, then that would be as well as not. She would insist he use some sort of walking stick. But surely she no longer cared to prop him up; she'd learned that much. He was not a person whom she'd ever try again to lead about by hand. But yet there was his bulging makeshift sandwich in her pocket. She cast her eyes the other way, toward where he lay, and saw a sparkling line of surf. Ah, let him eat. They'd talk. And then she'd find the way.

Behind her, Diotoma spoke; "Please pardon. Shall we go back now?"

"What?" Vicki turned about.

"Shall we go back now?"

"What? You mean to the beach?"

"Yes. Everyone is waiting for what you say."

Diotoma stood there in the lighted door that cast her shadow out into the stony street. Behind her some of the others were watching too.

"They're waiting for me to say?"

"Yes, of course. And the boy is . . . mmm . . . whimpering."

Vicki touched her bosom where she'd held the boy. She pressed her hand to feel her pregnancy. If her child were male, she wished for one like him. Or were there twins? Then at once she knew this was a boy and girl. She felt the great potential and the danger too. To raise Phillip's son would be some job all right, but to also raise a being like herself? But she would do it. And, if necessary, damn the world. And yet she was surprised to find inside herself complete acceptance of the leadership these people here were inexplicably requesting. Why were they choosing her? She did not know. And yet she looked inside her heart and did not find unwillingness at all. She had stood up in that sinking bus, even when two saints had tilted over, and she had done what was required for them. If they now had to stick together for some reason, she could handle that as well. There wasn't far to go at all, just up the street and out between the fields. She knew the way. After all, she was a goddess.

"Diotoma."

"Yes?"

"What in the world do they want? I realize it's Friday night and it isn't really late but don't they all have homes to go to? Can't they just take taxi cabs from here? Why are they going to the beach?" And Vicki smiled. She wagged a finger at Diotoma. "And aren't you going to the country for some fooks?"

Diotoma laughed. She stepped out to the shadows of the street and took Vicki's hand then glanced around at everything for a lingering moment. "Oh;" she almost whispered; "I and Socrates have spoken. What did your fellow say? Abstaining, for a little while, it has good purpose. Yes? It helps you dance with them for they desire you more." Then she gazed out to the furthest distant hills in the same direction Vicki had been drawn. In the cooling breeze Diotoma wrapped her thin city jacket tight. She looked up into her new friend's eyes and spoke with firm conviction; "This night is different. This is a certain night. And these people who have stayed; they are the ones who feel its thunder coming."

"Please;" said Vicki; "help me understand."

"First we dance. Yes, we really dance and sing." Still looking in her face, Diotoma pointed toward the hill on the horizon. "Then we go to Elephesis. There."

So then a new revelation flooded in with vast enormity. She was with them, they with her; all their generations. What was done before would be done now with variations but without the slightest difference. The fallow fields would sprout with grain again and death and birth would turn. The great immortal world was turning round her. And all this fitted to the flow of life arising from that spot of land and flowing through her womb. And yet, despite the turning world, she looked upon this place with open eyes. There was surprise to find that while she stood here on her feet these vast infinities were adding up so neatly. It seemed to her that suddenly great chunks of knowledge could be managed by her reasoning. It felt as if great chunks of what she knew and wished to know might shift into new shapes of understanding.

Vicki spoke to Diotoma; "Such a world. This is such a world."

Diotoma answered; "This is why we are here, you know; to wonder at it."

So Vicki wondered what inside of her had broken loose at last. All of her life and all the world could now be thought on differently; but why? Some bond had split. Her children who would be. The girl and boy both made of egg and semen. She traced the chain of thinking back. Her yearning fear of men. She thought on that and felt again the shifting weights, so that was it. She had waited on their smiles and trembled at their frowns. Her innocent delight with them, so buoyed on the waves of fear as it had been, must be abandoned as wisdom grew. That seemed a loss but more was gained. And the impossibly ridiculous oblong sandwich in her sweater pocket; what was that? She gripped it in her fist and squeezed it rather hard as though it were his manhood snugly wrapped. Was she a slave? Was she a slave to such as that? Ah, let him eat, share his pleasure – the man had shown much tenderness and given of his flesh so that was justice – then she'd find her way.

Victoria asked her friend; "Why are they violent?"

"Who? The men?"

"Yes, of course. You know, Phillip is a king of them. He is. You see it every time. They envy him and yet they will obey if he commands."

"Ah, yes;" Diotoma answered; "he was so with Socrates today. Your fellow laughs and my fellow smiles. Your fellow waves a calming hand and my fellow calms himself. One leads; one follows. One fellow says where he is going and the other, like a puppy, hopes to show the way just half a step ahead and always looking back. A cross word is like betrayal."

"My fellow is a man of violence."

"What? He does not hit you? Surely. Not you."

"Oh no, I'd murder him. I would. I'd cut his throat in bed. And I haven't even ever seen him hit anyone. He holds it close. He seems to treasure it, this strange knowledge that he's killed people for no good reason and he could do it again. But this knowledge breaks out in sharp flashes sometimes."

"Oh?"

"Yes;" Victoria said; "it flashes from his eyes. I've always thought it was a weakness in him, but to men it looks like strength. You know that dirty little medal that he wears? You know it's for his wounds, because he was hurt in battle?"

"Yes, I thought;" Diotoma answered; "but that is an honest thing. There are good purposes for such a thing."

"I'm sure there are, but what I mean is this: Other freaks – guys I mean – sometimes they sneer at it. Sometimes they make a joke as though he was stupid being in a war. But all he does is flash this look and they shut up. Sometimes they kind of slink away or else apologize. Oh my gods! I saw him take a swing one time! In Germany! He did. Some idiot came up close and touched his medal and sneered and so he flashed the look; the stupid bloke said something else and touched his nose. Can you imagine? Poked his nose! Phillip hauled back a fist and took a swing; the stupid sod just dodged and ran away. Can you imagine?"

"Yes. They are like that. Competing for the leadership. They admire a winner just for winning. I believe that even the most gentle men, like mine, have this in them with which to struggle. At least your Phillip is the kind who leads them best because he is himself. He does not vainly boast, but only truth. He speaks; they know it is a man who speaks."

"Are th

(lacuna)

s; that is the heart's desire. And – relating to the question now in hand – it is a beauty women give to men, this recognition and acceptance of yourself in all. Left to themselves, men provoke each other into warlike brutes. And what they lust for most is that which sometimes strangely tames them. This seemed to her a most peculiar way to seek Divinity. But it did clearly show the sacred forest as a place of mating. All of these vast thoughts encompassed scarcely half a dozen breaths.

Victoria asked; "Well, are things different now than they were before? No. So I say, if it's up to me: The laws of Eleusis have not changed. The men may go if they are well prepared to see the truth. They take a different road, as they must, but still their destination is the same. And this is justice."

"Justice?" Diotoma asked.

Victoria held out her strong arms toward everything. "Yes, the truth which they must see is justice."

7: Episode Six:
The Beauty And The Beast

The babes in her were stirring to the trilling flute. The man who held her hand and followed in her steps was glaring like a hungry brute. A wolf's tight grin pulled back his lips to show his teeth; his posture had him creeping through some thicket underbrush somewhere. She held her steady hand that gripped his fist far out to shove him back. The moving circle where they danced was full of other folk but yet they nearly danced alone. Each of the lanterns in the horseshoe ring around them on the beach was flaring bright and yet no more resolved the forms of solid substance from the shifting shadows than a ring of softly glowing yellow flowers would have done. Just so the lanterns looked to those who chose to gaze into their flames because the night was all-absorbing.

He spoke to her, his voice quite lost in the rising and descending chant but visible on his snarling lips; "You have my son."

She answered loud; "Yes, and I shall keep this one."

He replied; "No, I will have him, you take her. I'll take him when he's finished sucking you."

Her final answer, by some chance, found an empty moment of the chanting voices so he heard it loud; "I'll send him to you if and when I wish, and if you're threatening me then you can fuck yourself. You damn philosopher king."

The moving circle took them round to the dark place where surf was washing on the sand so that a wave came up and pulled his limping foot from under him. He stumbled but her steady hand imparted balance and he stood and stepped again.

"I worship you!" he cried. "You are my luck!"

And, seeing he could say no more than that, seeing that was something he must think she'd think a gift, she promised; "If you're good enough you'll have the boy." And then, looking at some gleaming focal instant from some ancient tale that rose within her consciousness, and knowing clearly this would be a comfort to the man, she smiled and said; "If you're good enough I'll send him to you with six hundred men and horses I shall lend him."

Where were they now? It suddenly seemed to both of them that this was prophecy which echoed back or forward to them from a distant time. They realized that they had danced this ring on this same beach with these same folk before. He took the prophesy into his heart as treasure.

On the battlefield, amid the roiling dust that choked his breath and scratched his single eye with every blink, not far from there at all, a thunder of six hundred horses' hooves began to quake the ground beneath his feet.

He was crowded close within a tangled clump of singing warriors standing like a tiny island in a stormy sea, a sea which steadily ate away their bit of land, and he rejoiced in it. As the men in the front ranks fell, both friend and foe, the foe men strove to drag the bodies off so they could close their circle tight again. The band of singing brothers in the center of the press were ever pressing out and holding up their fighters in the front line from behind, dragging in their wounded if they could among the legs, letting go the dead then leaping up into their place to jab and fend with all the might which rage could conjure. Phillip counted seven of his men between him and the front; then would be his turn to kill again and die. At least there were no arrows and no spears as yet against them. He understood the desperate situation clearly and took fierce joy from his own wisdom in summoning them here.

But then a thunder rising from the Earth, far away at first, was surely coming near. He felt the fluid rippling power of the rocky land rise through his feet and legs to wash his armored guarded flaming heart. The prophecy that he had heard sometime on a different dancing ground than this would be fulfilled; and so a shuttered window of his heart shot out a ray of hope. He understood this for the first time then: this familiar awful and despairing warrior's praise of Lady Luck escaping from his throat, which he had taught his comrades from a dream, was nothing else except a hymn to Mother Demeter, Our Lady of the cut and winnowed grain. He understood that all these stalks of mortal flesh – of man or ever else that ripples in the wind – were nothing else except her barley. He understood that his salvation was the puzzling grace of one he scarcely knew and that he'd never reason out the reasons for the gifts she gave to him one time and then gave to another.

So let her beckon to her fertile perfumed bed whatever man or beast or god she chose and send away the rest. He could touch her but could not possess her nor command her nor could they.

Victoria saw a different vision.

8: Episode Seven: Priestess

First came the dazzling vision as a tall little girl in which a Shining Lady had emerged and smiled and touched her brow, from the verge of a waving field of golden grain even higher than her head. She was walking through that sunny day to arduous labor braiding straw for rope to bind the sheaves. And the Lady spoke a new name she should take: Victory. She stood and sucked her booboo fingers for a long while.

Then came the creased soft face of their eldest crone, nodding, smiling an open toothless smile that grew and opened out to beam the way a flower can sometimes, who had put aside the evening's spinning at her household fire to listen to the breathless tale. The girl had run the whole way there, excused by her mother from the cleaning of the supper dishes, Mommie's voice crying after through the dark; "Hurry, little 'un!" And there the old Matron of the Hearth had scrubbed her face and hands then led her in a thankful prayer. And so she gained another treasure: a place in that month's village ritual. The wide eyed and astonished child had simply stood beside the altar holding in her calloused hands a bowl of holy water, having been very sternly charged to stand up straight and utter not one sound, and yet to meanwhile look around herself from this new vantage point.

Her mother's death was there. On a narrow bed, the dying woman took her hand and took the husband's hand and bade the father deed this valuable strong healthy cheerful intelligent and even pretty daughter to the holy service which had chosen her. She bade him swear it and then sealed their bargain with a curse in case his resolution failed. Then the dying woman opened out her withered arms to hold the sobbing child against her bony breast until the end.

And then the years of lovely budding worship and the troublesome boys; it all came back.

The charming boy whom she first bedded begged her hand in marriage so unstintingly, with such maddening turns of wheedling and demand, that she grew tired of him entirely. She came to definitely understand that marriage would not do. And anyway, for a wealthy woman it might do to send the household servants scurrying while she took the hours to pray and rehearse and stitch her vestment gowns, then offer up the hymns on holidays. But a peasant girl with such a name as Victory apparently must choose. To be a wife, for her, would be too close to slavery. And then in fact, it came to pass; by the age of twenty-two her love affairs would dwindle down to brief and few, however earnestly she tried to wend the arts of fond delight. And though she yearned for pregnancy and seized on every opportunity to do the things that women do to gain it – and though her order's law most definitely encouraged it – still conception did not happen. Motherhood receded to the realms of fantasy and dream.

And yet there were the visions and the prayers and rituals and labor in enchanted fields and friends and books.

There came a vision of a drizzly day, herself with others, hoes upon their shoulders, walking out the Sacred Precinct's gate so that the sprouting fields glowing with Our Mother's bright fertility came into view. They broke into a joyful song.

She saw herself up on a platform built in a village square with all the townsfolk crowded round, she lifting up a basket from which an aged gentleman picked up a golden sickle which he raised up for the crowd to see. Our Mother's power flooded through the scene.

She saw herself and another girl toward whom she felt a deep affection strolling slowly on a moonlit beach with wavelets licking sensuously at their feet, discussing Archimedes' screw quite archly and the pregnant roundness of the Earth.

It came to seem at first as if this gentlest kind of temple priesthood, which quite agreed with her, would be a home of lasting peace. Those had been the lovely days of childhood happiness but as in any human life those days were all too few.

The Temple of Elfesis took her in the springtime of her mother's death – took her from her father and grandfather at the ritual of the scattering of her mother's burnt remains – highly recommended as she was, at thirteen years of age. That was the lowest limit by their law for one not born into the temple life.

She left behind, beside a lovely tumbling stream, an old stone shack that needed labor, high on a woody mountainside, the tanning of the pelts and salting of the fish and all of that, the little ones all set to spoons and needles or trusted with the eldest brother's whittling tasks. "There's two that I can set to it;" the brother might have said; "Grandpa learned em good!" And holy visions saved up for the darkest hours of the night. And all the hired labor she would do among the valley farms, now with her mother's babies growing by her knee, so that she'd sit there with the mothers at the cooking pots and basketry and there would come a man.

She'd catch some fellow's eye.

"My pretty Miss; if I may ask, where is your shawl?"

"I have no shawl as yet, good sir; I am legally virgin."

"But Miss; inform me please. I've watched all morning. This is your place to sit at pots and basketry and spindles and these babes are yours by all appearances and yet you are still called virgin? Why is that then? Don't your bright eyes turn your clear heart toward an able well set man like me?"

"Sir! I am an eldest orphan virgin sir, if that's your business. Eldest orphan virgins sit among the women for our cunning skills and heavy duties but we have not borne the heaviest burden yet. That is the true rule of law. And may you not ask silly questions next time when you speak to me."

The laughter of her listening friends, the good man's smiling pleasure.

But, thankfully or mournfully, none of that would ever be.

First came a simple meditation ritual the day she entered. Great beings came to open out her grief and cleanse her grief of anger and the innocent childish guilt; they seemed to promise future joys.

Then, all spring and summer, came examinations. They'd call her unexpectedly from the garden work (she being then exempted from the farms) or from her tutor's knee, or from the evening's fireside amusements, twice or thrice each week. Every holy vision she had ever seen must be recited to the frowning Company of Elders with the most intelligent discussion of the details that her swimming brain could weave. Every detail of the rites and tales that she had learned so far was probed and prodded to improve her depth of understanding, as they said. They firmly requested that she memorize her "most important" dreams for them to hear, whatever that might mean. Why do you suppose, dear child, the Lady touched your brow but not your knee? If you had to guess, why would you say the winter altar is adorned with fir but not with pine? What do you know about the Sacred Well, the one inside the cave? Why do you think a pomegranate appeared to you, and that boat with broken oars? And on and on.

Of course she did not understand as yet how carefully that first summer's stress was weighed out for this very promising girl. They must simulate the challenges of adulthood to some extent, along the particular path that her particular life might properly take, and not to do a bit of lasting hurt. Looking back, she would appreciate and try to emulate how carefully the women and men who were her childhood Elders weighed out their frowns and smiles and kisses and caresses to gently put her in a proper state for what would come with autumn: the Hall of Mysteries.

And that stupendous thing had done its work in her exactly as they wished. The afterglow of that first experience inside the Greater Mysteries would shine all through her girlish soul until adulthood truly drew her from those days. Each ear of barley was a miracle to her, each thunder storm the manifested voice of deities, each flame of lamp or hearth a doorway to infinity. Each childbirth where she merely wiped a sweating brow or bundled up the bloody towels or lent a sturdy shoulder for the lucky laboring one to walk about; this was Goddess giving immortality to our world. Each autumn in the Hall brought deeper revelation. Each increasing duty which they put upon her head was joy. They set her supervising this and that. They taught her how to heal then, even better, how to teach. They told her every secret that she learned a secret well enough to guess.

But then at length they set the tall girl something new: to tie the basket of the Sacred Pregnancy atop her head and lead the whole folk of Athens in their tumultuous parade up from their city to Elfesis. This was a promise which the Elders had carefully held up for her to grasp and now at last fulfilled. That day they told the task, her age then twenty-two, she stood for half an hour in the Sacred Precinct's entry court and gazed up at the twin tall stately statues of the Basket Priestess there.

But that was the autumn of the awful year when Phillipus the Barbarian had come from the west and taken Athens. And he had taken Athens with such a shocking and infuriating ease, in his onward march toward ever growing glory, that by that autumn the people stood uneasily upon the brink of bloody riot. And Phillipus was the sort of pious conqueror who must cement and sanctify his work by extorting blessings from every great temple in every land through which he tramped. Phillipus, resting in the occupied city, announced with haughty confidence he would attend the rite. He would do it properly, in the main at least, at least marching unarmed with the rest in the beggar's shirt as was required by written law even though the three weeks of carefully graded fast was reduced to just one morning's prayer; and other unwritten customs just as badly broken for His Honor's sake; and all of this a stupid transparent scheme to gain the city's acquiescence in his wars. So now the girl must step out of the peaceful sanctuary, gather up herself and be a woman of his warring world.

And another memory came to her dimly at first then seemed to open out: a dreadful earnest conversation in a small room. She felt herself descend into the place.

In fact this was the Elfesinian temple inside the walls of Athens, a small place her order kept there as an embassy so various things pertaining to Elfesis could be done in easy reach of city dwellers and foreign travelers. She had gone there on errands several times in recent years and twice had done the march from its starting point there. There was a small beautifully decorated very quiet sanctuary. There was a narrow courtyard with a pomegranate tree and, on the sanctuary's small porch that overlooked the yard, a lovely sculptured painted altar where people often came with hats in hand to make their thankful offerings. They would then often spread a cloth beneath the tree to have a solemn picnic on the grass. There were a few store rooms and work rooms and modest living quarters where the small resident staff and frequent visitors from the Sacred Precinct like herself would stay. And there was a tall protecting wall to shield this cozy refuge from the teaming city and the even larger world around.

The small young matron with whom she was talking so very earnestly showed every sign of struggling against some mighty shock. Victory pulled the woman in and leaned against the door to press it shut and dropped the latch. They ought to sit but the woman's pacing wouldn't stop. In the light beaming through the bedroom's one high window, from the dusty afternoon beyond, the small young lady's handsome face, no doubt accustomed to calm dignity, was animated with dread for a moment then would freeze into a blank stare. She was as pale as someone in a faint. Her words would burst out in a tumbling rush and stop. She had staggered in at their gate, hanging weakly on the arm of a worried and bewildered citizen who had volunteered his aid along the way, she crying; "I must speak with Mistress Elfesinia at once!"

Now to every question she was only answering; "Oh no! Oh, why?"

She knew the small woman, or who she was at least, from the prior year. There was an annual delivery of certain objects, a ceremonial procession by visiting Elfesinians in lovely dress into the Agrai Temple's treasury chamber. Victory was sent along last year as an observing member of the delegation, given a certain small enameled antique box on a purple cushion to carry in. She and this woman had exchanged polite inquiring smiles, assessing one another.

The delicate pretty hands made frantic birdlike gestures then would subside to wringing. In this little room she paced about a space no more than three steps wide. She wore a fine white clerical gown and a shawl which had been properly wrapped about but now had fallen loose from the expensive lapis brooch which dangled from its open pin. Many long wisps of hair had escaped her matron's bun, probably all tugged loose by her own fingers which often reached to fret with it.

In fact this was the autumn afternoon before the fearful day when Victoria must speak her final prayers for aid in the lovely quiet sanctuary and then tie the basket on her head and take a young man's hand and stride out regally to lead the shouting singing throng. In fact this priestess who had fled to her was Matron of the Agrai Temple by the river just inside the city walls where all new aspirants for the great initiation must present themselves for cleansing and instruction each preceding February. In fact the whole crystalline process of the rite seemed fractured now already; the proper sequence of the thing stood twisted like some wizened tree for mere convenience of this conqueror Phillipus of the Macedons. He, alone of anyone in memory, had been admitted to a special private cleansing just one day before the march. There was no written clause of law to stop his mad desire. There was no military force then under arms to challenge him.

The small woman's pacing brought her into reach and Victoria grasped her shoulders firmly, gave a hard shake to wake her. She spoke loudly; "You are Matron Diotoma of Agrai Temple!"

The small woman trembled, nearly stumbled, but then stared up into her eyes. "I am."

Hoping that the woman had been brought into herself at last, Victory pulled the shawl properly about her shoulders and fastened the expensive pin. She demanded; "Now please tell me what has happened." It would be the sort of news her Elders had been fearing.

"The Barbarian. Something horrible happened at the cleansing." She was standing still at last but cast glances all about as if there might be spies in every corner. She put her hand to her lips but then removed it. She spoke with a startling flat calm as though about tomorrow's marketing; "Swear you won't tell anyone or else the city will go up in flames. Swear it."

Appalled, her empty fasting stomach falling through the floor, Victory made a hasty oath. She'd tell no one for a month at least except her Elders and the trustiest companions here, however might seem needed.

The woman shook her head as though in disbelief. "It's not against the law for them to touch you. Heavens no. When you lift the towel off their face and they see a human face for the first time, after everywhere they've been, they'll often want to hold your hand for a moment. That happens all the time." She paused. "My hands get sore in fact." She wrung her hands again and paused again and seemed to be subsiding into dream. "Or they'll reach up and touch your cheek." The stunned lady touched her cheek.

She was beautiful and the Barbarian was famous as a womanizer with a special appetite for priestesses; he'd even married one to be his queen.

"Oh dear Mother!" Victory whispered through clenched teeth. "What did he do?"

The Matron gently pressed her bosom. "And the children sometimes really need to touch the breast. Naturally I don't mind that. It is an honor, really, and I don't mind that at all. Sometimes – the cripples and the dear simpletons especially – they're so close to holy things – they'll kiss my hand." She held up her hands to gaze at them.

"Oh dear Mother! What? What did he do?"

"You look into their eyes of course. You understand?"

"Yes. Yes, yes, I can imagine."

"You're mainly looking for a certain kind of sparkling water look of course. For real cleanliness with a certain power in it. You understand."

"I guess so. Please! Go on!"

"Sometimes you see the spirits haven't finished with them yet but you thought they were done because they're resting."

"Please!"

"I have some little prayers for that, when that happens, and I'll just put the towel back." She absently pantomimed. Clearly she had been so overwhelmed in the midst of spiritual work that she had not entirely returned to the physical sphere.

"Matron!"

"You understand?"

Victory seized her shoulders again and shook. That
worked before. "For my sake Honored Matron! For the deities
both of us serve – for the whole world's sake dear lady . . .
Spit it out! For Our Mother's and Sister's sake now; spit it out!
Did the Barbarian rape . . . someone? Or did he strike you?"

To rape a priestess was unthinkable offense and there had
been no case of it in Athens since three hundred years before.
For a man to even strike a serving clergywoman likely would
bring death, surely banishment at least, without some
astonishing defense. All such felonies were classed as
desecration and desecration was the vilest kind of treason to
a city state which knew its fate depended on the gods. For a
foreigner, any foreigner, to assault an active priestess –
perhaps some blundering sailor in his cups imagining he'd
found a whore – would raise a cry for war among the citizens.
And here it was a hated tyrant. And there this woman had
been in the very purest act of ministry.

In answer to her question, Diotoma only stared up in
her face again.

So now Victory desperately tried to gather up her
thoughts. The earnest conversations with the Elders for this
sort of thing, the hours of prayer and song to have this holy
thing progress in proper peace; these came boiling to her mind
as if she had to do them all again. She found herself quite dizzy
from the sudden awful tension stirred into her fast, but
struggled to make sense of the event, tried to see her own task
within the steaming brew.

She thought: Athens very likely would rise in rebellion
and get burnt for it. He might declare them all enemies and
devastate the countryside as well. But then, keeping it a secret
would mean letting Phillipus do the march, postponing
confrontation till she brought him to the gate. Being there at
hand, the Sacred Precinct would then feel his wrath. She would
secretly send word ahead of course. Evacuation? That seemed

to be some hope. So which of the ghastly choices would be better; thwart the man immediately or later? What should she do? Would it violate some sacred law for her to let the city burn? Maybe not. But anyway, she had just now precipitously sworn an oath to hush the dreadful scandal up. Her lips were sealed.

And yet he must be stopped. The presence of a felon with such a crime as this hanging on his soul tomorrow night in the Hall of Mysteries would bring disaster to the human world. The man had assaulted an unoffending priestess while she ministered his needs as part of the same holy ritual in which he then took part. The gate of Elfesis might swing shut forever. Victory could almost hear an echo of the creaking hinges now. The shadow of a fevered scheme rose to her mind: assassination. Do it in a secret place then send a cry for the citizens to form up their battalions before the foreign garrison had got the news. He must disarm to make the march or else she could point to her book and forbid him on that ground. There was his appetite for priestesses. A stealthy team of enemies along the way; she'd lure him with erotic hints to where they waited.

Oh gods! The man was not an idiot. She'd better conjure up a plan to actually fuck him just a little once or twice along the way, with prearranged but seemingly unwanted surprising interruptions; thus the final lure to the secluded grove or gully or goat shed far from the crowded road would gain his willing trust. Intercourse would violate her fast of course but for a person of her rank such small concerns were optional. But yet she must be lusty, actually feeling bodily arousal in the act and then frustration in surprise, to make the thing convincing; she must lean back against some tree in his embrace and pull her sacred garment up and wrap one leg around his waist and arouse his manhood with her hands and with her open swelling sacred moistening flesh and smile into his one-eyed face while doing it. She must find him beautiful. But she could summon Kore for that work all right. Kore would find him beautiful all right and grin very lustily at such a willing royal sacrifice and give her special fiery blessing.

Or could she simply go to him today for some convincing reason, draw him to a couch merely as a willing woman, perform whatever act the situation might demand, and promise more tomorrow? Perhaps.

But either way, could she lead the march as Kore's priestess instead of Our Mother's? Or, really, with such a plan afoot she would be suffused with Kore, be that awesome thing herself in person. Could she? Yes. That would be proper if done for proper purposes.

But an assault along the march was desecration in itself even if it could be all arranged in time without publishing the outrage to rally up a team. But there would be no desecration if he came away from the march to a really distant ambush voluntarily. But then she thought of blood gushing out to stain the sacred shirt of an aspirant to Elfesinian initiation, even an improper one. She suddenly realized that no Hellene except a priest or priestess of her order or else the marshal of the march or marshal's men upon the marshal's order would ever dare to harm him in the costume of the holy tramp, even if it were in fact a forgery. She thought of pulling off his shirt before the cuts were made, her official ritual rejection, encouraging the killers. She thought: How could she get the sacred garment up off of his head and arms? He would surely be aware of its protection. Perhaps she'd be leaning back against the tree with him already in her; then a pause when she demands to pull his garment off, persuading at his manhood with her cunny; then the killers pounce. Thinking this, she spoke aloud; "Sister Kore, give me strength." Was she going mad?

A random hope: what if she had his child? Promising to breed him; some bargain to peacefully dissuade him from attempting this disaster. Salve his pride and offer compensation. Would he see that as sufficient blessing by Elfesis on his work? Surely not; Phillipus had a son he loved already; Alexander, his brigadier of cavalry, child of a priestess in his own barbarous land. And him begot in holy ritual.

Well, could she murder him herself, take the dire responsibility onto her head? She might be banished from the Sacred Precinct for a term of years or for her Earthly life, in proper balance for the necessary desecration. She might be forced to flee or forced to death by the great Barbarian's friends. She might wander far, sleep in dusty corners, sell herself for any use to any bidder, starve alone. But her initiation in Our Mother could not be wrested from her soul by any power ever without her own rejection of its terms and the Company of Elders in Paradise would surely welcome a faithful daughter regardless of the Earthly circumstance.

So she was willing. But how? A simple knife thrust in the back? Impossible; Phillipus was a famous duelist. Poison? Utterly unlikely; he'd be drinking from the public jugs. Fuck him till he dozed then cut his throat? An hour at least; how would she find the time among her duties?

The scheme was crumbling.

At last she spoke to Diotoma; "Could we cook up a lie, some other reason why he can't go? But no, that serves no purpose; the thing is to make Phillipus accept his rejection, not the citizens. But he might accept divine authority if we can prove it with a book. He must be stopped."

But Diotoma, now leaning heavily in Victory's arms with a hand up on her sturdy shoulder, sighed heavily and said; "Dear Mistress; don't you understand? My temple's law does not reject him."

"What!"

She sighed again; "Oh my dear, may we please sit and rest?"

So, apologizing most sincerely, Victory helped the woman lie in the cot. Her body curled up like a baby's.

Victory sat by on the floor, breathed deeply for a while until at least a bit of calm emerged, and finally begged for a fuller explanation of the horrid incident.

Lying there, looking toward the window, one hand as a pillow and the other listlessly fingering her hair, Diotoma spoke slowly; "It was on the river bank. That's where we always do the cleansing. Only him this time, lying on a white ram's skin of course, because he is a soldier, where there's always at least a hundred. My husband and I – he's our high priest – we were watching from the porch. It took an hour. Not surprising. Ah; why?" She paused. She resumed; "We were reading clouds. I saw a running wolf take shape just above and then, just then, Dionysos whispered to us both that it was done. Even though I plainly saw there was no peace upon the man. And yet, of course, obedient to the god, I went and knelt beside him and lifted off the towel. Oh why!" She pressed her hand to her eyes.

"What did you see?" Victory asked.

"That look in his eye! That one staring eye!"

"What did you see?"

"A wolf."

"Not the kind of sparkling water cleanliness your law requires?"

"That is not our law. Our law says the look of the aspirant must be pure and divine, not sparkling. It was purely divine! But stealthy, running, hungry. Not Divinity in any shape that I have ever seen before! And so our law does not forbid him."

"You said he struck you!"

"No. He did not strike me. He did not . . . assault me. If he had forced me, dear Mistress, I would not be here. You may be entirely sure; I would have gone before our altar at once and cut my wrists. What other way would be in my power to give undeniable testimony against a conqueror? No. A moment later, yes, I lost my balance and I fell; I nearly fainted from that look and, with that, from what he did; but he did not strike me. No."

"What did he do!" Victory well and truly shouted.

"His eye came open. He looked at my face, darting that hungry look about my face, and in the next instant he sprang up and knelt beside me and embraced me and . . . and . . ." She lost the words or else the wish to speak them, but pressed her hand here and there upon her bosom.

"By the gods, he started feeling you up!"

She nodded slowly, slowly reached to touch her neck, behind her ear, her cheek, her lips. "He . . ."

"He started kissing you."

Once again she nodded, then she pressed her fingers in the center of her lap.

"He touched your Aphrodite grove."

"Yes! Why did he do it? I fell. My husband, he came running. He pulled me up and held me. I had nearly fainted. Phillipus, he got up and walked away, saying nothing. Why? What was it for? Has the god betrayed me?"

"No! Lady, pull yourself together!"

For a moment Victory certainly wanted to cry out something much more harsh than that. The little lady swooned because some stranger grabbed her tits and made as if to stick a finger in her cunny. And the woman ran a Dionysos temple! If she ever had to dance the Dionysos Revels at a country town she'd die. And from this overwrought reaction Victory herself had flown into a fantasy of murder. But in a heartbeat more of course she saw that this was nothing but her own overwrought emotions finding a release; in fact the thing was absolutely out of place. The man had gone very close to assaulting a clergywoman in the purest act of ministry and tomorrow he would seek initiation in the Hall of Mysteries. It was improper. Not a felony perhaps but certainly improper to the grossest degree. And the woman's shocked reaction was not some stupid vapid city modesty at all, or only partly that; part of her soul had been dislocated between the spheres.

Victory took a deep breath to further calm herself and spoke; "Honored Matron, pull yourself together. Please. The bastard's a barbarian so try not to take it personally. But tell me; surely this disqualifies him from the march?"

Finally gathering herself enough to sit up on the cot with one leg folded underneath, smoothing out her clothes a bit and thinking carefully for a long moment more, Diotoma finally shook her head. "Not by our law. My husband searched the book. It is legal for the aspirant to touch. And I must testify he had a look which was purely divine."

"Arrrg!" Victory cried. She grabbed two handfuls of her hair and yanked to vent the dire frustration. "The son of a mule!" She didn't want him on the march. Everything she'd thought about disaster still was true but even worse. So what if the Earthly gate of Elfesis closed forever? That seemed like little turnips now. A wolf! He musn't go or musn't get there. The whole procedure of the rite was to take mortal humans into the manifested presence of all Earthly life and death, not take a being who was imbued with some conflicting immortality already. He would bring his war. He'd conjure up some phalanx of ghostly spearmen. He might burn down the Sacred Precinct on the hill in Paradise where it really stood.

Victory shook her head. But then she shook it hard. Shit; something happened. Reality seemed to shift and suddenly the awful nonsense of the minutes past came into focus. Murder! Revolution! Was she crazy from the fast? She must be! She hadn't had a solid meal in what; a week? She leaned forward, put her elbows on her knees and pressed her face into her hands and pressed her fingertips quite hard onto her closed eyes to see the little spirits dance. Still looking at the little dancing insect spirit things just for a moment's relaxation, discovering once again that this was even a little bit of entertainment too, she sighed very deeply to release the tension. She needed a massage. Really; a good massage. With warm perfumed oil, lots of it. What scent? Toasted poppy seed! No, Egyptian roses. Yes! In fact, under a blooming arbor of Egyptian roses. Done by some athletic mature gentleman with a nice smile.

Then she said; "For goodness sake, I'll take the fellow along and if he doesn't do anything outrageous, and if he looks all right, then when we get there we'll let him in. That's all. Let the gods decide. Tell you what; I'll pray hard. I'll ask them to speak."

"Can you reject him on the march?"

"Well, yes; it never happens but I have that power." If she had to, if it were divine command, she would certainly find some means to kill him. If nothing else, she could incite the mob. Well! That was simple! Why hadn't she thought of that before? Because it was a really really bad idea; a bloody riot on the march. Shut up! she told herself. She took her fist and banged it on her head. And those lurid fantasies about this ugly king! Thinking now, she almost blushed at her stupidity; it seemed as if she were some randy little snip instead of the queen whom they had sent her out to be. Well, she thought, in her own defense, how long had it been since she had a man? Not since the springtime revels, and he was drunk. Aloud, she said; "I'm going crazy."

"What!" Diotoma cried in real alarm.

"Oh, nothing. No, really; it's just my fast. My head is spinning. I'm hardly in a proper state to make these big decisions. Let the gods decide. We have a ritual this evening where we pray for guidance. Then afterward I can set the apprentices to it. I'll have them go on chopping at it all night long but I have got to sleep. I'll watch my dreams. I'm going to eat."

But Diotoma was not a bit relaxed. She reached and found Victory's forearm, grasped it very hard. "My husband has gone out seeking certain friends. He is respected. He is in the Comrades of Heracles, Chief Cowherd you know. He says if you decide to bar him from the march, then he – I mean my husband – he will raise a company of worthy citizens to stand guard here at this temple. He is respected. If the Macedons attack the embassy of Elfesis, then there must be a fight. There must! True Athenians must stand! Or else the city will earn eternal shame. If the city burns, he says, the reasons must be clear."

"Oh no! He musn't do that! Everything will be all right. The gods protect us!"

"Mistress Elfesinia . . ."

"Please; we are sisters. My name is Victory."

"Oh! Victory! Such a name is such an omen!"

"No! There will not be a fight. You must make sure your husband knows: a battle tomorrow would be desecration. I'll take the fellow along and see what happens."

"But you will seek guidance first!"

"Of course! Yes; this evening's ritual. And I'll set the apprentices to praying all night long and I will watch my dreams."

"I and my husband and our people will watch the sky. We will watch in turns, at least two awake all night."

"Yes, I'm sure that's fine. But please have faith in those who guide us and protect us. I will set out from here at start of noon, of course, just as I should. Please let there be peace at least till then. Let there be peace at least till then."

"May our senior temple staff begin the march from here?"

"Yes certainly."

"Victory, may we walk with you tomorrow?"

"Diotoma, I would be honored."

"Victory, I admire your courage."

"What? Why? What are you thinking?" And Victory found her new friend staring at her rather in surprise to be not understood. Victory asked again; "What are you thinking?"

"Oh. Didn't you know? Haven't you seen it? Didn't I say it? Well, dear, the Barbarian. Once he sees you, I am very sure – I have this from my daughter; my daughter went to our altar immediately and prayed for understanding; she saw it clearly in a flash and it is so perfectly obvious anyway – the Barbarian will go after you."

"What!"

That night she hardly knew her dreams from restless waking thoughts and then, when the morning's light startled her awake, could scarcely tell if she had slept at all. Those fevered fantasies of sex and murder seemed to haunt the room. Had they been mere phantoms of delusion as she hoped or else a solemn inspiration from the gods? The fast which had so dazed her, after all, was dedicated to the powers who inspired the rite. And the dire warning of the threat to Elfesis – that the Earthly gate might shut or even that the Precinct on its hill in Paradise might fall – was that merely some ghastly misunderstanding of reality on her part; or was it real?

The evening ritual had only given everyone a firm conviction that the rite must be done, that its blessings were, as always, quite essential to the human world. She quizzed them but that's all she got. She had not confided to anyone about the outrage so they all simply, in their bland naiveté, accepted the ritual's thick palpable radiant atmosphere as just one more thing of awesome beauty.

And then the only strong clear consistent thing that she had seen all night had been a little square of parchment with some words and pictures on it, repeatedly folding up then drifting from her hand. It drifted off to westward every time.

She relieved herself and washed – as usual a slightly messy business after resuming a solid diet as she had the day before – scrubbed her face especially hard, and stumbled to the kitchen, realized that she had not combed her hair nor changed out of her rumpled nightdress, but nonetheless slumped to the nearest chair and accidentally farted. She leaned her head down in her hands. While stumbling in, her bleary eyes had told her that the room was empty – it nearly was – and so she went ahead and let another one. Oh well.

Cook came over extremely quietly to set a bowl of porridge and a cup of milk before her, also their nicest sort of embroidered napkin and the best bejeweled silver spoon they had.

She had perhaps till noon to figure out the interlocking riddles of what to do. The table top was hard on her elbows. She eventually discovered that her eyes were shut inside her hands.

"Mistress!"

The world unaccountably came into focus much more slowly than it startled; she had to rub her eyes and cheeks. Here was a young apprentice, a beaming boy, seated there across the table.

Looking at the glowing face, she thought; Which one are you? So she pinched her lower lip and tugged it out and twisted left and right; that often helped. Let's see; fifteen, entered the temple last winter, scheduled for the Hall tonight. Yes. Quite intent and earnest to show a job well done; happy at discovering kindness; good at arithmetic; sharp eyed as a hawk about people; but also absent minded as a . . . as a what? Preoccupied with unspoken thoughts. In love with her lately. She doodled her lips with a fingertip. A frog? No, that was silly. A frog is not remarkably absent minded. Absent minded as a . . . mouse? Hmm. But anyway he looked more like some kind of fish.

The beaming lad was overjoyed; of all the places in the world, she had chosen to sit right here with him. And now she was even studying his face.

From her spoon, held in her other hand, porridge dripped to the table.

"Yes?" she finally answered.

"Today!" he cried, as chirpy as a bird.

"Huh?" She felt an itch and scratched her head. "What? Today?" Suddenly she realized a hair was drifting from her fingers through the air, westward toward the door.

"Yes! Today! We're going home. You know, the Hall of Mysteries."

"Ah." The hair had quickly disappeared. She closed her mouth. She looked at the boy and nodded but could not smile. "Yes, believe me . . ." his name refused to come to mind ". . . I do know."

So then, awed by his beloved's depth of wisdom and her consequent solemn mood, this lad of fifteen years fell silent. And yet he soon took up squirming with his erotic yearning for a chat.

So she vaguely wondered how to start him going, what to ask. She must ask for results from last night's vigil, maybe with some reasonable hope of hearing something useful from this thoughtful lad, but some light idle chatter would certainly be the best to start, considering her own distracted state. If this were one of the others then she might have delicately inquired into their dabblings in the pools of Eros; but this one was in love with her. Meanwhile she found the spoon in her other hand and started in upon the food, slowly and uncertainly at first. There were raisins in the porridge, and some honey.

"Well;" she finally mumbled around a mouthful; "where's all the rest? I guess it's late. Phaedrus?" Yes, that was it.

"Oh yes ma'am! They've all gone to the garden prayers. I was helping Cook. So I get all the food that's left!"

Cook's gruff voice, quite like the peasant wife she once had been, came rumbling from the back; "Good one too, Mistress, this one is!"

Now quite delighted with this recommendation to his lady, the boy started in cheerfully waving his spoon here and there, chattering about the different foods that he and each of the other boys and girls liked best and why each person did. In truth the variety of his diet had considerably improved since entering the temple and his better humor was in part a consequence of it.

She shrugged a couple of times at first but then decided that was probably a poor choice of gesture to keep him going; she took up slowly nodding between the mouthfuls of the sweet sticky wettened stuff instead. "Uh huh . . . good . . . good." But the bottom of her bowl appeared quite suddenly and unexpectedly. Feeling disappointed with this turn, she waved to Cook and vaguely gestured for another. But then she had a thought and called, holding up two fingers; "Two apples also please. Two apples."

The food was brought immediately. She polished up one apple with her napkin, gave it to the lad and felt invigorated by the renewal of his beaming grin. She had to smile when he embraced it to his bosom, making the smile as beneficent as she could rather than amused.

"My dear boy, weren't you praying all night?"

He leaned his head in adoration. "Yes Mistress; it was wonderful."

She thought; Why on Earth are you so cheerful? She finally took a big crunchy bite of her shiny yellow fruit. Trying not to spit, she shook a finger at the boy and spoke quite emphatically; "Phaedrus, you must get a nap this morning. You must."

"Yes ma'am."

"And the others too."

"Yes ma'am."

"And if anybody asks, you tell them I said so."

"Yes ma'am."

"So all right now, what happened?"

"Oh, it was beautiful!" he chirped again.

"Wait." A thought had taken shape. At this point in her life that seemed remarkable in itself. "What . . . uh." She held up an open hand. What was the thought? Oh; this chirping boy of course. "What is that story about a little bird? The lady gives this bird a lock of her hair to take to her lover as a token. What is that story?"

The boy's jaw fell open. He didn't speak.

"Look;" Victory said; "don't worry. I don't seem to know it either."

"Mistress." He was whispering with wide eyes. "About last night."

"Yes?"

"A little bird flew out from the temple. That's what was so beautiful. It glittered every color like a bug."

"Oh?"

"We all saw it. It was really there. It had a leaf in its beak though, not some hair."

"Oh?" Now she bent close to him and grasped his hand on the table top. She turned her head somewhat to listen with her left ear mostly. "Please be very careful;" she held up a cautionary finger; "be exact. What did you see? What did you hear? Were there any smells?"

"Roses!"

"Roses? Oh!" Oh no. That idle momentary thought of the afternoon before flashed back to mind; an extremely sensual and satisfactory encounter for a change. Some athletic mature gentleman she had said to herself at the moment, with the picture so alive that she had actually thought it into well formed words. Now she saw the man of that momentary thought again more clearly; amid the close cropped hair and beard with starting streaks of gray, his face was ugly with a puckered sunken scar in place of a right eye. Lost to a spear, people said. Yes, it was Phillipus. Victory had not seen the king in the flesh as yet; she had come to Athens on this trip only just a week before and then had stayed secluded in accordance with the custom of the rite. But now she understood that she had seen his soul. And by the gods, his smile was nice.

"What else?" she asked the boy.

"Oh. Well. Well." He tugged his ear. "Well." He chewed a fingertip. "Uh." He chewed a different fingertip, gave it up and bit his lower lip. She was about to suggest he try pinching and twisting his lip instead but then he blurted out; "Oh, well, I'm the one who chased the little bird out to the courtyard to see where it would go!" And of course he pointed vaguely west. Somewhere over there lay Phillipus' country.

Phaedrus stopped, thought, nodded, smiled in satisfaction with his recitation.

She said; "I see that you are doing very well. I see that."

"I am?"

"Yes you are. But now I need to know what else there was about this incident last night."

"Please Mistress!" he suddenly cried. "What do you want to know?"

"Oh, well, you see;" Victory answered; "all I need to know is just whatever were the important details. That's all. Just please tell only the important details, all of them." And now she shrugged deliberately.

Of course that suggestion might seem impossibly vague but she was very fondly hoping the apprentice could respond to it. That was the very truest way to explain the art of reading omens. If this student came to understand its central secret now – and especially if he instinctively felt that he had gotten hold of a big thing by the scruff of its neck – then no more actual instruction in that art would be required, only the helpful hints and rules of thumb. And this child had already, in some way that she did not recall, impressed someone on the senior staff, at some time, as having a good ability at reading people, enough to make it part of his verbal dossier the senior staff were building. That ability at reading people usually sprang from the same inborn type of the gift of divine inspiration as did the art of omen reading. So she felt optimistic for him. And surely it would be a great reward to her and to her order if he could take this art all fresh and new into the Hall of Mysteries tonight.

And he did respond extremely well without equivocation. He said at once, "Oh, I thought the color of the leaf meant something."

"Yes? The leaf in the bird's beak? What color?"

"Just like parchment."

"Yes! You are doing well!"

"I am! And the music!"

"What music did you hear?"

"It was the Little Mermaid Hymn! But I haven't heard it like that before." His voice fell at once into an unaccustomed silken softness and his eyes wandered round as the sound returned, faint to her but clear to him. "I've never heard that tree in there before."

"A tree? In the Little Mermaid Hymn?"

"Yes. From the needles. It was a fir. Rustling. Like somebody was shaking it. Ooh." The ending exclamation was a tiny mousy squeak. He put his hand to his mouth and spoke behind it but was looking straight into her eyes with the real immortal gleam of Eros shining deep in his. "There were lovers standing at the tree. You know."

"Yes, I understand."

"And just the one other thing; one other thing was important, I thought."

"What's that?"

"The little bird. It was sitting on Our Sister's hand."

"On the Lady Kore's statue?"

"Yes, it was sitting on her hand before it flew."

"Ah! Well!" she cried. "My good boy! My very good boy!" She was nodding and reaching out a hand to touch a lock of hair upon his cheek. His hand went up to touch her hand. In fact, she was gazing on his face with a mother's deep affection. "Yes, that's what I need to know."

"Mistress?"

"Yes?"

"That was important, wasn't it?"

"It was indeed."

And now the boy stood up and began to shift on his feet.

"What's wrong?" she asked.

"I don't know, Mistress." And yet a joy replaced his puzzlement. "It just feels like I ought to go somewhere."

"Yes you shall. I'd like to send you on an errand in the city. Can you find your way around here?"

"Yes ma'am! I was born here. I am Athenian!"

"Very splendid! Can you do without that nap this morning?"

"Yes ma'am! I'm sure I can!"

"All right then, you're to take a note to someone. You will be my little winging bird. It's to King Phillipus of the Macedons, somewhere in the city." The boy made a startled cry and so she reached to place a finger on his lips. "First fetch a pen and ink and such, and a bit of parchment just the same size as the leaf the bird was carrying."

"Yes ma'am!" He vanished in a wink.

There scarcely was the time for her to gobble down the second bowl of porridge and finish off the little pool of milk it left then sit in hopeful contemplation just a bit when the boy came rushing back. He had a little box of writing things and placed it very carefully on the table.

"Well done my child. The beings who protect us are at work. Now go put on your beggar's shirt."

"My beggar's shirt? Already!"

"Yes. You see, I want to make it completely clear to this king that you're on a sacred errand from Mistress Elfesinia." She thought how much to tell him, not to put the boy in danger, but she must. "And yet you are so young that no one will suspect you are my spy."

"Oooh!"

She pressed the silencing finger to his lips again. She fell to whispering; "You must have your eyes and ears and nose open and really see and hear and smell all the important details at his house. Can you do that? I think I need to know what he's going to do today on the march. And see how he responds to the note."

"Yes ma'am!"

"So go put on your shirt!"

He vanished once again.

Now what to write? She did not even know the import of the message let alone the words. Without being asked, Cook came with a cup of water and went away again. And so she wetted down the ink then sharpened up the pen then finally dipped it, then held it poised and simply spoke aloud: "Sister Kore, come to me."

The pen dashed here and there at once, jotting and splashing on the little page. Scarcely two heartbeats and it was still. She laid the pen down.

Cook came creeping up behind, surprising her from concentration. The woman leaned down beside her shoulder.

"Do you read?" Victory asked.

"No, Mistress, but may I see the shapes it made?"

"Definitely." She held it up for the woman to peer at, very careful to hold it flat of course until the ink was dry. "What do you see?"

She pointed at a group of letters. "Well here, Mistress; here's a wolf."

"Yes?"

"And back over here, that's our own blessed hill of Elfesis and this road goes to it. Here's the farms along the way and here's the beach."

"Yes?"

"And this over here, that's a tree."

"I see."

"But maybe then again, the tree's a woman. That's all I see."

So Victory now quite peered at the splotchy irregular lines of tiny lettering and read aloud; "There is a grove that hides a stream. If the beggar king can truly beg and truly rule a special blessing can be made."

9: Episode Seven Point Five: Arithmetic

My dear reader, if I may – for I would not do it without your permission – I will here digress yet again to an earlier scene, although now, unlike before, just a few months earlier. I do apologize for any disorienting temporal distortion. And please let me assure you there is very good reason to include this episode here; it may help you understand the following and preceding Episodes because it very often occupies the thoughts of our young Phaedrus who is currently on his errand. But on the other hand, I cannot simply describe his thoughts for you because I want to give a larger view, something of a panorama. I want to conjure in your imagination a larger reality than that which Phaedrus carries in his memories concerning his adoption by the temple. A larger view? Well, at least different.

May I? This is a few months earlier than the preceding and following Episodes. May I set the scene?

Here is a bright afternoon half way down from noon to dusk, just past spring and certainly not summer yet. But it is warm enough. Here is the beach of pebbly sand where Elfesis Hill lies gently down into Elfesis Bay. There is a clear green gentle surf. And there are lots of humans.

There are a wide variety of them – ages, shapes and sizes – without exception naked as their day of birth – except for the straw hats and canvas sandals many wear, and the occasional towel across the shoulders – and all very glad that this first day of suitable water and weather has come again this year. In fact, Elfesis has officially declared a holiday. It is growing cool with the declining sun but none of them are keen to pack it in. These people are quite accustomed to weather from lifetimes outdoors.

Here a granny lady tiptoes out knee deep into the clear green sparkling gentle surf to help some youngsters toss a ball.

There a wife strokes her husband's hair. When he wakes, she suggests that he roll over so as not to burn.

A little group is walking round and calling, recruiting umpires and contestants to go out for yet another swimming race.

Over there a teenage boy, urged forward by his fellows, bows to a teenage girl who sits up on her blanket and accepts from him a flower. Her friends are laughing but they talk. Leaping up, she runs away out to the water.

There is a lot of young male prancing and young female glancing. Those who wish to kiss go hand in hand to seek the sanctuary of a conveniently located nearby sacred grove.

Up on the beach, up near where the hardy grass over tops it, really very happy with the soft breeze and clear light, gesturing with a big straw hat in her hands, the sandals untied and rather flopping as she walks, hair loose around her shoulders, Victory is strolling with a student, teaching.

The student is a senior apprentice, a young woman with red hair and freckles, eighteen, recently married, one of Victory's personal charges for a long time now, and they are friends. But the apprentice is speaking in deadly earnest. They are discussing agriculture, mainly how to manage sheep in a dry year. Victory is contributing general advice on the philosophy of farming.

Victory's eyes are flashing here and there. And there, ahead, she thinks she spots a recently admitted student whom her colleagues say requires attention. If memory serves, he needs a boost to get out of his shell. What is his name? She can't quite recall. Fifteen. There's talk of putting him in her care. But is this him? The poor child's back is toward her as they approach but this is definitely the skinny one. He's lacked a proper diet for awhile. But then the boy jumps very nimbly to catch a ball which she had thought was out of reach and when he throws she sees the profile of his tense determined face. It's him.

She stops. She gestures with a hand to halt the conversation.

The apprentice, the red head young woman, is startled to be halted in mid-sentence but shuts her mouth immediately. There's evidently something to be done. In the shadow of her big brimmed hat, curiosity lights in her eyes and she nods. She will observe.

And Victory calls, projecting her voice in the boy's direction; "My good lad!"

He turns. His jaw falls open. He's not accustomed to seeing females, outside of home and family, without clothes. He's not yet accustomed to the idea that all these people here are now his family. He is used to nudity himself, even in mixed company with strangers – for boys in this society are encouraged to parade their manliness – and even used to snide remarks about his poor physique, and used to gazing ruefully at shapes that he could never hope to touch outlined teasingly within the shifting flowing drapery women wear, and even used – by this time on this day – to not looking very deliberately indeed at these astonishing girls on this astonishing beach until he's absolutely forced to sneak a peek. And the stunning goddess of the place has summoned his attention!

The ball comes sailing back, clocks him in the head and bounces off. A look of vague annoyance briefly stirs his face but he keeps staring. Another boy runs up to fetch the ball and runs away.

She and her friend walk up to a proper speaking distance. He is small.

Normal decent courtesy, naturally, would have a person say "Yes Mistress?" or "Good afternoon ma'am" or make an equivalent gesture with the hand, or at least nod. He stares. He seems to be examining her left nipple.

Victory is not surprised of course. She tells him, "I have heard that you are very good with arithmetic."

He tries to say "oh, no" but only manages to mouth the words and bow his head while shifting his gaze to, approximately, her navel.

She smiles very pleasantly indeed and humorously shakes a finger at him and says, "That's what your mathematics instructor tells me."

In fact, word was that the boy had come in with a clear grasp of the fundamental methods of that skill and then shot through the memorization tasks. Arithmetic was said to be his tip top subject. But could she penetrate the daze of erotic loneliness for long enough to buck him up? Well, she thought, there was something that ought to work in this case.

The boy was finally speaking, blushing too but saying, "Well, yes, I guess. I'm good at that. I am." He was nodding with his eyes on her pubic region.

She began, speaking quickly and emphatically and a little loud to startle a bit; "Very good my friend! As you know, real humility is honest but false humility is not and it does make sense to be as honest as we can. You do know that! So this is quite excellent my friend! Now, just to start in with the figures, would you kindly tell me . . ." She poked out her chest, not too much at first, almost just as though to take a deeper breath, and made an almost normal gesture of the hand that actually definitely caught his attention and directed it to her own upper torso and her friend's as well. Then, as she began to speak again she stuck them out farther. ". . . what is two multiplied by two?"

His head bounced to left and right as if he had to count them several times.

To keep from bursting out with loud guffaws, the red head woman clapped both hands to her mouth but could not stop a high pitched squeaking giggle.

"Four!" he cried, and looked up to his teacher's eyes at last.

"Yes! And four times four?"

"Sixteen, and then two hundred fifty-six!"

"You are quite correct! And can you do two hundred fifty-six by two hundred fifty-six?" She hoped he could. Was this a risk?

His mouth made chewing motions. He was watching transformations in his mind's eye as the steps of the problem clicked. "Sixty-five thousand, five hundred and sixty-three."

"Ah, well, but look" she answered, and held up her breasts, "if we started out with two then the answer always is . . ."

"A female number?"

"Yes! And so, again, two hundred fifty-six multiplied by two hundred fifty-six . . ."

He turned the little pictures in his mind and saw an error in one of the boxes. He flatly stated, "Sixty-five thousand, five hundred and thirty-six."

"You are intelligent." Victory said.

"I am?"

Victory's apprentice nodded so the boy looked in her eyes too, and she told him, "Oh yes."

Then there was silence. He was looking inside himself now and inside his memories.

He turned away.

He turned back, even while he walked away, and said; "Good afternoon, Mistresses."

They watched him go and sit where boys and girls were looking out to watch the swimming race begin. One of the girls touched his knee, spoke to him and pointed out there. They saw him look out there and look at her and answer.

Victory's friend, who was her apprentice, whispered loudly, "What in the world did you do?"

"Shhh!" Victory took her arm and led away. But presently she answered, "I told a dirty joke."

"Dirty! That was dirty?"

"Wasn't it?"

"For Heaven's sake, Mistress, to be quite serious, if you are being serious, I was laughing because I put myself in his place. Or something. I think it was something like that. I'm sure it was."

"But that's you." Victory answered, "Why did he brighten up?"

"Oh of course. Hmmm . . . All right, tell me. I give up. Don't make me guess again. Really."

"Because a woman he wants to fuck told him a dirty joke. If they're strong enough, that gives them no end of confidence."

"Oh."

"Of course, if they're weak it's awful. Now what were you saying before?"

10: Episode Eight: King

Of course young Phaedrus was trembling with his great commission. And yet the confidence that his beloved had placed on his head tugged him upward so that, although he trembled, his feet scarcely touched the paving stones. He seemed to fly the whole way there, winging through the solemn air of a city very quietly awaiting Mystery or war.

In truth he was not entirely sure where he was going when he strode out through the Elfesis embassy temple gate – having heard of the residence of this Phillipus just one time a week before – and yet he found himself in scarcely half an hour's time standing at the door of a mansion just across the square from the great marble stairway of the Acropolis. Up there atop the broad stairs there stood a number of the burly armored Macedons all watching him. He felt quite sure that in this house there would be found their king.

And of course the boy had never been out in his sacred shirt before, never worn it at all except a single time last month at the ceremonial fitting. He had drawn some stares from people in the nearly empty streets along the way, further strengthening his confidence with pride so that, here now standing at the door, he firmly grasped the purse which hung from his belt, wherein the sacred parchment and the sacred apple had been tucked.

A very confident yank at the bell chain, a wait, another yank. A very tall and broad and proud butler came and pulled the door aside, his massive body really filling the narrow open space, and then glared down.

"Deliveries around back!" the butler commanded in a foreign slur, hooking his thumb toward the alley.

That made Phaedrus tremble again, of course, so he was surprised to hear the words rather trumpet from his lips quite loud; "Official temple business! Message from Mistress Elfesinia herself to King Phillipus!" Actually his voice had cracked at the end so "Phillipus" came out in a rusty screech. He cleared his throat, puffed out his chest again.

And then there was the dark shade of the spacious alcove just inside. A quarter hour wait. He found himself nearly dozing on his feet but sternly told himself that would not do and shook himself awake. Oh well, he'd use the time to study the art work here.

And with that thought, one particular sculpture suddenly irresistibly drew his attention; Heracles wrestling with the giant snake. After several moments of careful scrutiny he became quite sure this was an exact miniature replica of the big one on the pedestal at the city's main gymnasium. Then he felt compelled to take three paces back from the niche in the wall where the statuette stood; suddenly he saw it surrounded by the house and understood the oppressive atmosphere of this whole place. He realized that here was the same exact feeling that imbued the great gymnasium. The stupid boys who lorded in their petty power. The stupid men with their stupid blindness. And a particular memory rose up vividly: One of the teachers reciting a famous poem about this statue to the boys all standing in their ranks; all of the others oohing and aahing at its deep profundity while he alone stood there struggling not to laugh behind his hand. And so then of course the whistling rods had spoken the same simple-minded sort of verse upon his back.

So by the time the butler led him in to the sunny atrium where Phillipus sat at a small table, a scroll open in his hands, with half a dozen other men hovering about behind, young Phaedrus had found a new dignity that was rooted in his own experience and was therefore his own possession. He stepped right up before the king and, with nothing but an ordinary courteous salute, pulled the small square packet of the folded note from his purse and held it out. "From Mistress Elfesinia sir." That's all he said.

One of the men behind spoke up; "Your name, boy?"

"Phaedrus" he answered with scarce a glance at his fellow underling and without a "sir".

The one-eyed ugly king frowned at the bit of folded parchment and let Phaedrus wait, still holding it out. But his hand stayed steady.

There was suddenly, apparently, a mere flick of Phillipus' wrist and he had it. He held it up before his eye, turned it slowly once, began examining the seal. He laid the book he had been reading on the table and turned to give a silent glance toward one of the men behind him.

This fellow came and bowed from the waist, leaning down to examine the red wax stamp on the yellow parchment. This muscular fellow, alone in the crowd, wore along his tunic cuffs the embroidered insignia of a nobleman of Athens. "Looks right." he said.

Phillipus bade the man back to his place then held up the folded note between two fingers for all to see. He finally spoke to the lad; "What's in it?" His accent too was barbarian, stretched and slurred, scarcely Hellene at all.

"Sir, it is a note."

"Ha. You have a sense of humor boy. What does it say?"

"I don't know sir. Surely. I've only come to bring it. She did not ask for a reply."

"Hmm."

And all this seemed so far really little more than Phaedrus had seen before: a day his father took him along to learn their business, delivering a very big bill to a nobleman for some fancy boots their shop had made. There are polite ways to be rude and pushy. Could it be this easy?

Phillipus for a moment made as if to break the seal but then cast a look on Phaedrus again. "Won't do for you to stand;" he said with a dim suggestion of respect; "messenger from the temple. Have a seat." He pointed a forefinger firmly at another chair which was there opposite across the small square table.

The chair was large and heavy as little Phaedrus drew it out, its feet squeaking on the tiles. Climbing in, he realized that this too was meant to be humiliating; the chair was big enough to suit a champion wrestler. His toes just touched the floor. But on a sudden urge he chose to relax. He leaned back into the creaking leather. He even took up idly tapping fingertips on the chair's thick arms in the rhythm of the Little Mermaid Hymn. Exactly why? He wasn't sure. But then a glance up told him that this air of ease did seem to disconcert the king a tiny bit, just a tiny bit, invisibly perhaps.

Phillipus asked; "Are you the boy priest king of the parade today?"

"Oh no sir! Not me! I'm not even initiated yet. I'm just one of the Mistress' new apprentices."

"Ho ho!" Phillipus cried. For just an instant his mutilated face formed a lovely friendly smile that seemed quite genuine and warm. "Good lad." His face went serious again. And yet he said again, even giving a bit of a nod; "Yes, good lad."

And so then a few hot words blurted from the boy's heart before he even took the instant that he usually took to weigh his speech; "I am Athenian!"

Phillipus' friendly manner did not change in any visible way. The boy even thought he saw the king respond to this declaration by sincerely trying to open something deep inside himself.

"Yes, good Phaedrus;" Phillipus said with an air of deep thought; "I can see that. You are Athenian. And Pausanes here;" he hooked a thumb toward the men behind him, doubtless meant to indicate the fellow who had come and bowed to examine the seal; "he's your fellow citizen. Pausanes is a good man, a brave man, or else I wouldn't have him." He paused an instant but Phaedrus made no response. The king went on, spreading his hands wide; "He's honored himself by giving generous hospitality too; he's lent me his house here at no profit to himself."

No profit to himself? And the words even bore a tone of sincerity. But the lad only nodded. If that were sincere then he could certainly see the self-deceit in it.

"Son;" the king said, leaning forward as if turning confidential; "you're only an apprentice, I understand, but you are an apprentice of Elfesis." He waited for an answer.

"Yes sir."

"Are you planning to be a priest there, a real priest, for your whole life?"

All of the lad's fond yearnings rose from his heart and he found himself imitating the sort of phrases he had come to understand so well in just his first few months in his summer of awaking love. His gaze lifted to meet the king's gaze quite plain and straight as he said; "I pray the gods will find a place for me there." And, quite powerfully in these words, he felt a certain unaccustomed mature calm dignity; even though he also was surprised to hear a sweet boyish tone more clearly than he'd ever noticed in his voice before. Of their own accord his feet began to stir, to dance just a tiny bit, a lifting of the heals and wriggling of the toes as in a dance.

"And;" Phillipus said; "even now, on this auspicious day, you have the honor to be a messenger of your temple."

"Yes sir!"

"Why did your Mistress choose you?"

"Oh, sir, I know my way about the city."

"It must be more than that. She trusts you."

Rather overcome with this, knowing it was true, Phaedrus cast his eyes down and saw his callused hands and thought that, yes, his beloved knew that he could do a job of work. She had said that he is good.

The king went on; "She's commissioned you to observe things here."

"Sir?"

"It's all right. It's your duty and you've come here resolved to do it."

"Sir . . ."

"No doubt she's charged you to report back on my reactions to the note . . . yes?"

"Sir . . ."

"Because of your youth few would suspect you are a spy . . ."

"Sir!"

". . . and yet your dignity itself has given you away. Yes? It's quite all right. If you were mine I'd entrust you with similar orders." And the king idly fingered his close cropped beard to patiently await a true reply.

"Sir . . . well . . . yes."

"Well then, seeing that she trusts you, I wish to trust you with a confidence myself. Nothing grand, really, just a bit of news your Mistress might like to hear; but it is from my lips exclusively to her ears for the present. Yes?"

"Yes sir?"

"You should tell no one except her, until the news comes out to the public eventually. Can you accept that stipulation? Within your honor?"

The boy did not realize – not yet – that the man was plucking on his tender sensibilities as skillfully as a fine musician would have plucked a tight strung harp. He did, however, understand Phillipus' actual genuine motive in this particular small detail of this sport. Phillipus genuinely wished to make a good impression on the order of Elfesis and was genuinely offering a friendly gesture to that end. That was true and the lad, even in the fog of misdirection, did understand it. And Phaedrus certainly also felt the honor which was his as messenger in these affairs of state. But he did not see, not yet, how very competent a king this was. The man who had already conquered most of Greece was sitting here on a busy morning, with his officers waiting, bending all his skill to win the loyalty of a fifteen year old boy.

Why? Objective and strategy.

In fact, Phillipus loved a proper fight but mainly wished to conquer so as to rule, and to rule wisely. In sport he was well known for generous treatment of any beaten foe who would simply show respect; but also for a famous ferocity toward any who would rather cheat than yield. You should know what you are doing when you fight. In making war he fondly hoped to rule with wisdom, thus to step beyond the common rank of louts whom the gymnasiums of Hellas cranked out in multitudes like so much sausage. That, he hoped, would be his lasting fame; that he was a thinker, a philosopher king. And one essential element of this beloved scheme was to win over the orders at all the great temples. All of them. They conversed with the gods. They conversed with the people. They had most of the books. And rich treasures were entrusted to the care of many of them too. Their acquiescence in his conquests was essential. And as well, in his secret heart, he deeply feared some outbreak of wrath which he might stupidly commit if one of the temples someday chose to thwart him; by going to them of his own accord he hoped to win some magic antidote to rage. Some temple somewhere had some medicine that he should take. Perhaps some morsel of divinity itself. The current gods of Hellas did know anger but, unlike the gods of earlier days and other lands, did not themselves succumb to rage. And so he fondly hoped for this particular day to pass by easily and yield some profit.

And, in any case, there was the startling fact that the Athenian militia had nearly beaten back his personal battalions.

In any case, Phillipus saw two specific reasons to lavish personal attention on this child who had unexpectedly entered his busy morning. First: This was a smart lad who, like as not, would hold a senior office at a very major temple in ten or fifteen years. Thus he looked like somewhat of a prize himself. But much more importantly: With the ghastly thing Phillipus had done yesterday he now felt as if he'd hung up some sort of huge ax borrowed from some ancient Titan by a thin thread above his own head. Looking back, trying to see it clearly, his amazing act beside the river seemed to be exactly the sort of inexplicable nightmare of divinely inspired self-defeat which was the only thing he really feared. He thought the Gods of War had made him do it but had no idea why. And this note now in his hand was obviously a proof of the resultant situation's gravity. And so he hoped to impel this unknown lad to carry back a sincerely glowing report of his sincerely friendly intentions.

And so far the king was successfully stringing the boy along. Now the lad was carefully considering his honor and deciding that as his lady's trusty spy he must certainly treat with utmost confidence any information that he gleaned. But yet one thing did seem to be required. He said; "Sir; I can't keep secrets from the Elders. Of my order."

And the king pointed at him as though he'd made a very worthy philosophical choice, and nodded vigorously while saying; "Oh! Yes! Of course that's right. Of course you're

right about that, good Phaedrus. Point taken. Agreed? Very
well then, the news is this;" and his tone fell suddenly almost
to a whisper to impart a sense of startling urgency as he also
tapped the tip of his muscular forefinger hard on the table in
the rhythm of the phrases; "Pausanes is raising phalanxes here
to march beside the Macedons! As we go onward! Against
our common enemy . . . Persia!" He even pointed eastward
as a bit of grand finale.

But this supposed confidence made a quite different
impression on the boy than Phillipus intended. For one thing,
it was old news. Athens had been buzzing with it like a hive
of bees for a fortnight ever since that traitorous nobleman
Pausanes first began circulating discrete inquiries for officer
recruits. One particular unimportant lad named Phaedrus had
heard the story immediately after he'd arrived with the Elfesinian
party last week, from his shoemaker father and shoemaker
brother who had come to visit at the city temple. For Phillipus
to tell it in this way was just a blunder, unaccustomed as he was
to the ceaseless grinding of the democratic city's rumor mill.

And for another thing, the lad had felt disgusted with the
news of aggressive war ever since he'd heard it. His brother
and even his father had been a bit enticed; they had chatted
warmly at some length about this prospect of a well equipped
adventure into the fabled Oriental empire of erotic luxury and
wealth. But he, sitting at their little family picnic in the
temple's narrow yard, had looked up in vague hope of some
omen about his own future; and he had seen the spreading leafy
branches of the pomegranate tree here close at hand far below
the sky. And a breeze at that precise moment came up so that
the leaves rustled as if they spoke, if he could understand the
message. And then afterward the chat about the thing among
his fellow temple youths had quite confirmed his thoughts; their
temple was a place of simple work and simple love and home
and peace. That was the message of the pomegranate. He was
not a soldier nor would he ever look with favor on soldiering.
He would be rather like a woman.

And yet the philosopher king spoke on; "Yes! The Helenes will march united once again just like they did before! And their capital of Athens will become a capital of the world! Oh, Lady Luck will march with us. Oh, even more; I say Lady Victory will fly above our march and hover above our ranks just as she did above the field of . . ." and here he fell into the gruffest possible manly whisper; ". . . Marathon!" And so his fist struck hard on the table.

Young Phaedrus, needless to say, was not impressed by Marathon in quite the way the king had wished. Finally, this coarse and belligerent use of Lady Victory's name as merely Luck, she his beloved, whose name he himself uttered only in inmost thoughts and then with the deepest kind of tenderness, struck him as vile desecration. He let his hand find his purse which bulged with her sacred gift, the golden apple. He silently shook his head. Her kind of victory grew from the heart's struggle with the soul's hunger; this he knew. His impulse was to leap to his feet and cry out that his Mistress never could bestow her favor on this bully as she had on him. But that impulse was immediately tempered by remembrance of his duty. He now realized how far he'd been betrayed and lured away from duty. He began to wonder if the silent buzzing left upon him by his victorious night of meditation had left him weak here in this Earthly sphere. He should have been noticing everything and secretly ticking off the most important details on his fingers, not being lectured by this would-be Heracles like the puny athlete he had been before, standing in the ranks at the big gymnasium.

And with that reawakening of duty, the boy began to feel for the first time how constrained his life would be. This sort of king would shape it. Every duty of the Sacred Precinct had been a joy ever since that first day's ritual of entering the place had opened and sweetened his callused bitter heart. He had walked about there ever since in love with everything; but now he saw it as a man would see. And so he thought he understood the purpose of the Sacred Precinct's wall: to keep this fellow out. This sort of fellow shaped the boundary wall wherein his life would pass. He thought whenever duty sent him out again he must go armed, perhaps with holy power instead of iron and bronze, but armed and armored as he had no wish to be.

And the king was still here set to speak some more. Phillipus' mouth was even open with some word not yet uttered, his fist hanging in the air between them with the meaty forefinger pointing at Phaedrus. And yet Phillipus was studying the bitter sullen look on the boy's face and suddenly realizing it was no use. He'd somehow lost the boy, even despite the elegant rousing carefully constructed speech which was, he thought, so well composed to twang the patriotic heartstrings of Athenians.

And so the king's fist withdrew. Different words than he'd intended rose, drenched in his own bitterness; "Ah, boy, you're too small to make a proper soldier anyway."

And young Phaedrus, looking off to hide the pain that caused, retorted; "Just right to be a priest." He gripped the arms of the big chair and twined his ankles snakelike underneath.

Thus with anger full in him, king Phillipus finally threw his body back in his chair and bent his fingers to the folded note in earnest. He broke the seal and lifted up a corner; and to Phaedrus it seemed at once as if a beam of spirit light glared out from the open corner of the note and bathed the ugly snarling face in a blast of crimson darkness. And Phillipus most certainly felt it. The king's hand for an instant trembled and his jaw fell; he reached to cover the sunken puckered scar of his missing eye as if that eye could see the light. But then, by a strong effort of will, he steadied himself. He murmured; "By the gods!" Slowly and cautiously he lifted up the other corners too and so, visible quite vividly to Phaedrus, the red black glare seemed to overcome the sunlight of the open garden courtyard room.

Steady now, Phillipus turned the note this way and that, holding it out to seek a focus, holding it close so that, to Phaedrus, it looked as if the glare must burn his skin away. But he could not make it out.

Phillipus turned to beckon one of his men; Pausanes stepped forward but he waved him back and called another; "Alexander, your eyes are strong enough. Read this to me."

And a young fair fellow with flowing hair and the slimmer shape of a champion horseman rather than a wrestler came at once by Phillipus' chair and did not bow and took the note carefully between thumb and finger. He peered into the dark light with open youthful eyes. After just the first glance he reported quietly; "Sir, unless I'm a fool, some deity wrote this." But then, after somewhat longer scrutiny, he bent to whisper briefly in Phillipus' ear.

"Ah!" sighed the king with his face turning toward the sunlight that glowed so dimly through the open center of the roof, and with his expression seeming to sink almost down to nightmare. "Again!"

Alexander whispered in his ear again, a little slower and more distinctly.

Phillipus sighed; "By the gods; does it mean what I think?"

"Shall I call one of our prophets?" Alexander asked.

The conqueror vaguely held up a weak waving open hand. "Later. Later. I think . . . Read it to everyone."

So the fair young champion turned to the others and with a clear strong voice read this: "There is a grove that hides a stream. If the beggar king can truly beg and truly rule a special blessing can be made."

Phaedrus understood it. The Grove of Aphrodite where he, Phaedrus, had not yet found the stream of rippling bliss; the stream which he had sought one time so far in flesh but only found in dreams. And this was promised now to whom?

A king who dons the beggar's shirt in earnest worship; one who rules with truth instead of lies. And the lad for that moment thought that he could stand that duty better than this conqueror could.

Turning back to the king, Alexander spoke with more familiarity; "Father, this is clearly a challenge."

"Yes, do you think I'm stupid?"

"But she's offering a great reward."

"Don't you think that's obvious?"

"It seems essential. This is some deity of Elfesis and she's offering a way to sort out the mess."

"Shut up!" the king fairly shouted. "Did you ever fuck a goddess?"

"No sir. Not yet."

Phillipus visibly trembled. "So shut up till you have. First thing you learn: you're not a god!" And he stared up toward the morning's light again and said; "Your mother. Our wedding night, to make you, and she burned me. It was to make you."

And Alexander only nodded, knowing the story well.

Another one, an old soldier by his looks, stepped up quickly then and pointed toward Phaedrus with a hand with several missing fingers. "Phillipus!" he said.

"Huh?" the king responded. "What?"

"The messenger is still here."

Phillipus immediately shook himself and looked toward Phaedrus. He said; "Oh." And it dawned upon him how much he'd shown a spy. Really with a snarl he said; "Eh, boy, got what you came for?"

Phaedrus felt quite dizzy with the storm that had erupted so unexpectedly in this quiet place. And a vast day and night still lay ahead. He drew himself together as well as possible and chose some words as carefully as he could; "Sir . . . Shall I leave now?"

Phillipus, rather slumping in his chair, glared back at him in stony silence for a very long moment. But then he looked away and shook his head about his own thoughts and said; "Tell your Mistress this: I will speak with her on the march this afternoon. No; tell her I will ask her permission for a talk."

"Yes sir." And so young Phaedrus pulled himself forward, got his feet upon the floor and stood. Was there anything he ought to say? Did his duty call for parting words? He struggled to make sense of all his thoughts and found them far too personal to speak. What he felt was vivid livid resentment that this lying treacherous bully might possibly, by force of arms, extort from the beloved Lady a prize which he himself could scarcely hope to ever win; to lie in the shadows of her inmost holy grove. And so he only mustered up a silent ordinary courteous salute and walked away with his sandaled footfalls seeming to echo loud on the tiles.

"Wait!" Phillipus cried.

Phaedrus turned.

The king was leaning forward very tensely, gripping the arms of his chair, his face knotted up in pain. "Tell her . . ." he paused. He cleared his throat. He seemed to force himself to nod and then to force some strength into his words which began strong enough but then trailed down; "Also tell her I will seek the blessing which was offered."

Phaedrus saw the old soldier who was apparently the king's genuine friend stand up straight on hearing that.

And then a bit of revelation opened to the youth. This man was seeking Destiny wherever it might lead. The path he walked was ankle deep in needless blood and the fire of holy power might burn his flesh away before it lit his soul but he was set for all of that. The Sacred Precinct's wall was not to keep him out at all, but only turn him back toward the proper sort of spiritual victories so that the gate which could not be forced could properly let him pass at last into the Mystery which stood at the center of the giant forest. In truth the Mystery was meant for all. And as part of that, given who this fellow was, the Mistress of the march might see fit to lure him on with a promise of a passage through a different grove along the way. Not in words this understanding came but he did see it clear.

Resentment burned hot in the young man's flesh but he gathered up all the honesty he could and said to himself that his Lady would bestow her favors when and where she chose. The Lady might be, and had been already, touched by his own hand for a passing moment but was not his to command any more than any other's. For some reason that he did not understand – and yet Phaedrus saw in general the very proper shape of the test that she would set – she was offering a prize for this other man to try to grasp.

Phaedrus suddenly realized there was one proper thing for him to do. It would be a personal sacrifice by him as acquiescence in her sovereignty and, as well, a benediction which a future priest bestowed upon this struggling king's lost and wandering journey. The boy's hand went in his purse and grasped the Lady's golden apple, souvenir of the Hesperides. The countless secret meanings of this sacred symbol rose up to his mind although he scarce could comprehend their roiling shapes. The few steps back were quick and he reached to place it standing upright before the king who sat there staring utterly astonished and dumbfounded at the appearance of this shining thing.

Fear, even terror, fled across the conqueror's face. Whatever meanings of the golden fruit he knew were evidently quite a statement of the Lady's power.

And when Phaedrus walked away he was a man more than a boy.

11: Episode Nine:
Up From The Human City

All seemed ready. The holy statues waited; Our Mother, Our Sister, Our Brother. There they stood in their shining vestments of silver wool and snowy linen, crowned and draped and heaped with wreaths, ensconced securely under the gauzy bit of awning on their lavishly adorned brightly painted large wheeled cart in the softly glowing autumn noon of the narrow courtyard. Their gauzy yellow roof billowed from its wreath wrapped poles in a shifting breeze that ruffled at the floral decorations too. The team of men from the Sculptors Guild stood ready in the harness, now being conducted through their customary hymn by a famous ceramics artist and export entrepreneur who had won the prize to be their captain for the day. The pair of trumpeters from the Stage Performers Guild stood to attention left and right of the gate that stood shut still.

Standing on the temple porch before the altar, Victory surveyed this crowded little place and moment which she loved so well. How many times had she been inside this scene? Only twice, actually, but the moment echoed through infinities of time. It surely always changed but always was the same. She had not seen it from the porch before. The sculptors found the lingering quavery cascade of notes that led them down to silence. The courtyard itself was very silent now and so she listened for a moment to the muffled humming buzz of countless others out there in the street outside the wall.

Diotoma and her husband were also there beside the gate, among their senior temple staff whom they had brought along. Their group included several frowning men equipped with tall remarkably heavy walking sticks. Unarmed? Unarmed like Heracles. She frowned. But Heracles himself had done this march. There might be need for him somewhere along the way to this day's end.

And Matron Diotoma, half an hour before, had rushed to her for a private word about the prophecy their staff had read in last night's sky and been surprised with Mistress Elfesinia's disappointment. In the night sky's stars and clouds they had seen exactly the same map to Elfesis with the wolf and woman-tree which Auntie Cook had found in the note a few hours later. Nothing else, except a giant snake was coiled about the woman-tree just as you might expect.

Victory turned to glance back through the open door into the shadowed sanctuary. That lovely quiet place; would she ever see this Earthly copy of it ever again?

And there were the Elfesinians where she herself had been for these few fleeting autumns gone, just a few steps down from her but seeming far away now, clustered waiting in their precious shirts behind the cart and turned to watch her now. When this day was done would she be one of them still? Perhaps. She might be here up on the porch again next year, this year become one of the echoing memories. Perhaps some day, three score and ten, she might be standing in that courtyard again in her dear shirt again, the fabric full by then of very careful patches.

But now she wore the Basket Priestess gown and if one thing or another happened, she might be standing soon among the spirit company instead. Or this day's dusk might find her huddled hidden in some corner of a barn or in some cave with distant flames somewhere on some horizon.

Phaedrus was there among the rest. He took a step or two to reach out and rest his hand on a thick swag of barley straw that draped down from the cart in the shape of a human smile. Then, with the bit of strength that gave, he gazed up to smile at her with a weary look that seemed like confidence and resignation.

Victory nodded, smiling too, glad to see him safe after the fearful mission, glad to see how well he'd grown in just that morning. In truth, she'd hardly looked at him as he himself while listening to her spy's terse detailed report of the visit to Phillipus.

Ah, well; the morning was over and the time, as it always seemed to be, was now. Why was she hesitating? Even the final prayers were done. The few to stay behind were waiting round her on the temple steps; Elder Eisistratos who was their superintendent here, his wife, beloved Cook, the rest.

Wizened wise old Eisistratos even now was holding ready in his withered arms, against his bosom, the Basket of the Sacred Pregnancy to set atop her head as though his shrunken flesh still could offer such a gift.

Her boy priest king was by her too, a lad named Petronus, nineteen, naked but for shoes as was the rule for him to start on the parade, hair hanging down in heavy artificial braids around his shapely shoulders, makeup round his eyes to make him look heroically antique, jogging in place for warmth now as another breeze came by. The ancient face seemed quite a contrast to the lithe young desirable and distinctly male body, here seemingly in easy reach of any casual gesture she might make to touch.

This Petronus was a genial sort who thought himself entirely ordinary. Although he was a noble, still he'd sometimes thump his chest and quote from the official notice that was nailed up on every public warehouse scales in the port facilities of Athens – posted there by the official scales inspector's ancient and revered directorship – Petronus sometimes shouting of himself declaring he was "fit for common trade". Victory quite liked his clever wit and knew him personally; the custom was that he be picked by lot among the better families, sent through the rite one year and then serve in this ceremonial role for two or three years after. This was his third and surely final time. He was, of course, engaged for marriage to a wealthy girl.

Good Petronus had enjoyed coming out for scenic educational retreats at his little kingdom hideaway twice or thrice in each of his regal summers. Who wouldn't? They had to make him work the garden though, not just hang about whistling on a little flute to bring the mermaids and the jinn, to smell their steamy smoke – and other suchlike pranks – but he rather liked the pots and pans and making soup. Truth to tell, he was a mischief round the place and master of the other mischiefs.

He'd once this summer brought along his blushing fiancee to gain bucolic privacy – and, as part of that, to gain a host of little willing helpers scampering through the place by day and night, all quite intent as any mob to carry onward to completion the devious erotic scheme for which he'd written out the most delightful scripts and assigned the parts and brought along his priceless copy of The Guildhall Book Of Holy Sketches, dog-eared by that century and even parted at the seams – and to be greeted hand in hand with his semi-official temporary queen by his country family as he said. The Board of Elders, for the occasion, declared a holiday and voted him two new titles. And the happy couple had enjoyed each other pretty well before the end of Chapter Two with just a few startling twists of scene and plot.

And then one lovely afternoon, well ahead of schedule, this pious nobleman of Athens did a ritual of his own devising in the shady Grotto Chapel. In heartfelt thanks for future happiness, quite relieved and glad to find that his future bride loved to fuck with the same degree of artistry and philosophy which he loved devoting to that activity, he pushed across the altar there a codicil he'd written out to deed that famous precious magic scroll, with its emendations by a dozen previous proud and happy thoughtful owners, to the temple library upon the deaths of himself and wife and then forever more. And beside that slip of parchment was another larger one he'd brought for dedication as another treasure of his future home, both documents expertly executed on the finest vellum, this one in a polished frame. This was their nuptial agreement done in loving verse with the last lines freshly inked.

Why was she hesitating? Was there something still that she must do?

On an impulse, turning to Petronus, she reached to pinch his bicep, spoke to tease him; "You've been building up?"

"Yes ma'am!" he answered.

"Oh, well;" she said; "you'll gladden the trembling heart of every maiden in Athens. They'll spread your fame. They'll all be watching."

"Mistress!" he cried, cringing comically from her hand. "Thanks so ever much! There's a thought I really needed, yes indeed."

She laughed; "All the courtesans too; they'll drown you in a sea of gifts."

"Oh yes;" he said; "today my fortune will be made."

She grinned; "Don't worry, you don't look half bad."

So now he laughed as well. "Which half?"

She thought of carrying on the joke but then suddenly understood what she must do. "Here's something serious."

"Yes ma'am?" His half smile showed he didn't quite believe it.

"King Phillipus."

His face fell to an angry frown as quickly as a stone dropped into water. "Huh?" he said. "Him? What about him? Is there going to be some trouble?"

"Let's pray not."

"Curse it!" the lad said with all sincerity, holding out his empty unarmed hands. "Here I am like this!"

"Keep a hold on yourself, Petronus. This is your sacred duty! Listen to me." And she called up one of the lessons which he must have learned; "Why are you naked, here in the city, starting out? Why? It's the way our old ancestors went into battle isn't it?"

Rather grudgingly, he answered; "Yes; I see the point. To prove the gods protected them; to prove their courage. But they were armed of course."

"But Elfesis wants peace!" And then she rather struggled, seeking a way which he would understand to say the thing. She fell to a whisper; "Petronus, I know you will remember your honor – and your city's honor – but you must remember the honor of Elfesis too."

He was still reluctant but he nodded; "Yes ma'am, I see the point. Elfesis wants peace. So I'm here as a peaceful warrior, whatever in the world that means. I'll try."

"You'd better try. There's something you have to do."

The lad very creditably drew himself up straight.

Victory said; "Phillipus and I exchanged messages this morning. He wants a talk with me along the march. The thing is, he's got to ask permission very courteously first. His message said he would be courteous and he must be."

"Of course he should." Petronus answered.

"He must. He must ask permission for a talk. Him, he even thinks it means he has to beg. And a very courteous request has got to be the first thing out of his mouth or else I won't even stop and listen."

"Oh!"

"You understand?" Although, in truth, she hardly understood herself.

He responded slowly; "Yes, maybe."

"And if that's not the first thing out of his mouth, to courteously ask permission for a talk, then you shall inform him that it should be."

And perhaps a glimmering of the coming scene was coming clear to her.

"Me!" Petronus cried. "Me?" He looked around as if to find some other dupe who might be recommended for the task. "Can't I just cut his throat instead?"

"You may not. We want peace. We do want peace. And the words you say will help us find it by showing him his proper place."

"Me?" the lad repeated. "Why me?"

"Please don't be dense. You're a king today. You're his equal."

"Oh ho, sure!" He snapped his fingers. "Just like that I'll tweak his ear and tell him mind his manners. The city will be very proud of me. They'll vote me city honors too; funeral games no doubt."

"What! Do you think a weapon would protect you better than your naked flesh?"

"No, its just: what on Earth should I say!"

"I'll leave that up to you."

"What! Mistress, I'll do it but tell me what to say!"

"Haven't we taught you anything?" Her tone was suddenly icy, sarcastic, even almost scathing.

"Mistress! Elfesis has changed my life. It has. Surely you know that. But what on Earth should I say to the Barbarian? My rhetoric tutor gave up on me, you know. He did."

"Are you a priest?"

"Oh, well, sure." He waved his hand. "Quite the priest I am I am."

"Then I suggest this: When you speak to King Phillipus – and it is very likely that you will – first call out to our deities and ask them what to say. Then just repeat what you're told."

"Oh Mistress, you make it sound so easy."

"That is your duty. I'm telling you that is your duty. Will you do it?"

"Mistress, you can't be serious. Me?"

She let the buzzing silence answer.

And so he gathered up his confident resolve. "Yes, Lady, I will do it. May Our Mother help me!"

She answered very firmly; "And Our Brother especially and Our Sister too. Call them and they will help you."

He nodded and nearly whispered; "Yes, I'm sure they will."

So now she thought that she must offer comfort to his courage. What would he understand? "Look here my friend;" she said; "if you are killed today while you're doing your duty to Elfesis, then I myself will conjure up the holy powers who will do your vengeance. I must and I will. Or if I die the Elders here or else in Paradise will surely do it. Our deities will protect their own."

Now he was looking deep into her eyes with all respect. "Friend?" he asked. "Mistress, you honor me."

"Only what you deserve."

"Mistress, I pledge the same to you."

She nodded solemnly, just as she must do to show she took the stupid bargain. He had given an honest promise in sincerity; their gods must surely find a place for it in any of their plans.

But she was suddenly really quite impatient with the time which had been spent on all of this so now she found the trumpeters with a glance, saw them watching her like all the rest, and waved a hand in the gesture to proceed. Just like a perfect stage performance, both at once raised the tall bronze instruments to their lips, tilted them up into the sun, and blew a single blast that seemed to echo everywhere at once throughout the spheres.

She turned to Eisistratos as the reverberations settled down. "Now sir, if you please."

That excellent old philosopher rather struggled with the tall cylindrical basket so others on the porch came crowding round, reaching out ten hands to help. Victory stooped a bit and yet kept straight. The little crowd of the Elfesinians around her settled on the soft but awkward burden, upright and quite precisely balanced now. How many burdens had she carried on her head? They had grown larger as she grew, but none like this. It seemed very light but very heavy. Her people tied the various ribbons into bows. It seemed no weight at all for a person of her strength and posture; in fact it only held a few small secret bits of this and that all nestled carefully in folds of crimson linen. Cook found an instant's opportunity to rise on tiptoes and kiss her cheek and speak a powerful blessing to which she whispered thanks.

The ribbon under her chin might, she thought, inhibit speech somewhat but the thing itself was made light, simply to be in miniature the same proportions as a robust woman's torso. She reached one hand to test the burden, found it was secure, and stretched into her tallest stance. The hike ahead was slow but just one hundred and twenty stadia, and even with stops for rest. And she had eaten.

She looked to Petronus; "Are you ready, king?"

And in his awestruck eyes Victory saw the image she now showed the world. She was all women. Reality seemed to shift and break like some pot of stew lidded tight and burned too hot, then find new form, opening out the inner truth of everything. So now she saw in him the greatness of humility in every man. She looked out on the little courtyard, saw all sacred places everywhere, saw the statues on their cart as all of Divinity progressing through the mortal world, and saw all these folk as all who seek the utmost beauty. Into her memory there rose the two great statues of the Basket Priestess who ruled the distant Sacred Precinct's entry court; how her childish eyes had gazed so often up in rapt adoring study of their radiant womanly forms and faces; how those meditations had prepared her with a multitude of clear and vibrant messages for the work now in hand. Now they were she and she the third of them who walked in this world.

So down she stepped in queenly grace, the king beside her keeping pace, till they were standing at the gate and so she raised her hand again. The trumpets blared their seven final reverberating notes. The husky fellows from the Porters Guild drew wide the doors then, dashing out into the street, pushed back the hushed and whispering crowd to make sufficient space.

Victory cried out loud, in a voice that seemed to her to echo through the Universe's spheres and spheres quite as the trumpets had; "To home, in peace!" So out she walked in utter confidence that all who seek the beauty of the world would follow.

The greeting cheer drowned out all sound except an inner voice that clearly spoke these words: "My faithful daughter." And too, the breeze that rose to touch her cheek was Mother's kiss.

A hymn of Mother's charity took shape among the shouting crowd as the big wheeled holy cart came out and turned into the way, pulled by the singing draughtsmen. Soon the words of praise came clear enough to make her feel buoyed on along the narrow street upon a wave of prayer, Petronus tugging firmly at her hand to act as guide here on the Earth while she was striding elsewhere too. An almost random thought: she could not conjure up the route to mind in such a state as this but he would find it. First to the city's marketplace and then from there one certain path would take them home. Meanwhile she would gather up the souls they passed and lead them on along the spirit road. Consigning all her trust to him, she turned her eyes to the blue blue sky as clear as rippling water.

In fact she clearly felt the souls she gathered up along the city streets, they coming from the doors and gates; those in the beggar's shirt most vividly of all. Among the throng of pious revelers these holy tramps appeared in glowing light so that, although she gazed up where the sky rose from the city's roofs, she reached a giving welcoming hand toward every one of them. She was the flowing depth of darkness in the sea and in the sky beyond the light where swim the glowing fishes and the stars. She was Our Mother's Daughter; she was crowned and blessed Kore.

In fact the moments passed with blurring speed. Petronus soon was glancing all about in growing worry that they strode so fast. Around into the larger street and then it was downhill from there and soon he saw the cart and all the rest had really fallen back so that he could not even surely glimpse them anymore. The new arrivals from the doors and gates and the connecting streets were filling in the opened space much more than they should; in fact a whole phalanx of common trade whores was just behind them suddenly, four ranks deep, linked arm in arm across the whole width of this whole wide street, already drunk on sacred beer or holy ecstasy, in fact well rested by their week long annual holiday from work now almost ended, dancing with their skirts tucked up into their belts to free their kicking thighs, all of their open tugged up bosoms quite a bounce and nipples gaily finger-painted, singing Mother's praises boisterously. It seemed to be their wave of joy that urged the Lady on. He realized how far they now had come; already past the city's favorite brothel.

He thought the cart should follow closely on the queen and king, and then the Elfesinians with their invited guests, then the beggars mostly, then the rest. That, in his opinion, was the one arrangement for a proper order. He very fondly hoped the marketplace would somehow give a chance sort it out before they hit the rutted road where the holy cart must definitely slow down, but there in the marketplace was where the real mob of pious revelers were waiting in their thousands. He'd done this job two times before and there had always been a calmer spirit in the previous Lady. He linked his arm in hers and hoped some hope would soon appear. And, he thought, where was Phillipus?

But then one of the happy sluts, a redhead girl a little older than himself, came bouncing up beside and for a moment pulled up his free arm across her back, molded that hand around the breast from which she had completely pulled back her dress, and gently pulled the arm a little so he leaned a little on her. Looking at her now, he thought with great surprise that here was the one his father several years ago had hired to take the sacrifice of his virginity and she had done it with a proper private ritual behind a bolted door, with prayers to Dionysos and Aphrodite and with incense smoking. And yet in fact she was a country girl accustomed to lascivious parades. And though his eyes popped wide and all his conscious judgment quailed immediately at the indecency it must present, the girl's hand found his naked manhood and, as they strode along, she plied the skill she knew to stiffen up and reassure the human male. And she was grinning merrily up in his face.

Just a passing moment of his life this gesture took before the girl retreated to a place among her sisters – some of them shouting gleefully to see the sudden change in his posture she had made – and yet it made of him a thing which he had never been before. At once he felt and knew Kore's awesome fierce beauty at one side and at the other side reminded of the homely beauty of a lusty wife who echoes her. He felt himself chiming like a bell between then bursting open like a ripened pod of poppy seed that bounces on the breeze to toss its magic powder round about. Suddenly he was Our Brother Dionysos come to show his power in the mortal world. Suddenly this was the harvest time parade in country towns where a laughing plowman king is wheeled in a common wagon round about, with an enormous knobby bull-like cock adorned with ribbons, carved from an olive branch, strapped at his crotch, the huge thing bobbing up and down upon a rope that runs up to a pole and thence down to a pedal lever, with a leafy wreath of grape vine tilted on his brow, bees buzzing in a cloud, tossing fruit and drippy honey pastries to the jostling crowd from the heap of wine jugs where he sits enthroned.

Oh, he had heard philosophers discourse respectfully upon the country rites. And he had made a point the year before this last to be residing at his family's farm at Dionysos Revel time in a vain hope that he might have the luck to tup some really pretty girl amid some fragrant blooming arbor. But in the village square he'd looked up from that jostling crowd and, callow boy he was, had thought the laughing plowman king to be some lesser being than himself, king as he was then of the Greater Mysteries. Not anymore.

All things conspired to conjure up the dual powers of Nature and of Craft together in him. His love of beauty and of friends, the humility and wish for justice he had taught himself, his striving to do the best he could toward proper goals; his good humor; these were the simples of the brew. Then when the happy cunning redhead girl had plied his Old Man in hand so skillfully that his whole instinctive body suddenly jerked upright with its wise lust and told him her beauty, then all those virtues came roaring out from his various parts where they were rooted and they boiled into new power. Within the roiling steam that filled his brain, he saw it all in timeless time. He saw Our Brother's gift: to heave upon the plow so that the furrows turn aright; to whet the sickle sharp so as to ease the reaping work; to lay the stone walls straight and lift the roof beam high; to gift his seed into a human woman's womb then hold the children in his callused hands. To shovel out the graves as well. To laugh as heartily as he must weep. He understood now what it means to be the Peasant God of endless ages. And he was striding home today.

Here was the marketplace of Athens.

These were three acres on a plain below some hills, the space below a sleeping woman's breasts, where much had happened. This was the place where human liberty was codified in law and yet where countless slaves were bought and sold and too where Socrates was given death for being free. Here Pericles first preached the full beauteous spiritual graces of the Parthenon but then called up the empty honors of a long and pointless war. Here were the luxuries of distant lands and yet the fish and meat and fruit and bowls and pitchers and knives and spoons and saws and nails and bolts of cloth and shoes and hats and little statuettes and buzzing flies of ordinary daily life, the hawkers singing out their wares and too the puppet shows and cheap refreshment stands and acrobats and instrumental bands. Here for generation after generation came the folk of every sort to simply elbow through their lives as best they might. But not today.

Today the booths were folded up and all the goods and gear were put away. Now this noon the place was packed with all the city folk awaiting deepest Mystery or possibly a call to arms against an alien king who stood there near one corner of the place within a small square of alien armored guards. Resentful rumors rippled out from those near the growling soldiers, whispers that their presence here itself was blasphemy, subsiding in the worried hush of those who wanted peace at least today.

And now, bursting in upon the only open corner of this space, right down upon the spot where that king and his startled soldiers stood, here rushed a goddess and a god quite visibly incarnate in the flesh amid a joyous festival of dancing whores, pressed on by the many hundreds more who came behind.

It's fair to say the marketplace of Athens had not seen the like of this in quite a while.

The crowd erupted into waves of pandemonium. In truth, Pan in his titanic hirsute glory stood above the place, his panpipes roaring, come to celebrate his brother who was striding home with Victory. Ecstatic cries that never had been heard inside of walls before, only in the misty mountain pastures and beside the tumbling upland brooks, rose first from souls who knew such things but then were taken up by souls who in that moment learned them. Sixty thousand hands rose in the air; thirty thousand bodies swayed in a wind of overwhelming weird triumphant beauty. Twenty foreign soldiers, all members of the king's elite battalion, all at once without command, crouched, held up their shields and drew their swords.

Naked young Petronus had today been pulled into the very center of the Hall of Mysteries for well and good. He had gone three times by now among the awestruck folk who file into the Hall and find their seats around the outer walls or close around the border of the clearing, then cling to one another murmuring in the darkness as the torches all go out and the doors swing shut. He had already peered three times into the darkness in among the tall thick marble tree trunk pillars of the Hall that make the giant grove, seeking with his blinded eyes the patch of sky above the opened roof and then that little marble house below and its small door which hide the central rock. Three times the thunder rolling from some distant place had quaked his being. Three times the huge sheet of flame that was all holiness, erupting as the little door was opened, had consumed his flesh and gathered up his soul to swim within that flame. Three times he had been led away to a clean cozy bed in a quiet lamp lit room then wakened to a day of simple rituals that led him out the gate into the human world again. Not anymore. Now and henceforth he would always be a being with a proper place right at that central hearth which glows through every sphere. In fact this day he had become a priest. It had been his immortal sister's joy, striding by him through the timorous world he knew, which had pulled his soul into the world of confident joy he feared to know, at the moment when a mortal sister pulled his mortal self into the highest joy a mortal self can know. He strode in several places all at once. And so the spirits packed into the marketplace seemed as real to him as would a crowd of ghosts.

And for her part, for Victory, the day so far had been a vast assurance of her name. She understood at last why Shining Hera long ago had touched her brow to open up the inner eye; that she might see this day for what it was. Now she saw a host of spirits from across all time and space converging toward the consummation of this rite, those now in flesh as real as any others.

To the folk here in their flesh the two of them, striding hand in hand out from a hidden street, suddenly shone with the darkness from the heart of light. Their figures seemed enormous. Through that confounding trick which often happens when a vision shines from another realm to ours – at those moments when the veil between the worlds goes transparent and becomes a shimmering lens – through this trick they seemed to tower high so even folk back in the farthest edges of the crowd felt that here were great monumental moving works of art. And the dancers swirling round seemed to raise the dust of ages past and yet the dust of stars into a roiling thunder cloud above, golden brightness in the midst of which bolts of power blazed crimson dark. And yet the eye could not behold this powerful ethereal stuff so that the trembling colors flashed and changed their place and overflowed into each quaking heart. Powerful sounds seemed to echo in every ear. Voices could be heard amid the shouted song. The wind seemed full of every potent scent.

To the thirty thousand this was blessing; to the royal bodyguards the sounds and sights seemed like the magic threat of a gigantic sorcery.

But Phillipus and his son, both pious men in their own way, had also felt it coming. Both of them had, some minutes past, fixed their eyes on the opening of the street from which the day's parade would soon emerge and Phillipus asked; "Alexander, what is that? Do you hear it? What is that, incense? By the gods, do they have Persian war drums?"

The route to Elfesis lay just a little way across the marketplace. It ran just across that corner of the open space into a short street which then led out directly to one of the city gates then onto a rutted road. Every other year the queen and king would pace across in stately manner followed closely by the sacred cart, the Elfesinians with their invited guests, the beggars mostly, then the rest, the thousands slowly merging in a bit but mostly coming on behind. But not today. Every other year the folk would bide their time among the halting moving throng with songs and chanted prayers and clapping hands and tapping feet, with dances where they found a bit of space, with parents faithful their lost children would be well and secret lovers vanishing together in the crowd, all this spanning the range of earnest worship, impromptu fun and free entertainment. Decent folk would always stand aside to let a person in the sacred garb go on ahead. But none of that today.

Among the tensely waiting tens of thousands, all were hanging back because the company of heavy soldiers stood there in the path. The grand parade could scarcely pass till they withdrew. The military plan, indeed, was thus to force a momentary halt. The conquering king would then immediately step forth and shout a little five-word speech which he and his officers had labored over – "I kneel to Our Mother" – and the king would even actually kneel an instant, as befit the perfectly tailored beggar's shirt of Egyptian cotton he was wearing. Then, unless the Lady had some words to say, he would immediately step in among the folk behind her and his son would quick march the little phalanx of royal guards away. That was the plan. But none of that.

As the human swirl of movement flowed into the bit of open space before them, with the weird awesome figures towering above, it did not stop but only kept on swirling, the etheric thunder cloud of power slowly turning, the clot of soldiers standing there in battle crouch with weapons drawn as though their company were some uprooted thorny shrub which fell into a stream and for a moment dammed a flooding wave. Those who came behind on the narrow street were pushing in as well in hopes to glimpse the miracles, and finding ecstasy and linking arms and joining in the swirling mob.

Alexander, seeing that his father was entranced – as he properly ought to be – exercised command at once. He judged Phillipus was already in the thing head deep, already was entrusted to the gods and that the gods were here in glory, so the time had come to leave him. Now they must either shoulder space enough to march away in file or else attack the mob or else be overwhelmed by press of numbers. Which? Alexander tried to speak with Phillipus for a hurried moment first, tried to shout through his father's ecstasy, but only got a beaming smile and laughter of surpassing joy as a response, his father laying hands on his shoulders and trembling violently with physical excitement; it was certainly time to go.

His father stood there in the center of the little square of men, pointing at the stately tall queen with the mythic basket on her head, pointing with a trembling arm, gazing raptly at this beautiful woman's face and shape.

Alexander thought in fact he'd love to toss away his cares himself and join the fun but duty called. And yet he saw there was no hope of marching off at all. The crowd was surging all around them now. The best thing he could do was bring the twenty fellows through the flooding throng in straggling single file as though it were a perilous ford. And first, above all else, he had to ease their fierce anxiety to stop some dreadful accident. And so the young commander with the flowing hair pulled off his helmet, slung it at his belt, began to shout and wave the order for the besieged clot of armored men to stand at ease and sheath their weapons. He shoved a way to each who showed reluctance, shouting in their faces so they must obey.

And that was just another link in the curious chain of incidents that day. The next was a particular man who stood there in the Macedons' front rank against the towering work of sorcery; he together with a certain one of the Aphrodite Sisters who, flouncing by and seeing that this unknown fellow stood so tensely at his ease, chanced upon the instant's urge to pity his anxieties and throw herself and drape herself with arms about his bull-like neck to try and draw him into dance. She looked up in the shadows of the helmet; he looked down on the panting grin and heaving painted bosom pressed against him; and they recognized each other.

Now, this particular fellow had a story of his own as we all do. He was of noble line but for his father's crime the family was impoverished and put to shame. Two kings back there was a palace coup in which his father, then a captain of the guards, had shrugged and tossed a coin and made a quite unlucky guess. And so the boy, when grown to youth, must enlist into the common ranks then try to scrabble up again through every sort of valor, loyalty and right behavior. But it was going well. By special pleas of relatives and special oaths the boy got in the royal guards. By taking charge whenever things looked bleak, he rose to sergeant. More ensued; he earned a sprig of holly on his helmet crest and then a sphinx medallion on his chest. Then, just a week before, when the captain of the company of which this twenty were a part dropped dead for no apparent reason, the order came promoting him into the ranks of gentlemen.

The custom in the king's battalion then – as a measure toward healthy fraternity – was that an officer who rose in rank would spend generously from his promotion purse to host a dinner party for others who held the rank which he was entering. And this particular fellow, being anxious to improve his family's sullied reputation, even borrowed more and went deluxe. He took himself at once to the city's favorite house of hospitality, talked it over there, and ordered orgy number two; consisting of a private dining room with very sturdy furniture, food and drink in ample quantity but of the common sort, personal attention by the manager, ladies who would stay awake till dawn, three musicians for two hours, a comic doing animal impersonations, and a bag of honest dice. Broken crockery cost extra at a stipulated rate.

And then, thanks in particular to this particular lady here, the evening proved a great success. When the festivities were lagging, after midnight passed and all seemed spent by the festivities which were printed in the program so to speak, she took it on herself to draw the host up on the table top into a pantomiming dance, a sort of operetta, which revived the company into gales of laughter. The lucky host found himself following on her lead enthusiastically, wafted by a growing confidence that his investment in professional development was wisely done. All of the guests had stomped and clapped and banged their cups in time and shouted out the choruses. They had toasted the performance. In the weeks since then they'd shown him new respect and tendered dinner invitations of their own. In fact, in his opinion, this lady made his reputation as a royal officer, vindicating all his family's hopes. Next day he'd borrowed more and bought and sent around a necklace as an extra gift. He'd even thought of marriage.

It was The Eunuch's Shame, a well beloved old barracks tune wherein a thieving peasant dons a eunuch's gown to sneak into his master's house for robbery but finds himself attending at the noble lady's bath. Comedy ensues. He yearns and yet dares not, no matter how she bends and rubs herself or clings to him to do the steps, no matter how she kicks so high, no matter how she sighs for her absent husband and a lengthy list of paramours all gone to war, reciting as she sighs a very detailed and unlikely catalog of past delights. She got her dress onto him first of all, its strings untied to stretch about his burly hips and hairy chest, coached him to the company's great delight on how to mince his walk, to extend his pinkie fingertips and turn on tiptoes, to pull up his skirt on cue to show the audience the thieving peasant's true identity, all of that, meanwhile keeping up the steps and verses. It ends, of course, with her surprise. Discovering his purported scrubbing brush has found its way into a certain orifice and rather tickles there, the lady looks about with eyes popped wide and hand upon her cheek and does her level best to trill the final line just like some warbling song bird might. She only wore a serving bowl herself to simulate a quite unnecessary hat.

Now she's clinging on him once again and doing all she can to make him dance again. He tries to tell her he's on duty but she cannot hear. She's got the necklace on an ankle and she kicks so high to show it that she gets a foot onto his shoulder, showing all. And these fellows here today are not the captains of his new acquaintance nor lowly privates either. These men here with him now are all the sergeants of his battalion, now for today under his command, picked and promoted for each one's ability at individual initiative just like he'd been. And just to left and right are a pair of tough old sharks who used to be his friends. They start to laugh and urge their new captain on into some stupid lapse of discipline, shoving at his back and neck until he stumbles on an outstretched foot, lumbers forward a little way, falls down amid a cloud of dust, and one of them hops quick to expertly kick his helmet off his head into the crowd.

Lying like a floundering fish, wriggling round face up but struggling with his shield that's pinned beneath, flailing with his feet, he's groping toward the unseen helmet. Luckily the nimble lady falls unhurt into the arms of several other priestesses of love who now come swirling round; she jumps astride his chest at once, laughing that he's much too eager when he hasn't paid. She pulls part of her skirt across his face and reaches underneath to tug his beard. He's desperate what to do that would comport with honor; his free hand grabs a buttock so she slides right down and reaches underneath her thigh to grab an ear. Looking back, the lady sees his armored leather kilt is up and reaches now to grasp his nether parts as well. In fact this is a proper wrestler's hold and she has got the best of him unless he decides to actually fight. Suddenly he's overcome by yearning, wants a woman just like this to be his wife. Gnawing gently at the smothering cloth and flesh, kneading with the hand that's got her butt, he thinks of sons.

Meanwhile, amid the roaring noise, a command is being passed for them to file away. It is unusual indeed, not the regular kind of terse clipped formula of words they know and so – especially since they see their captain's disappeared among a dancing singing ring of grinning Aphrodite Sisters all with nippled bosoms quite a-bounce and gleaming thighs among their hiked up skirts – some of the fellows wrongly understand it as an order to dismiss. Willing as they are to follow in the gale of war, they are also more than willing to follow into this. Passing mouth to ear, the order's magically transformed into a joyous cry of "Chase the whores!"

Their small formation quickly starts dissolving rank by rank with all in back pressing toward the action. Their encumbering shields are cast away, first by those in front and then by all. Fumbling hurried hands that try to hang their helmets at their belts in fact just let them fall all clattering among their stumbling feet onto the fallen shields and paving stones. Seeing how the first who disappear into the crowd are badly hindered by their swords and belts and such – seeing how the laughing women grab their gear to yank them back and so their laughing prey flies from their grasp – the fellows now assume the order must include a uniform that's more appropriate for the duty. Eagerly they help each other get the ties and buckles loose so armament and armor drop away as well. A few brave souls pull off their tunics too to go into the fray more gloriously garbed as hairy naked warriors.

Today there is satyricon here in the marketplace of Athens. The great god Pan is blasting on his pipes above. This was the first encounter and the Lady won.

And Alexander, leading off no more than three obedient men, turns to them now, sees their lusty looks, grins despite himself and cries; "Dismissed."

And Phillipus, standing now amid the heap of gear, gazing at the priestess whom he glimpses through the crowd, blind to everything but her, starts to walk her way.

The laughing people part for one who wears the beggar's shirt. One of them – it is little Phaedrus – comes beside and reaches up a hand upon his back to urge him on.

So there stands Phillipus, conqueror of Greece, among the swirling mob, at last before the crowned and blessed Lady whom he's always sought. To him she is an awesome thing, a goddess in the flesh. To her he is a ghost from somewhere come to this event for no other purpose than to properly consummate the rite if he is able.

He speaks. Of all the turmoil in his heart and soul; of all his yearning toward the immortality of fame; of all his vague and wandering hope for wisdom; out of all of this one question now arises to his lips. What is the blessing that she promises? What curse is threatened if he fails the unknown test? He says to her; "Why did you send the apple?"

And now she seems a blazing thing to him. Why does she blaze? He does not know, but feels his lust rise with her heat. This lust to be one with her and then to blast his greatest power into her, small as it may be – he's sagging on his feet but people hold him up – that lust is now the concentrated point of everything.

The Lady's look is fierce within the burning aura round her face. She does not speak.

"By the gods Phillipus!"

He turns suddenly to see a most peculiar figure by him. Somehow here now is some ancient king of the Hellenes. Can this be Agamemnon?

The figure reaches then to tug and twist his ear so rough that the tough scar across his missing eye is pulled; pain both sharp and dull penetrates his foggy senses.

Rage rises in Phillipus. The familiar Gods of War speak in his tortured ear; yes, he'll find a sword or spear and go to battle now. He even hauls back a fist to strike but suddenly understands this figure here is naked like the greater gods. And in this nakedness there is a dignity more enduring than the most famous of the famous kings, some ageless simplicity of sweat and semen watering the Earth, the depth of which Phillipus now can see but cannot fathom. A sparkling haze of power round the ancient face glints and gleams through deepening darkness into both of his eyes somehow.

And the god-king-peasant speaks again, full of scorn; "Mind your manners! You will beg before she hears you!"

So Phillipus was struck dumb with shame to be discourteous. His fist opened to a hand that pressed his open mouth. And then the shame is guilt: he's wasted this fine chance to do his duty to his honor and advance his scheme. And next he thinks a most familiar thing: the gods he knows have led him into stupid folly once again and so a greater deity rejects him. But then – with all his self so open wide that all familiar self-deceits are phantoms to be swept aside – a different thought arises full, a thought he's often felt but always banished out of consciousness and fended back with other thoughts put up as barricade: "Nobody knows me." Now that is truly pain. Our Mother does not know him. Nobody knows him. He must force and bargain anyone to gain some love. This is loneliness and grief in endless measure. And all his glory seeking now is naught but lost and aimless wandering far from home like old Odysseus, naught but a vain attempt to find some recompensing balance for the truth which withers pride.

In fact now Phillipus, conqueror and king, is marching toward Elfesis as he should. He's come a step ahead with this. In fact he'll follow her along the way in silence – fleeing all who speak and hiding in the crowd, finding how to stoop and limp quite like some hard used slave would do to hide his regal stride, rubbing dirt onto his face and shameful fine Egyptian cotton shirt, watching her until his lust has grown again so that her silent glances and her grace and his tender swelling member, standing up so alone and yearning as she looks upon it with the fixed stars in her gaze – until these lure him farther.

In fact the crowd was moving. There across that corner of the marketplace the gaily painted sacred cart was standing in the farther opening of the street that led out to the city gate and folk were flowing round it, going on. The sun burnt captain of the pulling crew had donned a sailor's cap he'd brought along and now stood high up on the cart, clinging to a green and flower wreathed corner post with the gauzy yellow awning billowing behind him like a sail. He was shouting, beckoning to all. In fact this master of the kiln and glazes and the artist's brush was a wily master of much else. He had gotten his crew and magic boat and holy passengers clear round the marketplace by alleyways.

The goddess queen and her brother king passed on.

12: Episode Ten:
Garden Of The Hesperides

Up from the human city through the sacred gate; out upon the sacred road among the orchards; there at last the great procession somehow by the will of all was sorted out into a different proper order.

The queen and king and sacred cart today were floated on among a tight-knit crowd in sacred garb who warily watched about themselves – some Elfesinians mixed in with some of their invited guests, some with walking staves like clubs of Heracles, crowded in a tight watchful cluster round the queen and king and cart – then the whole folk of the city and the travelers of the world. This year the beggars felt the power of the holiness they went to meet so powerfully that some must even walk in a singing crowd a little way ahead.

The wide bridge next was easily passed, and then into a space of land that really made the city dwellers feel their walls were left behind; fields turned by the plow and waiting for the autumn's second sowing, rows of grape vine marching up the hills. The hymns of compassion and charity gave way to songs of Nature's fertile beauty.

But then the narrow bridge was seen. For many on the march – in fact, for most – this was the one real test. It was well known to all, for every year it was the same, and yet it was a thing which very few would ever claim they had done well. It was a test of wise humility some said, but others said it was a test of sturdy pride, and other arguments of greater philosophical refinement too were made.

A team of Athens' famous comic prostitutes stood up there on the knolls to left and right above the far end of the narrow bridge to mock the folk who tried to hurry past below. The folk came on across just three or four abreast and somewhat slowed by fear of stumbling in the press. That's all it was. And yet to have one of the vulgar beings point at you and screech and make some motion of the most obscene insulting kind – and then to know that the least small protest on your part, your least small hinted expression of outrage or disgust, would be greeted by your fellows on the march, and even for the next year in the city, as a weakness in your character instead of strength – this brought disorienting turmoil to the proud Hellenic heart. They tried to hide and tried to brazen through and tried to spy upon their neighbors. And they thought about it.

For Phillipus it was hard. And yet it took him one step further on. As he came hurrying by between the narrow high railings, feeling all the thousands coming on behind but slowed by those ahead, looking up, he saw one of the women definitely looking down at him, even pointing. Then she clearly signed that he let other men fuck him in his missing eye. That's what her pantomime had meant, with no mistake.

He wanted first, of course, to storm the little hill and strangle her; the others too but that one in particular. He truly thought upon it. This perpetration stained the honor of his wound. His honor was the only beauty that he had. And was he not the conqueror of Athens? Was he not a lion hiding here among this drove of sheep? Such a homicide was justified simply in the name of sanity; whatever ancient priest had dreamed this up was mad and so too were the nation who sustained this abominable custom for all these years.

Just past the bridge he stood at a little spot beside the road while others hurried on to get shut of the place as quickly as they could. He wiped the road dust from his sweaty face but he was in a cloud of it. His face was blazing in a blush. Of course his better judgment did provide restraint. He simply stood beside that rushing road – actually standing at a little resting spot provided for this kind of contemplation – breathing as deeply as possible, while the murderous rage subsided, gazing up at the unguarded backs of the jigging gesturing women on the pair of little hills that flanked the bridge. He blew the dust out of his nose then put his hands upon his hips and gave himself to thought.

This damnable thing had been explained to him last month by a perfectly sane philosopher his staff had hired to come in for a seminar. Everyone was mocked. It happened every year. The honor of the thing lay somewhere in accepting it without complaint the way a labor slave or abject peasant could be broken down to do. Where was the sense? The hired philosopher had likened it to a sudoforic used to balance down the system, but that analogy seemed dense. Thinking on it now, Phillipus thought that from his point of view this narrow bridge was part and parcel with the note this morning and the strange king who'd tugged his ear, all riddles he could not unlock. There was a vague thought that all the pointers of the riddles seemed to point at him. Could he personally gain any profit from this thing? He had no notion how. Yet there it was and he had bought it with the bargain. Solemn holy oaths had long ago bound him to the noble task of bringing glorious adventure to the human world, et cetera. Adventure surely led through Athens. If he wanted Athens longer than a year or two then he must have Elfesis. Rocky as it was, this was the only path. This was his duty.

And all of this was deep confusion. Honor somehow was dishonor; the reverse as well.

Weariness came on him and pain glowed in his leg. He looked about and found there was a large rock provided to be sat on and he sat there by the road, which still of course was flowing fully with the crowd. This ritual was a greater and more peculiar strain on his resources than he had expected. Half way to the Sacred Precinct, more or less, and he was tired from the stress. These wafty wispy joys of these spiritual pursuits were certainly hardly the palest shadow of the vibrant carnal exhilaration of a properly conducted bloody battle. Where was the reward?

That woman! That struggle sparked his carnal appetite. No doubt it was the danger. By the gods, one look and he had wanted her. He had to think his body's lust to copulate with hers was something with immortal reasons. The thing he really wanted was to blast his soul into her, not an image that he quite remembered ever having had indulged in, certainly not ever with such enormous passion. Not to get her pregnant either, really, but just as though a key would fit some lock and turn, as though some door between the spheres would open. Even now his cock swelled up again just thinking of the moment when he first had seen her. But damn! He'd made a solemn promise to himself to never fuck another goddess. Once burnt, twice shy and he was burnt one time indeed; he'd lain abed in agony for days. And from his bed he'd had to scotch a plot among the council to charge his wife with sorcery; she'd done the ritual at his behest to get a holy child and there were factions in his court who didn't want that. And yet, despite the horrors of that experience, he wanted this one now. Right now, today. Afterward, tomorrow, would not be the same. Where was the sense in this?

Phillipus had to blow his nose again to breathe. And yet that suffocating smell of Earth penetrated through his senses. It gave a feeling almost that he had been buried here alive, immersed in dirt.

Now what was this? Some sort of ripple seemed to pass through everything. He looked about, looked outward from his thoughts, and found the world had changed. Looking outward from his nearly overwhelming yearnings now, he found the billowing air and shaking ground were somehow glowing with his passion, and in the same confusing blend in which he felt it. A moment then of disbelief but then an understanding that he looked now on the world as true magicians do. It seemed preposterous, not in a temple with the incense and somnambulistic chants and animated statues and that whole load of crap, but here in some ordinary open space of land. And yet the same incomprehensible vibrating hum was in this place that he had sometimes felt in solemn rites. He reached to press his hand onto the ground and felt a power of Divinity in the countless rushing steps.

He looked then at the narrow passage with the people streaming through between the little hills. Oh yes, he thought he saw, the hills were tits. He could read the symbols. Oh no, the hills and bridge made up a cock and scrotum. No? Yes? And thus he saw the purpose of this bit of landscape: confusion. Break the bonds between these people and the normal world. It was a magic gate. This whole land from here was a labyrinth and an outer forecourt of Elfesis. And it had snapped his bonds to everything he used to know before he stepped onto that narrow span. The power in this day was more than he could hope to comprehend. Nothing else to do but go on forward.

Wishing now to rise and disappear into the crowd again, to seek somewhere a little further on some clarity, he found his aching hip would not respond. That was the damndest thing. Seeking to rise, he rather fell back on the rock and even seemed to strain his lower back. Where had this lameness and the stooping of his shoulders come from? He'd thought at first that he had taken on the thing quite voluntarily as a disguise to ease his passage through the hostile mob. But more and more he yearned for a sturdy walking stick and for some merciful deity to lift off his back the burdens of the struggling wandering life in which, in actual fact, he tramped the Earth.

Trying once again to stand, he slipped down to the ground instead and felt the depth of weariness. Despite himself, he leaned back on the rock but found some hard sharp point was stabbing at his evidently bruised lower back. So he crossed his legs as comfortably as possible and leaned forward with elbows on his knees and with his face pressed in the darkness of his hands and gave himself to prayer.

He did not try nor care to name the deity to whom he prayed but only knew it was the one who walked in her today, whomever it might be. He saw the woman as he'd seen her in the marketplace, saw her fascinating womanly form and face reflected in the shining aura round her, and now again gave himself to rapt adoring study of that glittering countenance.

Phillipus formed his yearnings into words as he so glibly did so many times and, though he felt the worthlessness of eloquence, he spoke to her; "Lady, mistress of my soul and body, I am yours. I beg whatever you may wish to give. I humbly beg the honor of giving what you wish to take. Give me better life or take this life I have from me, whatever is your will. Only let it be, I humbly beg, a shape and form of blessing I can understand, to be a beacon for my journey or to light my thoughts in Hades' halls, or to be a memory in future lives."

The moments passed. He held himself into the task of prayer as best he could, found that he must concentrate attention on the holy face and on his plea by turns, not both at once, or both would start to slip and fade.

Something thumped onto the ground beside so that he almost started from his work – as though this were a battlefield where tasks of every kind must be attended to at once – and yet he pulled himself back to the job again by force. And yet the thought of that unknown something falling at the roadside by him would not be chased away. Suddenly the Holy Lady very clearly in his vision frowned. Her hand appeared. She pointed there. He was supposed to look.

He took his hands away and then he turned his head to look down by his side and then he opened up his eye.

By the gods! It was a crutch! It was a knotty twisted kind of peasant's crutch roughly carved from a fruit tree branch.

Just a mile or so beyond the narrow bridge there stood the noble house of the Agrai Temple's ruling family. A large parcel here on this side of the stream was their estate, handed on and on to each of that temple's ruling couples for the last few hundred years.

Here each year's crop of new holy beggars must come into the high walled courtyard for the revelation of the opened basket and the oath.

Diotoma and her husband and their staff had everything in perfect order here. Of course. Around their house an olive orchard stretched at great extent with brooks and paths about and meadow pastures dotted in. In these pleasant fields thirty thousand people once a year could rest and even bathe if they wished, and certainly drink deep of the sacred beer and sing and dance for two hours or so of leisure. It served to get their spirits up again. Small shrines of various sorts stood at spots where folk of earlier times had felt a call to build them. Here the Stage Performers Guild each year put on an ancient pantomime of the ritual's sacred story, clergy led fervent prayers and harper poets strolled about. All of the regular stock were safely shut in barns or herded off to neighbors' farms.

And by the house, near the high walled courtyard's entry door, a smaller place was perfectly prepared as well. This space was cleared of all a country mansion's usual bales and heaps and broken vehicles and lumber, making ample space for that year's hundred-odd new vagabonds to wait their turns to make the oath. Benches were arranged to let them contemplate the Universe at ease. There was a long stand of water jars equipped with taps and towels hung on pegs, the gravel ground around it nicely drained. A path with nicely lettered signs led to a proper jakes. Beside the courtyard door the cart stood waiting like a ship come in to dock, its holy statues gazing beatifically upon this place of blessed prayer and rest. Beside the cart a little stage was built, its railing hung with swags of barley straw and floral decorations like the cart; there the Master of the Agrai Temple briefly stood to instruct them in the clear and reassuring tones of his paternal pride, a speech his father-in-law perfected some years back, repeated several times as they came straggling in. Repeated without the slightest hint, the Master proudly thought, of this year's turmoil.

Female servants of the house went about this quiet shady yard pouring herbal barley beer from pitchers and handing out free souvenir cups to those who had not brought their own; it was the custom that these simple small round clayware cups, each decorated in one of five roughly painted standard little holy motifs, would be held among a family's heirloom treasures, bundled with the shirt, and gifted to a worthy child.

And back through an arbor was a lovely garden spot where volunteer prophets and prophetesses sat at little tables with incense burning, equipped with little baskets of colored pebbles and the like, advising any of the vagabonds who might require a consultation on this lucky afternoon.

This lovely garden was surely one of the finest places any city's people ever made. But then inside the high courtyard walls; there the people of Elfesis Hill held power.

The entry door would open and an eager or reluctant vagabond be beckoned in; or, if lame, carried in the door by men from the pulling crew. (In recent years Eldress Eurycleia with her fabled memory ruled in this; she knew exactly at a glance who had been and who had not.) The door was shut behind them. A white curtain then was lifted back and there stood the boy priest king with his ancient face, clad now in a glowing saffron yellow robe, beside an altar. There on this altar lay the Basket of the Sacred Pregnancy lain down to be a cornucopia, its folds of crimson linen very carefully spilled out with each of its sacred bits of this and that lain on the fluffy folds.

So came each holy tramp to be a priest or priestess for the fleeting moments which it took to lift each item in their hands, all instructed by a priestess (this they took in turns) who stood beside them, she speaking one key phrase about each sacred thing as each was lifted, each examined, each returned to where it lay before. All of this was meant to be Our Mother giving birth to all things in this world but all the words and gestures were quite brief; in the main each person must be trusted to behold the splendor as Divinity might show them in their heart, both now and later in their dreams.

When that was done (and it was quickly done) the aspirant was turned about and another curtain raised. They were guided through (or carried) round about a labyrinthine little path adding up to seven chambers of hanging draperies suspended from invisible poles and ropes, each chamber of a succeeding rainbow hue in keeping with Musical Electric Force harmonics, open to the sky above, until at last the purple cloth was lifted back and so they stood before the Lady who sat there enthroned between the spreading viney branches of an ancient apple tree, still fully leafed in green here in this sheltered spot. Of course all dying autumn leaves were snipped away the day before.

Here in this very private booth so far from the worldly entrance, with this goddess and this green ancient wizened bony tree and a tall ivy covered wall behind, the enclosing draperies here midnight black, here the oath was done. This was a drama in itself of course. The curtain fell behind; the priest who was guiding them would quickly speak the oath beside their ear, enunciating very clearly. It was no more than just a brief simple list of basic things they should have done to reach this point, ending with the question; "Have you done all this?"

Then the Basket Priestess would fix her eyes in theirs and speak; "Do you swear that you have done what is required?" More or less a hundred times she'd speak these words.

Sixteen different categories of their answers had been taught to her, each being a different mix of humility and firm resolve and anger and guilt, each sort of answer with the way she should reply so they might gain some understanding that they lacked. She must coach the individual if required, or usually just make a certain silent blessing gesture or a certain formula of words. There were just three of these sixteen sorts of answer which required the individual's ejection from the march and they were merely theoretical, you'd almost say; no aspirant in living memory had been rejected at this point. In really questionable cases her reply, which she must speak with utmost genuine sincerity, was; "May Our Mother (or Sister or Brother) guide you to your proper goal."

But still, it was a demanding task to instantly catalog each person's state of being by their aura and body stance and tone of voice and words into the one paragraph of her memorized instruction sheet where they best belonged, then turn that tap to let the best response flow out. And even then it was not over; she should observe the impact of her words and gestures and strive to learn from the experience. This was her duty.

Of course she'd ordered special treatment for Phillipus. When they'd first arrived, when her staff had finished rushing round to put the final touches on costumery and other gear, while they were all washing off their dusty hands and faces round a big tub in a hidden corner, she had pulled herself back to this Earthly sphere from trance and told them this: Do not seek him from the yard but let him come up for admittance as his will or chance would have it. Then delay him at the Basket Mystery, with some lecture on the sacred bits of this and that perhaps, or such, until the aspirant before is conducted out the exit. (The one behind also has to wait until he's gone.) Some one rushes to her with news he's next. The one who guides him would then speak no word and give no sign except to try to slow his passage through the chambers to a stately pace. That is, delay him. Finally, before lifting back the purple cloth, his guide tries to fix the conqueror's gaze with theirs and then, with a final dramatic look and thought when it's open, would turn his gaze toward her. The guide must not betray surprise regardless how she's posed herself.

Then the two of them would be alone until she either called or clapped her hands three times.

But this was stagecraft frippery. This was not a plan. She asked herself, what would she do? He had approached her several times along the march so far but did not speak, like a lone wounded wolf who finds a fire lit camp and smells the hunters' meat then limps round and round the circling darkness in fear. Within the loose folds of his shirt his manly part had stood up more and more and so, being Kore then, she had felt herself staring at it, murmuring charms as though it were a snake, coaxing at that piece of flesh to draw him in. Then arriving here and coming to herself again, she had asked Our Sister what was next but got no answer, only that she must accept the holy presence on herself again when he appeared. She would obey as best she might – and, to tell the truth, she might enjoy a sunny autumn afternoon like this with him tomorrow or some other time – but what if it were sexual relations there and then on Mother's throne or leaning on her apple tree? Could she do it? Or could she do a homicide in this peaceful place? What if she must do both? She did not know.

And then two hours of ministering to the holy tramps; the passing minutes drew her more and more into the Earthly sphere. She began to find herself in a very physical yet nearly timeless moment with each one, truly gazing in the heavy cares and fears and heartfelt yearnings of this world. Then the next would flash into her presence. At least the dappled shade was cool on her hands and face and feet and her fine spun silver woolen gown was comfortably warm and loose. At least Our Mother stood behind her in the woody substance of the tree and through its rustlings advised her what to say and do or sometimes, when her growing weariness led to wandering thoughts, Our Mother would take pity and simply directly shape her words and gestures. Where was Phillipus? Would he come at all?

Outside the courtyard wall, he was sitting alone back behind the others, deep in tortured thought, awaiting what he did not know. Perhaps awaiting hope. At last a shadow came and stood beside his lonely bench. Awakened, he looked up.

There stood the Matron of the Agrai Temple.

Standing there with folded arms across her previously violated breasts, scarcely taller than his height though he was sitting, Diotoma spoke to him between clinched teeth with winter in her breath; "King, they're closing shop."

"What?"

"Have you come to buy or just to look?"

"Ma'am . . ." he said. And then he said; "I must apologize for what I did."

Icy stony silence.

"Ma'am;" he said; "I dishonored myself yesterday." He waited, looking in her face, hoping for the mercy of some reply. He finally added; "I fondly pray that I did not dishonor you."

And so she answered; "King, as far as I'm concerned you may as well eat donkey shit and die. I'd like to see you hung up by the thumbs and flayed with whips. I really would. I'd love to watch; I'd pay to see the show. Someday maybe I shall hear that you have died in slavery. Know what I'd do? I would go to my altar and give thanks for revenge. But still, I live by my temple's book and in that book it says that you are free to make this march if you can find the juice in your liver to do it."

"Ma'am . . . I do apologize. I do."

"Go fuck yourself."

"Ahh . . ." he sighed, looking at his empty hands.

She demanded; "Are you going in there to try the oath? I'm the hostess here so I guess I've got to ask. You're the last one. Every other thief and half-wit and whore and cripple here has done it. And every one of them has passed."

"Honored Matron;" he replied; "please, may I show you something?"

She paused. What, of all possible things, was this? Finally; "What?"

He fumbled in his purse and found the note. He unfolded it and held it up for her to see.

She took the little square of parchment in her hand and read it.

A moment's wait, Phillipus said; "Mistress Elfesinia sent it to me this morning. You can see, it's a very special challenge."

"Mmm;" she answered; "yes." Her friend had sent it to this man? And the jumbled letters shone with holy light; written by Our Sister's hand apparently, an invitation to her hard and hot embrace. That was repugnant and the reasons for it did escape her, but who was she to judge? Some high affair of gods and states. And the shapes of the writing did perhaps look like a map to Elfesis startlingly similar to the one she herself had seen take shape in the midnight sky. So she asked; "What do you want from me?"

"I don't know. Guidance."

"Not from me." She folded it shut and gave it back. "You want advice, go in there and kneel and beg for it." And then she could not help but add, with a sharp tone of vengeance: "If she wants you, do it."

He shuddered visibly.

She said, suddenly with a clear indication of her own strong preference: "Either that or else turn back now. Anyway, it's time to choose. They're packing up and moving on."

And so he looked up at the little door in the courtyard wall. And as he looked his courage rose. Though it was shut, it seemed to beckon. And as his courage rose he took his rude peasant's kind of crutch, and with the sturdy stick braced between the bench and ground, pulled himself up to his feet. He hobbled quickly as he could among the silent folk till there he stood knocking at the door. Three times he struck his fist against the wood, each time louder.

The peephole in the door slid open. The sun burnt captain of the pulling crew looked out.

"Sir;" Phillipus said; "may I come in? I think I'm ready for the oath."

The fellow shot back, in plain and simple tone; "Why are you here?"

He found himself shaking his head in bafflement while words came tumbling from his lips; "I do not know. Honestly. All I know is that I have to go as far as I can."

The captain nodded, slowly weighing it carefully. "Yes." he finally spoke. He opened the door and helped Phillipus in.

Victory was by now quite thankful that the stream of human shapes was slowing down. Sufficient space had come between each one to lean back in the cushions of the ornate chair and let her gaze idly caress the knotty intertwining branches of the tree above, to catch her breath and try to trace the branches in between the trembling leaves despite the blurring in her eyes.

There had come a crippled woman leaning on her son; to speak she'd stood alone as best she could. Our Mother gave the finest blessings to them both.

A rest.

There came a man with sunken cheeks who darted looks about; the Lady understood he was a thief in fear of justice snapping at his heels and yet the man gazed deep into Our Mother's eyes through hers and let his love come pouring through; "Oh, I do swear." She gave him merciful benediction number eight.

A longer rest. She seemed to doze. She thought perhaps all this had been a dream. Perhaps she was the tall girl now again.

Someone came and spoke to her. She did not understand but smiled and nodded as Our Mother said to do and gestured thankful acceptance number one.

A shimmering reflection in the branches caught her eye, something golden in a cloud of leaves. Was this just a trick of light or could it be an apple which she had not seen till now? What delight! What joy there would be in here to touch its warm smoothness and leave it hanging there in secret from the human race, to let that single one be given to whatever spirits rightly came to make a claim.

She rose, feeling as she stood that this was indeed one of those weary dreams where you can scarcely find the strength to drag your feet despite the way you are somehow invisibly supported; she made her steps one by one and came at last and stood close by the trunk as she must do to reach up toward the glimmering.

It was too high and yet she felt herself relaxing as she leaned to let her Mother's strength take up her weight. The sun was glittering down from it into her eyes so that in truth there was no up nor down nor left nor right. All of the stress of these last hours and the morning and the restless night and day before and all these months – the stress of all her life – seemed to quite dissolve into dark fluids and flow down into Earth. Her bare toes dug like roots and new brightly colored fluids rose fresh from the living ground to fill her up again. The growing grass was tickling at her feet like wavelets as you walk beside a moonlit sea.

The rough old bark was somehow very pleasant on her skin. How like is flesh to flesh? Oh, very like; all flesh is one. The sunlight and the dark and land and sea; human folk and beasts and finny fish and meadow flowers and thorns and snow and rain, all these are one. The thieves and worthy sons, the girls and priestesses; all these are one. She could not find a thought to speak the loveliness in this sensation so she lay full length upon the leaning trunk.

What is the greatest passion? Love. And what is love? Justice. And what is justice? Truth. And what is truth? Reality.

This delicious roughness of the bark where she rubbed her naked calf and thigh was full of Earth's coarse real sensuality, as full of sensuality itself as lilac on an early summer's breeze or fir trees' scent in the cold still hush of upland winter forest where the only sound is snow. And then she realized: this sort of potency made it absolutely clear that Demeter had changed herself to Kore. And by the glittering that took shape in her eyes, Kore seemed to smile at her very ardently like a woman who desires.

So, obedient to the holy will, she stretched to mold her thigh and hip into the curve. She gently twined and twisted as she stretched and rather climbed so that her naked belly then each swollen teat and then beneath each round firm breast and then her throat and cheek each rubbed as she turned and stretched; each felt in turn the lingering caress. Where were these things? She could not count these things about herself and found a pride and wonder in it. But now she found that thus to climb she'd wrapped one leg about and felt in this a very weird polarity. She'd never thought of this before, not even once. What were these colors in the air?

And yet she could not help but let her sister's body force her thighs a little more apart so that her tender parts were now parted open by her sister's sure demanding touch and she felt pressed there by her weight as though now pressed between a firm hand on the small of her back and the penetrating fingers of a very knowledgeable lover's hand. And yet a very gentle breath of breeze came softly tickling in the hair behind her neck. And with that breath a leaf came down to gently press her cheek so that she laid her ear down to the branch and to her ear perhaps there came a strong woman's voice; "My love, my sister, shall I teach thee all of pleasure?"

She must answer. She pressed her lips against the woody flesh to whisper "yes" but found them lingering in the texture there. And yet her other mouth was feeling texture too and it was answering. Passion in a great surprise; she pressed out hard; a rippling tremble and a flash.

Ah, reality is life and life is pleasure, pleasure love, so all is one.

And love came flowing from her tenderness through all her being. And then from out this well of love there came a sigh of deep release which pulled the strings from there to all her other parts and drew all remaining fear and weakness from her out through that place. And then into this tenderness and love and strength and courage came from all the world around awareness of all life and death, awareness that suffering and pleasure are alike and both are lesser powers than the pure desire which ever makes all things of every kind. With that wisdom in her inmost privacy came flowing peace.

So then, with all the dreamy strength of a lover gone to dreams of swimming in the streams of bliss, her arms reached out. Each arm stretched out strongly twining along a spreading branch. Her fingers stretched out far to hold the leaves into the sun.

In this dream she looked down on a lovely well shaped woman's breast which lay against the curving trunk and gleaming golden in the sun, green light on the flesh around, so like an apple on a leafy twig. This was a thing of beauty far past knowing. Here was the juice of life. Here was the fountain of Our Mother's love. Here was the nourishment of generations. Who might come and dare to touch?

Finally, into her human consciousness there rose a shock that she was waiting for Phillipus naked. The precious gown of finest thin spun silver wool lay down there on the grassy

Earth where it had fallen like a ring of tender downy mushrooms in the shade. A little fingerprint of awesome forces?
But this thought soon dissolved into her trust.

King Phillipus, standing at the altar with the bits of this
and that which make our world passing through his trembling
hands, could scarcely hear the droning explanations. His crutch
had fallen by.

Here was a thing the shape of which must be a fish seen
through the ripples of a shallow stream and yet became a
winging swallow in the air. Here was a gleaming pebble
shaped so like a human face that he could nearly see the lips
move and speak, and yet became the profile of some scowling
mythic dragon as he turned it round, and then became the
profile of a certain craggy mountain near his home when he
laid it gently down. Here was a thing whose shape he could
not even see but as he looked beheld a field of waving grain
with reapers moving through. Here now, when he picked it
up, there was a thing which most distinctly made the sound
of gentle rain but then, as he laid it by, rose into the pelting
downpour on the roof of the barn so fragrant with new mown
hay where he had first lain dozing in a girl's arms. Here was
a knotty little bit of wood and yet it was the gleaming silver
pendant on a string which he had knotted round his new son's
wrist that morning when he had sat enthroned among the whole
assembled court and when his wife had come to lay the three
week's infant in his lap. Here was the world.

And then, obedient to the carefully slowly enunciated
carefully gesticulated instructions of the old woman by him –
she whose toothless smile and sparkling eyes were so
beautifully full of her particular humanity – he had done it all.
Doing it most carefully to be quite sure he did it right, he had
beheld each little thing and placed it back upon the crimson
folds and now she bade him to behold this masterpiece of art
entire. Here was the basket she had carried on her head. Here
was the whole world spilling from Our Mother's womb.

Words were no use at all; Petronus in his ancient face and rustling saffron gown gave up on talk and came to grasp the awestruck fellow by the shoulders, turn him round and move him on. The crutch was useless too; this one must be almost carried. Eldress Eurycleia indicated she would come along to pull the drapes aside.

This half blind king was stooped and limping badly like a hard used slave. But why? Petronus rightly guessed it was a divinely manifested symbol of humility and felt an unexpected tug of sympathy as he got the big fellow's arm up over his shoulders, helped the poor sod slowly hobble through the chambers of the rainbow labyrinth. The king was staring dumbstruck at the cloths that rippled in the shade and sunlight of the autumn breeze. He must be pulled or pinched or shaken into wakefulness again with nearly every step. It seemed to be a journey to the far end of the Earth.

The purple curtain now at last.

Petronus got the fellow balanced on his own two feet, let him go and saw that he could stand for a moment at the threshold. As per instructions then, Petronus stared into this handsome face which was so mutilated by the horrid scar until the one brown eye stared back.

Eldress Eurycleia pulled the final purple drape aside.

Petronus flashed a thought, as per instructions, to the beggar's mind "Here, look at this!" and flashed his glance in toward the Lady's throne.

The place was empty.

Petronus blinked.

Where had she gone?

Becoming frantic, Petronus frantically cast glances all about, examined every shadow of the apple tree, each tiny bit of shade among the ivy on the wall. He rapidly blinked and blinked to make quite sure his sight was clear. She must be hiding. Amazing. Where? Behind the throne? Behind the drapes that made the walls? And why? Was he, Petronus, now supposed to understand the trick and play along?

Eldress Eurycleia tugged his sleeve. She gestured with her sparkling eyes that they should leave.

Petronus looked again; the Mistress was not here.

Old Eurycleia tugged again.

What were instructions? Show no surprise no matter how she's posed herself. Well, that was good. Conduct Phillipus in then leave them till she calls or claps. Well, that was easily done. He grasped Phillipus by the shoulders from behind and shoved. The fellow took one stumbling step. Petronus let him go and saw him sinking to the ground when the limping leg gave way, as the Eldress let the purple curtain fall.

Although she now really grasped a handful of his saffron sleeve and pulled, Petronus could not help but stand a moment more and listen. In that moment as he stood, a fresher wind came in above the wall so that the apple's leaves were rustling audibly. And yet inside of that Petronus seemed to hear another sound: a subtle hiss.

From the Earth, Phillipus, once a king – once, of all unlikely things, a conqueror – raised his dirty face to look about the empty room of rippling midnight curtains and an ivy covered wall. There was the empty chair, its cushions still pressed where the magnificent body once had been. He was alone now after all the weary journey with much more still ahead, once again now waiting for he knew not what. For hope? At least the Mistress gave this leafy tree to give its shade while a pilgrim waited. Slumping, leaning on one hand, he dropped his gaze and saw his other empty hand was dirty, wiped it on his dirty garment, realizing now belatedly that unclean hands had touched the sacred things. Should he apologize for that?

Thinking that the walls were curtains and people were certainly listening while he waited, he thought; "Should I beg out loud?"

"Youuu have already begged."

He thought it strange that he would answer himself in a voice like that. And he did not believe what he had thought. It was quite obvious he had not begged enough. He closed his eyes, forgetting somehow that he had but one, to try to find that voice inside himself again to argue with it. It had sounded something like an owl.

His eye was shut; he did not see the branches of the tree quiver in displeasure but he heard the rustle and the hiss.

A snake? His eye flew wide. And just then as his eye flew wide there may have been a slither on a branch! By the gods, it could not be a dragon! His gaze darted immediately here and there about the twisty trunk and viney limbs. He tried to calm himself. There are no monsters here; this is not the Odyssey. Perhaps a snake of course. Perhaps a really big one like they used to have at Delphi. People say they fed it fatted sheep that it crushed in its coils then swallowed whole. Or just the rustling leaves.

He looked up to the tree again; in fact this was a goodly thing to calm a person's fears. He tried to breathe. Here, now, he said to himself, this thing is completely real and lovely too; a wizened wise old apple tree carefully grown here in a sheltered spot for all these years, standing here to watch calmly through all of the human to and fro, still fully leafed with green, two golden apples hanging on a lower branch.

He spoke aloud; "Mistress, I am begging, please, that you tell me your wish. Is it your wish that I speak to you?"

"Yesssss."

And he was thinking that he really must now wake from the lovely trance that even now despite that bit of shock was still clinging on his thoughts like wraiths of fog. He was deciding that he really must really find inside himself that practicality which had been so very helpful all his life in every danger.

Struggling with these thoughts, he took a few deep breaths and tried to cast a practical gaze on this. What was the sense of all this now? Well, he thought, things here might be arranged to dupe him if he were unwary; of course. Those hidden mechanical contrivances which they used to have in ancient Babylon to swing the temple doors, and such. And these effects that he had seen so far were nothing half so grand as that and might be cobbled up easily and, coupled with the damn distractions, might easily make a fool out of him. But then he shook his head to clear that off; no point to that. The clever woman was sitting right behind her throne right now, no doubt of it, and had that boy of hers atop the wall with a rope or stick to shake the tree on signal; but so what? He'd do as much.

"Mistress?"

No answer.

In all sincerity, what should he ask or say? In all sincerity, what did he want? He wanted glory. He wanted to shine the light of glory like immortal Heracles had done into this mortal world. It was a medicine to give a balance to the suffering. That was his sworn career and he was here to make the best of it that he could. So he wanted Athens and for Athens he must gain the blessing of Elfesis.

"Mistress?"

No answer.

He cried; "What do you want from me!" Then he tried to calm himself from the sudden panic.

The voice said: "Truthhh."

Truth? Oh, he remembered now. "Oh, he said; I see." The note. "Your note;" he said; "I wondered at that bit; a king who truly rules. You meant a king who rules by telling the truth. Yes, it's good. I do that when I can." He found that he was trying now to make a joke; he thought perhaps a jolly laugh might flush the partridge out. "Good policy. Confuses friends, confounds your enemies!"

The branches trembled. A shimmering glimmering from the apples caught his eye. By the gods! They looked for that instant then just like tits in darkness in the light of lamps. And yet the lady did not speak. Why not? Because his stupid joke was far beneath contempt. He was a fool. He was a fool hiding in a show of bluster and it worked; nobody knew him.

And from this sudden misery, he could not help but look for hope. The lovely tree was fine, a sign of life going on and on, but what of human love? Oh, that pair of apples there; it was his longing for a mother's love which let his eyes see holy breasts.

And so he said; "I want love. My friends say they love me but all they ever know is the show I give them; otherwise they wouldn't. It's the things I do that make me what I am and that's all they love. Can't you see that?"

Still no answer.

"Look here;" he said, surging on along; "I want to be wise but what is wisdom worth if you haven't got the power to use it? That's the truth. And power means you have to lie, even to yourself sometimes. That is the truth." He raised a finger to tap his chest. "I will do the best I can. I have failings, I make mistakes, but I will do the best I can. And if that's not what you think is best, then I'll just beg to differ. Understand? Surely you can understand. All right then, understanding that, what do you want?"

"Truthhh."

First he shivered but then cried; "The truth! Well then, very well then, here's a bit of truth I want to hear: Why do I want to fuck you? Is that your doing or is it mine?"

"Bothhh."

"Oh Lady, what shall we do?"

He brought himself up straight as possible still kneeling, fearing still the weakness of his leg. He found a corner of his shirt to wipe his face as best he could. He wiped his hands again.

Clasping hands together, "Oh Lady;" he said, gazing to the sky between the leaves; "whatever you may be, whatever I may be, I'm yours. If you desire a toy, I'll be your toy. If you desire a king, I'll be your king. Kill me if you want. Take anything you want from me; I give it gladly. That's all I know. What else can I know? I am a mortal in immortal hands like you. Lead me forward if you want or leave me here alive or dead."

"Sssswear it!"

"Oh yes, I swear that is the truth."

The branches trembled now again but yet the rustling sound now touched his heart quite like cascading waterfalls of notes touched from a harp. The harper's tune was all of yearning.

And with her voice the notes said this: "Sssso tasste Our Mother's fruit."

The apples. Yes. The apple she had given him this morning was not here but locked for safekeeping in an iron chest locked in a guarded room with barred windows, an iron chest hid beneath his cot down in the city. But these were here. And so he struggled to his feet. Lurching like a drunk, he managed step by step to make his way.

And the harper's music played.

And the trance came flowing back like fog rolling down a mountain pass, quite like the dappled light in the tree's shade that rose to fill his gaze as he approached. On coming close, surprised, he saw there was a ring of mushrooms here below. Life emerging of its own accord from Earth. Yes, that was right. He'd have to watch his stumbling step. He reached out far to lean upon the curving trunk and in the trance his hand came to a woman's smooth inviting flesh which curved away to secret things. Looking down he saw the ring of mushrooms was in fact a silver gown discarded there. He knew not what to make of it but did not care; a glowing apple now was in his hand. Bidden only for a taste of this fine thing, he'd do no desecration; only carefully do what had been asked. He would not pick it. Taking one more step, kneeling down beneath, reaching up to balance with his hand upon a branch that seemed to rise and fall with breath, he raised his lips to the luscious fruit that was pressed in his palm and found a mother's nipple there and like an infant then began to suck.

Surpassing joy there was, such joy that none could know whose joy it was. Every color bright and dark flowed through all. Here was accepting thankfulness. Here was the juice of life and too the juice of death. Here was the fountain of Our Mother's love. Here was the nourishment of generations. This was a thing of beauty far past knowing. Somewhere was a shimmering veil, a door between the worlds that could be opened. Both had come and both had dared to touch.

And yet the moment passed away.

Filled with calm ecstasy of nursing him who was so strong, she could not help but reach with fingertips to touch the pitiful thing that was his hurt. His mutilated face. Then she could not help but smile when he looked up and saw her face. At least that made him smile his beautiful beaming smile as well, still with her breast so warm inside his hand.

At least his strong hand on her back began to find a proper thing to do as she began to move, his hand supporting as she untwined her bones from Sister's bones. Quite as a dancer might, she reached an arm about his sturdy shoulders, reached a leg about his waist and like a coiling snake came slowly twisting down around him, for a fleeting instant feeling quite as open on the smooth soft fabric of his shirt as she had been upon the roughened branch.

But that was not a thing for now. The man had sworn the oath according to the law all right but only passed half of Our Sister's special test. Progress there had been but he'd persisted in his self-deceiving lies.

She stood behind embracing him. How to tell him? Both things at once, she turned her head to whisper in his ear and reached to find his phallus, quite erect of course – and very pleasant it was too to squeeze it firmly in her fist although her body's lust had been slaked already very beautifully so that she felt no present need – and whispered in his ear; "Darling; not yet. Not yet."

In a single instant thus awakened to the possibility and then denied, he cried; "Not yet!"

She slowly let him go and there he stood reaching now again to lean upon the tree, his other fist hanging at his side opening wide and closing tight.

She knelt to fetch her lovely gown and, stepping one step back, drew the silver fabric that now glittered like a cloth of serpent's scales around her shoulders as a mantle, as a sort of matron's shawl, and found an easy way to tie it. She looked into his face quite strong and level.

Quite firm, she spoke; "You have passed the Elfesinian oath as well as anyone today has done it. You are prepared for more and you know you are and that is the oath. And you no longer need to beg, for you have truly begged and still find yourself here alive. But you have lied and persisted at it, even claiming to yourself that your lies are truth. You cannot know and cannot rule yourself like this. That half of Our Sister's test is not completed." And she shook her head and said; "So no; not yet."

Now he truly sagged with weariness. He was gazing on her breast, the one which he had kissed, as though he were a lone boatman with torn sail and broken oars, trapped in a flowing current, gazing on the last hope of landfall slipping past him in the dusk. He slowly reached his empty hand to it as though he hoped to touch hallucination or mirage and just his fingers softly pressed its blooming tender rosy tip.

So she took his hand and molded it to lie flat on her chest, on her heart, and laid her hand upon his heart and felt it beating. She prophesied; "Whatever destiny you try to chase will find you. So that is not the thing. And whatever good and evil you may do is no more than the world has seen before and will see again, for long ages outside our time. That is not the thing. No, what matters is the yearning of the heart. While you live, truly seek what your heart truly seeks, for it and only it belongs to you. That's all."

He could not speak. Nor did he comprehend.

She leaned to quickly kiss his lips; then she turned and pulled the curtain back and went away and let it fall. There was the sound of hands clapped thrice.

Presently some kindly people came and gave his gnarly fruit wood crutch and helped him on his way.

13: Episode Eleven: Abbot And Costello Meet The Four Barbarians

"What does your temple teach about reincarnation, good Petronus?"

The young man laughed. "Oh Phillipus! I'm hardly one to ask; I'm just an amateur. Phaedrus is a serious scholar; he may have a better line on that."

But Phaedrus, a mere apprentice in their order, merely shrugged unhelpfully.

"Oh Petronus, tush;" the sturdy lame old tramp who was the ruler of some far off land rather insisted, coming up reclining on an elbow; "please; you're their king. They must tell you things. I'm sure you've asked. It is a major question."

Little Phaedrus, sitting with them mostly in silence but all ears – waiting with them near the road above the beach between the brilliant sunset and the rising crescent moon climbing through the night's climbing web of stars and the infinite oceanic abyss deep beneath the ground, just where the cool soft whispers of the wine dark sea came caressing at the white dusty land where it reclined at last surrendering up its heat to let its pale colors sleep in darkness, among the buzzing waiting throng of human folk who sat and lay and milled around them in a thick carpet across that bit of land – there Phaedrus smiled across his cup. He did not feel one tenth so friendly toward this fellow as Petronus did, not even now, but he was thinking of a bit of mischief. The subject was reincarnation. He spoke up; "It's not one of the secrets."

"Well, there;" Petronus said; "you see? They don't tell me secrets."

"Ah hah!" cried the gruff old gray headed wanderer, pointing his finger at Petronus as though an amusing trap had sprung unexpectedly. "They did tell you about that then, about reincarnation? Please; I'm really curious. It's something I always ask everywhere I go. I'm not sure if I want it to be true or not. Phaedrus, will you tell me?"

"Ah!" the boy did say. Yes, he thought, the fellow likes to play and might be beaten. In his uneven fifteen year old voice, even scratchier than usual from the afternoon's songs and shouts to which he'd added actively, he roughly cleared his throat. He drank some of the fortifying beer. Then he straightened up his stance, prone as he was, with hands folded on his chest, and launched out onto the world in a miniature rhetorical composition. "Called upon to speak, I shall speak. But I shall change the subject. I shall tell you a different secret that I've learned, a real one. I've learned it on my own so I can tell. It's about secrets."

Phillipus at once held up a cautioning hand. "I don't follow."

"A secret about secrets."

"Oh."

"There aren't any. But that's a secret so don't tell anyone; let them guess."

Petronus cried; "By the gods! You've found the Labyrinth!" The pictured thing which had flashed into existence suddenly in his mind's eyes was now turning slowly inside out while he perused it carefully. "Is there a Minotaur hiding in it?" Unseen things were moving in his mind that he could distinctly feel more than see.

"Wait!" spoke Phillipus, holding up his hand again to make them stop. They were talking just exactly like two philosophers of the same sect or order usually do among themselves and he was far behind already. He was genuinely trying to catch up. "I know there are secrets. I even have some that I really do keep to myself alone." He tried to work it out, or at least to work out something not too foolish. Tugging at his close cut beard, he shrugged. "But, certainly, it might be said that if just one person knows them, even myself, then they're not really secret any more. Is that what you're getting at? More or less?"

Petronus shook his head. The vivid image in his mind was gone with just a sort of puff and a lingering shadow in opposite colors. Oh well. He answered; "No no! He's talking about the way they teach things here, at Elfesis. First you have to think of it on your own and then they tell you. Queer, true, but not too hard once you get the hang of it. And you really do learn that way, you see." But then he thought back over what he'd just then said, fingering his lower lip. "But that's not really quite it either though. That's how you go along through the Labyrinth but I'm really sure just now I did get a good glimpse of the whole thing."

Phaedrus offered another clue; "It's like the rainbow chambers in the courtyard back there. That made me think of this when I went through." They gave him no response except inquiring looks and it was growing near to real darkness when the dancing would begin so time was somewhat pressing. "Look;" he said; "there's no secrets but that's a secret so don't tell anyone. Everyone has to guess. Everyone does have to guess. But if you go on along until you've asked every possible question, and you've really struggled all the time for answers and none of them would fit, then eventually it just occurs to you that everything's been right in front of your nose all along. That's all." He gestured outward with his hands and made as if to glance around. "That really is all of everything. That's how to read omens."

So there they were where the wine dark sea comes caressing at the white dusty land which is surrendering up its heat, with the sunset maybe by then a little less brilliant but the crescent moon still climbing up the web of stars, and the deep abyss still down below, lying there among a crowd of thousands who are each experiencing an entire human life with everything that necessarily entails; Phaedrus has just made some remark that I, for one, find puzzling and yet intriguingly fraught with possible connections to all of this, and then this happens:

"Well you've got me stumped;" Phillipus said; "I look around and all I see is stuff. Lots of it, but it's all just stuff. I keep looking for something else behind the curtains. Or behind the chair."

That drew up sympathy in Petronus, like water in a well. Of course he understood the reference to curtains and chair quite vividly himself and he'd found the comment quite intriguing. He spoke from his sympathy; "But Phillipus, what you said before was true about this, just a different point of view."

"No." Phillipus shook his head, thankful for the courtesy but even slightly amused.

Petronus went on; "Really; nothing's secret because everyone can know everything. You were right."

"Well, if you say so, maybe; but if I get anything right in philosophy it's just by accident. But look;" he pointed at Phaedrus; "what he just said: That's all. That's what she said to me in the courtyard. That's all. She really meant: That's all of everything. The same way he did."

Petronus laughed again, delighted with this kind of chat. "Yes, and: It's all right in front of your nose. Well, it is." He reached up a fingertip to fetch a bit of the dry dark chalky makeup that was drawn in a thick line beside his actual nose, found that he must scratch to get some with a fingernail, and then inspected it closely in the deepening purple dusk. Smiling at them, he said; "I'm supposed to be Agamemnon you know, and a little boy too at the same time. So it's all right here for everyone to see; all the past and future ages."

So, if I may reiterate, there they were where the wine dark sea comes caressing at the white dusty land – okay with the sunset gone by now but still a magnificent display of stars which, together with the gleaming crescent moon, could knock your freaking socks off – and all the whole geography of Earth around them, and wonderful conceptions of the structures that lie below, and thousands of people right there who are existing amid all of this, and our character Petronus has just put into straightforward words a major idea about how to see all this: That you can see all this by simply looking at it for yourself with your own eyes.

"Alright;" Phillipus said, rather pouncing; "so it's come around again to the same question I was asking. Right? Rein-carnation. I really do ask about that at every temple I go to."

Phaedrus asked; "You're not sure if you want it to be true?"

"Right;" Phillipus answered; "first I say: We can't go on and on and on with this. With all this stuff. What's the point? But then I say: We can go on as long as we have to. Maybe at least there's some honor in it. Kind of like the narrow bridge. Maybe that's the point."

Phaedrus, now having truly beaten the fellow once and thereby gained in confidence, laid an arm beneath his head and frowned and asked; "But you're a famous duelist. You're even a conqueror too. What's that about, killing people, if you don't know what happens to them? Is all of that just too much fun for you to stop?"

Phillipus found he was embarrassed by the question. He rather shifted where he lay, but then looked up and answered directly; "Well, honestly, it is a lot of fun. It is a great sport."

"Oh, shame!" said Phaedrus.

Okay, now this is the last time I'm going to mention this, but there they are where the wine dark sea comes caressing at the white dusty land, the stars and moon and all of that – glory, glory, glory – and thousands of people, and this guy, as we have seen, is totally oblivious to it, but I do seriously suggest that you suspend judgment about the guy until you hear his side of the story and even then consider his potential for personal improvement.

"But look! I'm like an entertainer. I'm like a prostitute, the better kind at least that makes a fella work. I bring some glory to this stupid world and people share it. People have to fight me hard; no matter who wins or loses the world's a little brighter for it."

Phaedrus found himself completely unimpressed with this. The man was ruthless and manipulating, hungry for his pleasures, guileful to the point of self-deceit; but honest, humble, patient, generous, brave and maybe loyal too. All and all, he simply looked exactly like a man. He really was a king, whatever that was worth.

But good king Petronus went along a different track. "I'm not sure what you meant about prostitutes. Do you mean your work is something like a priestess? Death and making love, orgasm, that kind of thing? Have I got that right?"

Phillipus laughed. "No." He shook his head. "Not that complicated. Or, complicated in different ways." He had a bright idea and raised a finger. "But wait; I've got just the fella who'll explain the point." He twisted round and looked toward a huge lump of a man who lay close behind him. Phillipus called; "Captain Chimaeros!" But the man was facing the other way, deep in conversation with two others there, and didn't hear. Phillipus tossed some dirt. That didn't work. Finally he picked up his crutch and reached rather awkwardly to poke the fellow in the back, crying again; "Captain Chimaeros! Sir!"

"Huh? Oh, yes sir!" Realizing, quite embarrassed, that he'd forgotten for a while who was there, the huge bulky man, with a most surprising show of fluid grace, instantly rolled himself into a ball and then sprang up onto his knees, really now hulking above Phillipus, evidently ready and very willing to jump up farther to his feet. He was clad only in the rough linen smock that served the soldiers for their underwear. He dusted off his hands, repeating; "Yes sir?"

"Captain, may I ask you for your lady's name?"

"My lady sir?"

"Yes, your famous wondrous whore that everybody talks about."

"Oh her, sir? You mean the one what's got brains like Athena, legs like Artemis and hair like Persian silk?"

"Does she? I didn't know."

"Well sir, do you mean the one's got hips like a oak tree and armpits that smells like roses and she grins like the beaming sun? The one's got titties what tastes like pomegranates?" He was motioning on his chest; apparently they must large as well as tasty.

"Ha! Good man! Does she really?"

"If it's just the same one as you means sir." He scratched beside his ear. "Are you referring to the one what's smarter than the smartest crow you ever seen?"

"I suppose."

"The one knows every joke that's ever been told ever since anybody ever told a joke? The one knows all the songs? That one? The one goes whop whop whop with her titties on yer face?" And he pantomimed that.

Phillipus was now chuckling aloud with no wish to speak.

Big Chimaeros wagged a finger at him. "Sir, did you know she can play a three-string fiddle with her toes? With her toes! We're getting married soon as I gets a legal letter back from home about a farm my uncle promised me."

Through his chuckles, Phillipus asked; "Well, that's all very fine but can she fuck?"

"Fuck! Fuck! Sir . . ." He was looking round, searching for a good response, rather wriggling as he knelt there, and finally put his massive hands upon his massive hips and answered; "Sir, she'd be insulted that you asked."

One behind him called; "Sir, she fucked me half to death."

And the other; "Sir, she fucked me blind. She did. She really did, I swear. Damndest thing I ever saw!"

Chimaeros asked; "Sir, we'd be honored if you'd share some cider."

A fair sized skin came tossing over, landed on the king's thigh, drooped sadly there in its nearly empty flaccidness.

"Real stuff;" one of them back there called; "good old Memnon picked it up at a farm back there."

"Don't worry sir;" Chimaeros said; "I'm sure he paid for it."

Phillipus conjured up some seriousness, called out; "I hope he did pay for it; if not, he should have." Shaking his head, with an edge of serious warning to the word play, he advised; "If he didn't, I know he will." He pulled the stopper, took a modest gulp and shoved the stopper back. It was strong, something he had heard of from this country, apple brandy really. From the fumes he really had to shake his head and blink his eye. Expensive too, no doubt. For sake of courtesy he'd made it look a much bigger swallow than it was. He was not an avid drinker. He called, "Thank you very kindly, gentlemen!" and tossed it back generally in the same direction through the growing darkness.

But now that he was serious, he said; "Captain Chimaeros, me and these two gentleman philosophers here were discussing prostitutes."

"Yes sir?"

"And I naturally mentioned you as being an expert on the subject."

"Oh, sir, all I really know about the mysteries of the trade is what she's taught me, and that's just recently."

"Well . . . By the way, what's the lady's name?"

"I don't know sir."

Both Phillipus and Petronus laughed at that surprise.

"Well, see, she won't tell me. And I've asked all her sisters here this afternoon and they won't tell me neither." He took his purse that hung on a heavy strap across his torso and shook it; it was emptier than the brandy skin. "I give 'em all my money and they still won't say."

"That ain't exactly right." one behind him called.

Half turning back, Chimaeros really cried; "Oh yeah, they all tell me but they all say something different!" Turning to the king again, he shrugged in bewildered disappointment. "Last month, at my party see, she was boss of the show and made everybody call her Mistress. So then today I asks and she just grabs my dick and wiggles it and grins and won't say. So I starts in to asking people. First one, I puts a penny in her hand and points at my girlfriend and she says it's Lesbiania but of course that seems like a lie so I asked another, two pennies this time, and she says it's Nymphomania and on and on, shit like that. And every one was real polite."

A hoarse guffaw behind him.

"Well they was!"

"Phillipus asked; "You're getting married though?"

"Oh yeah, for sure. All I got to do is just persuade her."

Young Petronus, full of salt, cupped his hands around his mouth and shouted to be sure of being heard; "Captain, I guess you are enjoying Athens."

That got a hearty laugh from the two other soldiers over in the shadows.

Phillipus, lying there, reached up toward Chimaeros saying; "Sir, will you clasp my arm?"

A little startled, but guessing that his king now wished to rise, he grasped the offered forearm very firmly and braced himself to toss Phillipus to a standing position.

But Phillipus grasped the fellow's forearm still. He said loudly for all to hear; "Captain Chimaeros, you are a worthy man. You are a man like me. Thank you for your service."

"Sir . . ."

"And thank you for your guidance in my own affairs."

"Sir?"

"Congratulations on your coming marriage! May I attend the ceremony?"

"Yes sir!"

There was a space of silence while the two men beamed at one another in the night, holding each other thus quite the way each would have held a shield.

Finally Phillipus let him go.

Big Chimaeros dusted off his hands again and said; "Well sir, if yer wanting anything just give a holler. I'll be right over here with these two sharks. Awake this time."

"Thank you."

"If you don't mind sir, now it's really dark, I'm thinking we'd kind of tail around behind you just for safety's sake; if that's alright."

Phillipus was surprised this struck him as surprise. He fingered at his dust filled beard and tried to think it over carefully but found the day had gifted him with far too many doubts to let him easily find the quick normal sure resolution of a problem he expected from himself. He did not want to make a show of cowardice, certainly not; that would defeat all of his purposes in coming. And was there some slim chance of further privacy with her? A bodyguard would surely chuck that down the hole. And there had been no spy reports at all of any plots cooked up for execution on this trip.

Not knowing what was best, on the instant's impulse, Phillipus made a gesture of holding up the breast of his beggar's shirt and answered; "The deities of Elfesis protect me while I have this on. If you see me bare ass, then there might be trouble."

"Oh. Yes sir; good thing you told cause I didn't know."

"Why don't you good men just prowl around in the crowd within eyeshot and keep your ears open? Don't worry much about idle chat though; people hate me but the shirt is good protection."

"Sure thing. We all got knives of course. That's all, just little ordinary odd job slicers; but these two there, they're pretty handy fellas."

"I don't want action. I really don't. I don't want action. I hope you understand; very bad strategic move. Desecration; start a war we don't want now. Absolutely last resort. We don't want action. We want all Hellenes to be our allies from now on. The situation calls for very fine discretion. I don't want action. That's your orders."

"Anything you say sir."

"I can trust you. Can I trust them?"

"I'll hold em to it hard. Watch em like a crow. I'll spread the word about no action to the other loafers what's hanging about too."

"Good man. Make them understand the strategy. I don't want action. Absolutely last resort. If we do have action on this march then all our current plans go down the privy hole."

"Yes sir."

"Even ordinary stupidity may be punished."

"Yes sir. Well then, considering that, shall I rally em up in secret teams for discipline, to keep em still?"

"That's up to you. But if they fraternize with the yokels, that could be a good thing too. Might keep them occupied and anyway we do want friends among these people."

"Yes sir. Since you mention that, some of the fellas is really hoping for a fuck. Me for instance."

"That seems to be against the yokel law for now." Phillipus paused and rubbed a weary dirty hand across his dirty face. "Me too. Your discretion when and if to relax the order, not to cause confusion and not to break the yokel law; no rapes though. That will definitely count as ordinary stupidity. No rapes, absolutely."

"Yes sir. There's supposed to be a big camp tonight at the end of the road. Maybe there."

"Yes, maybe. Or maybe tomorrow."

Chimaeros shrugged. "Nothing wrong with that sir; tomorrow. I seen her looking. She'll want you in the morning too."

Phillipus now rubbed his hand across his dry lips, suddenly very thirsty for the flavor of her breast. "I don't know what to do."

"The gods will guide you sir. They always have before anyway."

"The problem is, she's a goddess. See? You know what happened to me the last time I tried that kind of shit."

"Yes, of course. But look here king; if any man can do it you can. Maybe two time's the charm." He reached a big meaty reassuring hand to gently pat his hero's knee. "And so what if she really does fuck you to death? Ain't it worth it? I bet it is. That one loves you; I can tell. She'd turn you into something someplace. Whoosh. We'll make a real fine song about it."

Petronus suddenly spoke up, surprising them; "So that's how such men are deified. A warrior's immortality."

And Phaedrus spoke up too, rather quiet in his scratchy hoarseness; "Just don't take off your shirt when you're doing it. Not tonight."

And then a cry above the buzzing crowd, out somewhere in the dark; "Agamemnon! Where are you!"

Phaedrus reached to grasp Petronus by the shoulder. "That must mean you. They're looking for you."

"My gods!" Petronus said. "Of course."

The two climbed to their feet to cast looks around. Phaedrus saw the little knot of searching figures stepping slowly through the sitting and reclining rather shifting shadowy mass of human shapes that made the landscape here, they peering down and round them as they stepped. The voice cried out again. There was something curious in the silhouette. It was the sticks they carried on their shoulders.

Standing now, Phaedrus pointed and Petronus waved and called. The little group then changed direction and approached with new resolve.

"Thank the gods!" the voice went on as they drew close. "Son, you're wanted. For Heaven's sake where have you been? You should have known. Don't wander off. There's work for you."

Here was the Master of the Agrai Temple, Diotoma's husband, he also being specially elected marshal of the march for this dangerous year, and also being long elected chief of the Comrades of Heracles, a very well respected fraternity in the city and widely known beyond, and also a noble keen to prove his worth and loyalty, and with him half a dozen other sturdy citizens under his command equipped with staves.

"Yes, good master, of course." Petronus now was answering as they came near. "All that is true but I have been tending other duties. I have been acting as a royal host, I have! And significant words have been spoken!"

He meant the manifestly genuine and obviously sincere order for peace that Phillipus had issued. He meant to vouch for it immediately

"Here now," Petronus cried happily, "look who's with us. Have you met this gentleman yet?" He gestured with a generous open hand toward where Phillipus lay.

14: Episode Twelve:
The Dancing Ground Again

The famous death of Captain Chimaeros of the Macedons was of course a terrific shock to the many innocent bystanders who saw the thing transpire through the fate or chance of being close at hand, being as they were engaged in a peaceful and profound religious rite. And the heroic nature of his end has earned the man a small but rightful place in human history through the honor that his final action shone in the eyes of the Hellenes upon the Macedons' adventure eastward. How many strong battalions did his famous honor – as the democratic city's general opinion gradually chose to see the matter – eventually raise for their amazing conquests? And the way it came to pass can even now perhaps be viewed as a miraculous salvation of the rite itself; in a legal sense it was not a battle nor a murder, not a fundamental desecration in the least, but a plain and simple fatal accident as though a pilgrim on the march had been jostled from the narrow bridge onto the rocks below or been struck down by a stone thrown by another pilgrim at a fox, or such as that, all of which had proper place in law and easy cures and did in fact occur occasionally. But the effect this soldier's sacrifice had on his king personally may actually be the thing which startles us.

The Athenian marshal of the march, who was also husband of the Agrai Matron who had been outraged, seeing who was lying there, in a sudden passion with a wordless scream stepped and swung his long hard oak wood stave from his shoulder downward at Phillipus with considerable speed and force.

Chimaeros, in a single fluid motion, mindful of his orders against violence, did naught at first but reach and catch the stick's knobby end dead still in a big meaty fist just inches from the royal head. But then, feeling in the ground or air the sudden movement of his fellow soldiers, who likely had not heard the king's orders clearly, leaping up and drawing their sharp knives and leaping then at once to reach the man who made assault upon their king, Chimaeros, not even glancing their direction, instantly sprang up and threw his great protecting bulk upon the man who staggered back a little way into the arms of his companions, so that the valiant captain took the fatal stab that entered high beside his ear and thus protruded downward through his throat.

It was the shouted order of Phillipus that brought a sudden stillness to the scene, a terse familiar formula of words to halt an action. The second soldier's arm with gleaming knife in hand was there held up in air, arrested in the very moment of descent toward a second blow. That polished blade glinted silver in the moonlight.

Standing there astride the king, the burly killer stepped aside and with the motion jerked free his blade which chanced to bring the dying body of Chimaeros turning, falling down to lie face to face upon the king

It was the spouting blood which bathed his breast and face together with the captain's distant gaze and smile of radiating grace that in the instant mystified Phillipus to the depths of his soul. And simultaneously Phillipus in that moment for the first time fully knew how well he had been loved. He felt the love break free inside the man and wing away into immortal realms, and in the final moment that was left to show responding love, Phillipus of the Macedons twined fingers in the man's coarse hair and pressed the trembling lips to his till they were still.

15: Episode Twelve Point Five:
Also The Dancing Ground Again

There was a moment when she knew her marriage bed and all of that would never be. Or rather when she knew that if all that were never done then still her priesthood would be worth the lack of it. Or rather when she first with conscious judgment chose her priesthood absolutely past all that, regardless what might be. It was so hard for boys to take a girl like her but by that time, that afternoon of choice, her dearest childhood chum already had a husband and a newborn.

A stitching bee. She was home for the holiday. Old Auntie Kettle plucked a random fussy little child from underfoot, examined it and knowingly declared "Oh, he wants to eat!" And with a glance about the little yard where they were sitting at the work she then of course thrust the hungry child into the bosom of the only healthy milking woman present. Of course, and yet . . .

Sixteen herself, her infant then days old, scarcely yet a week of life between she and the tiny one she loved above all else, and it her first, and never yet another child had she yet put to tit, and sleeping unsuspecting of this breach, this betrayal of a holy trust, this fracturing of sacred love, it sleeping unsuspecting nearby in a shady basket cradle wreathed with dainty flowers.

Old aunties know their work. There was a choice to make – community or selfishness – and now was time to get it made.

The young mother's face was blanched in horror and she stared.

And the priestess girl, the closest friend, the cousin tried and true, the intimate of bygone times, now come home for the holiday, was sitting just beside with mouth agape, astonished at the shock of such an ordinary thing. And her own tits were yearning to give suck. And yet she understood it all intensely without jealousy.

No spite and yet suddenly the tears burst out in panicked grief that such a life as this, of such surpassing beauty as this was, would not be hers. Where would her Goddess take her? Was she a stranger here already? The temple's early years – the years they gave the girls and boys who would apprentice back into the village rites – were almost done and no one thought that she would leave Elfesus. So could she ever again be home in this loved and dreaded village yard, this place of utmost courage? Was she a stranger here already?

Here was, in fact, the tragic fact that had and has informed great tragic song and poetry across that culture-world from Ur to Ireland. To live where they were living, with the means of living that were then in hand, humans must compromise continually between competing demands which were, despite the contraries of those demands, so doubtlessly innate to human nature or else so innate in the way that they perforce must live, as to be both, contrary though they were, doubtlessly sacred. These people danced a labyrinth with every step.

And then she understood that understanding this so well – that seeing this eternal tragic majesty of human life so well – was more than human heart could bear at such close reach. She was not made to be one of the aunties here where every instant of your life demanded so much acquiescence to the Fates. And this was just the very thing the village boys all feared of finding in her bed, this wish for knowledge over faith. This constant groping in the cavern of the well behind the eyes. This blaze of unaccounted thought. This laughter bursting from her weeping heart. Indeed, they understood her to be mad. And here and now – on this particular ground at this particular moment of this life – she was.

It can't be said the fit of laughing weeping took her unawares this second time. She felt it shadowed when she saw her well loved cousin start and stare. Then when the well loved cousin nodded, pulled the chiton down and held the hungry one to let the hands and lips seek out the teat, she felt it like a storm of knowing rushing up her spine. Then when an eager voluntary squirt dripped down the little cheek the fit came fully on.

She sat there slumped down on her stool just like the other time, the stitching things all fallen from her violently shaking hands and trod beneath her tapping feet, but this time knew exactly why she laughed and wept. The world was just so beautiful. And yet, what was the use of this? The dire frustration of these crippling fits – the inability to work, the liability it placed on her companions – all came exactly to this point: They who were so beautiful, how could she ever serve them as a lunatic?

But then her well loved cousin looked her in the eyes to gain attention, looked down at the child she had at breast, looked into her eyes again with dire anguish manifest in each contour of her face and silently clearly asked: "Dear priestess friend, is this a crime that I have done?"

Did they see she looked at things they did not see? Did they realize that this insanity was saturated all and all with holy revelation?

Apparently they did. For it was Auntie now who stood behind her quaking body, embraced to try to hold her shoulders still, and – even while her head was bobbing to and fro and even while the sobs and laughter barked out of her throat –

the old matron bent to speak distinctly in her ear: "Is it a crime what I have done?"

The fit then passed immediately and never would return. She sagged into the old woman's arms. She gulped and gasped for breath. She cried out hoarsely as the spittle flew: "It is so beautiful! It is all so beautiful! There is such courage! What is good is done!"

And in that moment she had chosen priesthood far beyond all else.

16: Episode Thirteen: Into The Hills

So up into the hills of whispering pines they found the moonlit shadowed path and climbed the gentle slopes, she in the lead with Mother's basket tall and straight upon her head. She called up strength and set a pace the tall girl would have liked. Petronus strode within arm's reach to right and Diotoma to her left. The path was wide enough and smooth and very firm with countless dark or glittering pebbles under foot, trod down tight into the soil by countless shoes before and later. The place was very beautiful indeed and full of its own soul.

She felt Phillipus close behind her. Before, this one thought himself a king and conqueror like so many others but he had now consciously risen to a place among the beggars in their very dirty shirts. She felt in him the mingled ecstasy and grief that is the very essence of human life's joyous tragedy, and felt him gazing round and felt him feel himself – with every breath of fragrant forest breeze and every step – now opening gradually more and more to the others there and to the stars and land. In fact, this place was somehow redolent to him of another forest, other land in different time. He used the crutch much more freely now, as a walking stick.

Presently, when he seemed settled well into this aspect of his proper work, Victory turned her head enough to show a profile of her face and cast a thought to catch his eye then beckoned with an upraised hand. Seeing this, Petronus courteously went a step or two ahead to make a space for him and looked back, nodding to assure Phillipus he was wanted.

When he was walking there, with the dark stain that soiled the breast of his holy shirt, and the seaside sand and roadway dust that made a hardening dough of it, as though for some strange sacramental bread – and with some remaining blood still stiffening his hair – and with a wondrous wonder fairly glowing from his pitiful scarred countenance – she looked straight in his eye, actually into his mind, and said in a flat plain tone quite loud enough to hear; "Beggar king, do you now rule yourself?"

The dirty tramp replied in rather great surprise just to be spoken to; "Lady?"

"Do you now rule yourself with honesty? Have you thrown off your self-deceiving lies?" She paused, awaiting more. She said, "Have you admitted to yourself the fear that used to drive you like an overloaded donkey, and the pain and weakness it gave you?"

Phillipus vaguely shook his head like someone waking from a most amazing nightmare and he said; "Oh Mistress, I was afraid of loneliness. Afraid that it would kill me. So stupid. Just nonsense when you look at it plainly, if you look at all of it, if you hold it up beside reality."

"Do you now rule yourself?"

He could not help but reach his hands to for a moment pat his thighs and chest as though to find some other body than the one to which he was accustomed. "I guess it's possible I do."

And so Victory said; "A stadia before the gate, in the last valley where Elfesis Hill rises up to fill the view, do you know the children of Elfesis come to meet the march, to dance for us?"

"I have been told that, Lady, yes. I understand they are costumed as ghosts. I'm wondering what's going to happen there. I mean, spiritually. I mean, for someone like me."

"There's half an hour or so available there and you have won your prize. And a warning: It would be stupid, frankly, to refuse Our Sister's blessing."

Phillipus gasped.

And so did Diotoma.

Seeing that he could not answer yet, not with his jaw agape, Victory waved Phillipus back into his proper place and turned her eyes up to that evening's glowing sky. She breathed deeply of the darkling perfumed air that rustled with the voices of the haunted trees that all came crowding round about them as they went. She smiled a smile of blessed peace.

Phillipus gradually fell back, burdened as he was with this new choice that never was before, to him, a choice at all.

Diotoma, glancing round to watch him vanish in the moving shadows of the silent striding crowd, waited as she thought she must but anxiously in the extreme. Presently Diotoma glanced to Victory then glanced away then looked again and said; "My friend, how is the evening going for you? Well or badly?"

"Oh my sweetheart;" the lady answered in a voice which almost sounded full of dreams; "it's very well with me indeed. I'm listening to the pines. Our Sister's singing to me with them. It is a much more lovely hymn than when I came through here last time, going down to the city. What was that? Last month? It seems like a long long time, a different world. A different life. But how are you?" Then with perhaps a bit of worry: "You must be tired; really I ought to slack the pace."

"Oh no! I don't mean that!" And Diotoma looked away again. She suddenly felt the coolness of the breeze and tightly wrapped her arms around herself. She felt the shadow of Our Mother's basket towering above. But the infinite life force inside it seemed hidden from her.

Victory insisted: "What is it, darling friend?"

The good woman shook her head. "Mistress, it is not my place to say."

"Is it something a bosom friend would say?"

"It is!"

"Then speak."

"Victory, you needn't do it!" Then Diotoma glanced around in the city way she had, as though to look for spies, and repeated just as urgently but nearly in a whisper; "You need not do it."

And Victory laughed. She said; "If we were standing still I think you would have stamped your foot."

Angry, Diotoma shook her head. "You're such a silly woman sometimes."

And quickly Victory answered; "My beloved friend, I only felt delighted with you. Don't be offended."

"Don't be stupid; I'm not offended by such a stupid thing as that; it's just that you're so blind."

"My darling dear, please tell me what you mean."

"You needn't do it. Don't you know anything about religion? The rite is full of substitutes this year. It is. Amazing. Haven't you noticed? Your Board of Elders shoved you in so suddenly and unannounced. My husband was voted in to substitute for the regular marshal. Me here beside you in place of someone from your order. Phillipus and that fool Petronus dodging in and out of each other's footsteps practically. And that ox actually dying for Phillipus!"

Petronus, certainly listening closely to this, surprised and certainly miffed by the unkind reference to himself amid his continuing best efforts, certainly spoke up. "Excuse me please. You needn't get personal. Of course you're right but yes, so what? If you know what it all means, then do tell us."

"Now you shut up!" snapped Diotoma.

He wagged his head in quite theatrical clownishness and quoted the classic line: "Oh, bugger me!"

But Diotoma would not laugh. She grabbed up Victory's hand and found that she was squeezing tighter than she thought she should. "Don't you know? There is someone right here who is completely willing and able to make any sacrifice at all in your place. To substitute for you!"

"No you couldn't. This sacrifice is mine." Victory shook her head emphatically which set the tall moon shadows of the basket dancing out among the all-surrounding shapes that were streaming by. "It's a question of balance, surely you see. There's been no felony and the rite was not broken and no recompense is required, but still a reverberation occurred of which we wish to prevent further reverberations in the future. The lack of a felony in itself is telling. It's not a question of restoring balance but of applying choice in a desired direction to overcome an undesirable state of balance. That's how healing works after all. That's what Musical Electric Force harmonics is, essentially, is it not? And we are now in my order's portion of this rite so it is my order's job to do it. And it's all quite plain from many things my Elders taught me."

Petronus shrugged. "You've really lost me."

Victory pulled her hand free of Diotoma's grasp so she could grasp one of Diotoma's hands instead. She pressed it to her bosom. Suddenly she sounded near to tears. "But . . . you offered. Thank you."

But Diotoma now was staring stark into her face with a look that bordered close to fear of the unknown. "Friend," she said, "I don't see your reasoning. Not at all. Our Sister's sexual activities are not concerned with balance and imbalance. Or am I mistaken?"

"Sex?" said Petronus in real surprise, glancing between his two companions. This was an interesting turn. "You're discussing sex?"

"Last time I checked, we were." Diotoma answered him. "Weren't you listening? We're talking about the fact she offered to have intercourse with that ugly man." But then uncertain, she glanced to Victory. "Aren't we?"

And right out loud then Victory burst into a merry laugh. "That's hardly going to be a sacrifice I think! Sorry I misunderstood!"

"What were you thinking then?" her friend demanded. "What sacrifice did you mean?"

"Oh no no no!" cried Victory and wagged a finger. "It's a secret of my order so you'll have to guess. I thought you had, you see. It's something at the Hall of Mysteries."

"A secret!" Diotoma nearly shouted. "Hardly!"

"But anyway," said Victory, "since you brought it up, about the sex: It's mine and you can't have it. What would your husband say if he found out? He'd have an apoplectic fit."

"That man!" cried Diotoma in an extremity of total disbelief. "I see he's changed but . . . You want it with him! You can't possibly! And what about Our Sister's trance!"

"Our Sister said that I can have him to myself. She'll only bless it. No fire or anything. She says I can get pregnant if it's good enough, if it rings the bells and toots the horns. Can't hope for much from a barbarian of course, have to take care of that myself, but still. She promised twins."

"What! You want . . . children . . . with . . ." and there her voice trailed off into the merest exhalation ". . . Phillipus?"

"It's been six months since I got poked, and that one was drunk."

"But . . . him!"

"He has changed. He's a respectful well set up mature athletic gentleman with a nice smile."

"But . . . him!"

"Well," Victory smiled and shrugged, "he is a man."

17: Episode Fourteen:
The Nun's Tale

"It's easily done." young Phaedrus said when Phillipus of Macedon came stammering, trying unsuccessfully to speak his business, there by the tallest flaming torches in the valley while the mob of mischievous costumed children were just then swooping down the dark slope that lay ahead, arriving for their ghostly fete, a stadia before Elfesis Hill. Phaedrus was straining not to be terse, rather ticking off in his mind the fellow's undeniable virtues. He did seem like a better fellow now. And this unwelcome duty was, apparently, a good thing for the temple and the city. And for the Lady. Really now, who else was of sufficient rank out in the world to provide suitably for the Lady's children? "She's waiting for you."

"But he needs clean clothes, definitely," Petronus said, "and more washing too, especially his hair."

So down to the little brook that flows beside that place and with a rag and borrowed robe a little bit snug they quickly got the bridegroom, so to speak, as ready as they could. All of this, of course, was just exactly to her plan.

"Is there still time?" Phillipus asked. At the moment he was standing in the moonlit stream with silver sparkling droplets falling round, rough hands handling his person roughly, looking down at someone's gleaming nakedness. He discovered that he did not care at all about the various scars. He did hear a fearful tremor in his voice when those words

"Is there still time?" drifted into open air but knew the subtle trembling in his flesh was its own very honest yearning. Could that be trusted? Was there time for love somewhere? Is there ever?

"Oh yes." they answered.

And they took him in, across the stream into the fragrant rustling grove, into the moonlit little clearing where there stood the sacred cart and she before it in the silver gown. She was now merely a strong tall human figure of breathtaking beauty, for the basket of the Sacred Pregnancy stood there erect on the cart among the sculptured deities inside the open precinct of their mobile sanctuary, the painted statues animate with flowing golden shadows, heaped with greenery and flowers, set off from this Earthly sphere by the large wheels and lavishly beribboned wreathed corner posts with their fat low hanging swags and the rippling gauzy yellow roof.

Fear, yes she felt transfixing fear. And yet animating desire. She stood there quite deliberately posed yet seeming quite relaxed, standing up quite straight with arms at her sides but with her hands, their fingers lightly entwined, gently gathering the glowing fabric to her lower belly, this to make the slightly parted thighs and the place between a visible invitation. This also was to heighten her sensations, as she wished to conceive.

With a reassuring nod the instant when his two ad hoc attendants disappeared from view, the Lady sang a pretty melody: "It's easily done." And so she hoped; although in fact she had her own attendant, Diotoma, listening from the shadows with an ax at hand as last resort in case of urgent need. With a very graceful gesture of open hands Victory beckoned Phillipus closer.

"But . . ." he said; "Lady . . ."

She spoke immediately for further reassurance, leaning toward the man a little, curving her neck gracefully and pressing both hands upward on her breasts to indicate a longing for his touch that was by now quite real; memory of another's fervent touch just hours before. "Our Sister will truly bless us but she will not interfere. She will not interfere. She told me this. She is giving you to me as my reward. And my demand of you is only this: give me pleasure. Will you give me pleasure as I instruct?"

It took a heartbeat's time for him to seem to take in this surprise, but then a deep sigh escaped his heart. He felt that he was leaping like a buck the few remaining steps and they were in each other's arms. Not yet a kiss; there had been another very different kiss that night so first he looked into her eyes and saw no death.

She was as tall as he and so the returning look she gave was level, very open, simple and direct. Mind to mind she told him this: I will not die. Nor will I harm you.

She saw and felt in him complete release of fear and, thus unbound, his hands could not be still but set themselves to fondling whatever curves of her they found. This felt interestingly rough to her in its ungoverned urgency but meanwhile his member – respectably erect for all these moments past – had been captured by a subtle movement of her hand within a soft fold of cloth and so was rather like some small thing like a bird, pressed against her near the spot where it was wanted most. And then it fairly quivered for a heartbeat.

That was a savory delight she wished again and so to try and make it quiver more she pressed her breasts against him and flicked her tongue inside his open lips. She felt the inner strings that held her inner organs loosening. Tonight was probably a few nights past her ripest time to make a child so everything that could be done along that line was useful.

And then again, to feel that phallus straining in her grip at least once more, with him now breathing tiny gasps and his whole face wide in astonishment at her skillfully massaging hand, and his whole body stiff, she growled into his face and bent her head down and bit the very muscular neck.

To think ahead: She had been told there is a certain state of female sexual arousal where your upper lips and tongue exchange sensations with their lower counterparts. Slight penetration in that state will yield a taste perhaps of wine or fruit or honey. Likewise, you may play the phallus with your lips and tongue and thus obtain a most delicious sense of ghostly penetration. What had the Eldress told about the hallmarks of that subtle state, so she might recognize an opportunity? Oh yes of course; that you will learn by doing.

She let the phallus go to force one of her legs through his, twining her leg around behind his knee and calf, his member thus nimbly caught again by the way her hip was pressed, and climbed up on him for an inch or two. Quite like a snake or dragon, she then bit his ear and hissed long and low between the teeth she clenched enough to thrill that piece of flesh with fear.

Then Victory spoke into his ear; "Do you want to give me pleasure? You must promise it. And there's very little time, very little."

He breathed, "You want to come real good? How can I make you?"

And so the plan advanced. His member did befit his stature in its thickness but not so really in its length and she was deep inside. She knew that in her case it ought to touch her there, and frequently, to rouse the energy her womb would use to summon spirits from the land of souls awaiting birth. She thought that she could numb the muscles above his scrotum that must eventually jerk to force the semen in, the nourishment of the spirit to be chosen, numb them till it was ready, and hoped to conjure stamina in him as well, to keep him going at it for sufficient time, till she had the spirit ready for its father's milk, but certainly he must quite rip down whatever dams he usually built across his stream of energy to keep on going at it for as long as needed. And she believed she could accept this comfortably.

And so she smiled into his face and raised her chin in gesture of fierce pride and heard her voice that was very very hoarse and gruff indeed as she breathed these words: "You must fuck me hard. You must."

To this he only nodded.

And she said: "I have a trick to slow your release for as long as we want, so do not fear. Don't hold back a single morsel of yourself. I want you all completely, every pleasure you can give, and deeply. Remember, you are my reward."

But that was not enough to please herself, the backwoods woman she would always be, and so she said again; "Fuck me hard."

What time had passed? How much remained? What next?

With him not knowing how she wished to start, she found the song again and sang; "It's easily done. It's done a million times a day."

She pushed herself out of the firm embrace and made a twirling dance just out of reach then pulled the ribbon ends so that the soft folds of the silver dress ballooned and then went rippling down to Earth across her tingling skin, she kneeling as it fell but then arising partly to begin a little pantomime of Aphrodite in the pool. She quietly sang a stanza of a harper's tune while reaching to the silver water, lifting up a handful of the sacred stuff above her head so as to pose most gracefully, and delighted sensually to feel it streaming down.

He stared, his fists clenching and unclenching.

Still in the kneeling pose, she did a lovely bow of open arms. Then she looked up and asked; "Are you afraid of being naked?"

"I'm not afraid anymore."

But still he stood there, despite the pressing time, not afraid perhaps, perhaps enchanted. Her fingertips could reach his robe but then what could she do that would not be clumsy?

She might rip it off with teeth and claws and then be on him. Stuff it in. Well, why not? She was aching. She was throbbing. Ye gods, she was randy. Or was he merely playing at reluctance?

She was on the verge of saying "Remove your garment" or the like but then perhaps the thought alone was prompting enough. Or else she now looked unmistakably like a lioness crouched to spring. In any case, the fellow now disrobed.

It was the scars he was reluctant to display. She saw this by his modest manner of undressing and the modest way he stood. They were a pride to him but he was here as priest and not as soldier. And yet he wished for her to see him. And the scars were part of he himself and he himself was priest.

He simply slid the garment from himself and folded it and laid it by. The muscles that had bulged the cloth so impressively became an astonishing sculpture, some artist's rendering of masculinity itself, all glowing in the softly shadowed light. And there he stood in her arm's reach, not smiling, not frowning, his stance as though he could stand here an hour or else stride out. There was a movement in his stillness. There was a patience in his pride.

Where had he learned this pose? Or was it natural? She thought it was. She thought that she would fall in love. His hands hung calmly open toward the world. It was a very proper pose to start a rite of blessing.

Kneeling still, she spoke: "I can conjure strength in you by opening all your power streams, so you can give me pleasure as I wish. This is done easily. It is done easily. You will be weary but unhurt. Is that a thing you wish?"

Surprised, he just said, "Yes."

A single step and she was standing, speaking, teaching: "You must stand very still, yes very still indeed, and yet you must definitely relax."

She got him turned about to face the east from where the sun would come, with back to westward where it would go. Left and right of course were north and south. The ground beneath his feet, the deep abyss below, the air and stars above, the stream of Galaxy around. She pressed her hands between his thighs to bring the legs apart again. She turned the hands and shaped them. She quickly lightly stroked his head and neck and arms and hips to tell him to relax.

"Exactly like you were." she said and he adjusted to obey.

"Excellent!" she said.

He was smiling. His eyes were very bright.

She felt a fine vibration in herself. Her inner organs hummed. Her sacred parts were wet and swollen, nipples firm. Her skin was prickling in the autumn moonlight breeze. Her mind was energetic and alert.

She paused to let him know this bit of it was now complete. She said: "We begin."

The erotic component is merely theoretical, you'd almost say, in the ordinary sort of blessing rite. Sex energy is a major part of human physiology of course, and must be clarified with all the rest to properly prepare a human for gathering and distributing galactic waves of Mother's electric life force milk. But ordinarily a blessing is emitted from the hands or face or upper chest so the person who sanctifies the blessor should give most attention to fluids there. Those are not primarily erotic fluids. How should it be done here? She decided this immediately: His semen ought to be the blessing stuff. It would be nourishing in the extreme. Its scent would raise a clamor in the land of souls awaiting birth.

And certainly her own arousal must be tended.

Then with the first gesture which she began, it all fell into place. In this piece of work she would ordinarily separate herself from him in many ways. She was standing back so that her hands alone were in his aura, reaching down with long electric fingers toward his feet. She thought and stopped that action. She carefully stepped closer, closer, very close, to where her eager nipples and her thighs tingled with his electricity. He felt the contact. The man was startled for an instant, eyes wide, but then deliberately relaxed.

She started over, a simple graceful gesture of her hands, and merged herself with him, and he with her. It was like a universe of sparkling fireflies.

He did not resist. He smiled. His member rose. It touched her there.

It was like a wind took them.

It was much more than she had expected. Had she lost count of her body parts, or gained new limbs and surfaces? Or had the wind blown them both to bits in some reality? The music of the wind was many colors. The taste on his tongue, to her, had coiling shape. In his mind she heard a hawk soaring in a mountain updraft.

The normal gestures then – she knew them well, the slow healing touches on the brow and shoulders, knees and abdomen – except that with each touch the spoken prayer was kisses. The energy of touch was breath. And when she spoke the final verse and pressed her open mouth to his, and tongue to tongue, and lingering, the phallus and clitoris kissed. There was a flavor that was scent of rose.

Then tiptoe up, an arm across his shoulder, hand behind his head, a leg around his back, the other round him too, the knees brought up. Reach down to press the tip into the center of her longing. Settle down a tiny bit and press it in enough to grip, a little deeper, more. Were they lovers now? Now the world had changed. She was thinking: She would never have to wish that she had fucked this man because she had.

She flung her head back.

It was very strange to just be fucking here in this wind and these flashing lights. A cock and cunny. Were they lovers now? And where were they?

At least in part this was the moonlit grove beside the holy statues' cart and he was walking. Did he know her plan? It was this: Those fat low hanging swags; sit up on one and he would enter from below. Find a way to bring her legs up wide apart to take him straight in deep to wake her womb. Numb her outer parts for sake of comfort when he thrust and thrust and thrust and thrust. And urge him on.

And here she was now, comfortably secure. There seemed to be a soft plushy fabric covering the grassy yielding swag that he had chosen for her seat.

The lights were flashing in his eyes. She gazed in deep, a corresponding penetration, and there were thunderbolts behind clouds. So something of the like must be inside her in the place where he was penetrating.

The wind was singing in her ears; what did he say? She shook her head "no" to mean she did not hear.

He said again: "You are the woman of my dreams."

But she was thinking not of dreams but of real real children now at last, now really now at last beyond the countless dreams that she had had of them; she shook her head again and answered; "Fuck me."

He pushed and pulled a little stroke, the phallus tugging at her grip, his body rocking like she rode a boat in gentle waves. He would have asked if that was good but she was smiling, nodding. With fingertips the woman touched his brow, caressed his cheek. The woman gazed on thickly muscled arms that held her gently. She bit her lip to keep from speaking love.

He slowly slid as far he could reach. It was easy.

Boom. A little one. That was surprise. She was randy. The blush was in her cheeks, the sweat beaded on her brow.

She breathed again. Her fingers dug into his shoulders so she braced herself and nodded, speaking hoarsely: "More. More."

So he began in earnest.

This was to him like other times but better. Far better. There was the hayloft of the hillside barn, the girl with gold rings in her ears, the meadows where they played. But he did not love her. She took a different fellow. There were the dewy morning springtime revels where they'd danced all night before. There were the tavern jades. There was his wife. There were the dangerous wives of other men. There was the famous courtesan who failed to charm his heart. But this was better. With this new thing in his heart it was all new.

To her it was a mystical experience. It is remarkable how well the body can attune to soul. Or is it better yet to say the mind and soul and body are all one? Somehow this act of intercourse, this thing of flesh that slid so rhythmically within her flesh, and so well fit, and how he rocked her like a babe, was like some thrilling music rising in her heart. There is a rising strain of flute or strings that bids the soul to know that it is beauty, bids the mind to open out.

And then some rhythm of her own awoke and sang a mystic harmony. In fact her body knew a trick her conscious practicing had never found. Each time the shaft was farthest in, a rippling of her muscles would begin so as it fled the passage held and loosed it in septonic overtone. And so: Orgasm came with every stroke: demanding and compelling shouts by her flesh toward all in her that might refuse. She was amazed at this at first – astonished that she'd somehow found this level of arousal which the Eldress said was rarest of all states – until the vision rushes in.

Now here was something known from dreams. In fact she'd never been on horseback in that life and likely never would. But here she was astride a horse at loping gallop. It was a stallion. The wind caressed her nakedness. It was bareback of course and each thunderous hoof beat throbbed her belly, thighs and cunny. The hoof beats swelled her breasts. Then, looking down, she saw the spirits in the ground all looking up with open mouths, roused by the horse's scent. This was the land of souls awaiting birth.

She woke herself, drew out a magic knife and pierced the cloud of dream that veiled her eyes and mind. The scene burst into sharper focus. At last, at long long last, she was really here.

She could not guide the stallion's path – he chased a pale sun in its course that was eastward here – and yet she knew it was her power to choose. She watched and waited while their gallop passed the fading moments. Then suddenly two little ones, embracing one another, flew to meet them. How did she recognize these two? From future life. She seized the little souls tight in her hand and thrust them deep into her belly. But there was no time to rejoice. They must have food or they would flee.

He must now flood her with his milk. They must now get his blessing. Her shouted prayer; "Ye gods now, make him come!" But then she realized it was she who'd stopped him.

Desperately she traced the circumstances back while little souls were crying in her belly. It was that touch she'd made below his navel. The stallion's musky scent was powerful indeed but he ran on and on and on. That touch had opened up the streams of power in his buttocks, legs and cock but put to sleep the little muscles that must finally jerk one single time. She had to wake those little strings of physicality, but how? With both hands now she held the little ones who were piteously weeping. How could she reach out of this distant realm to where the worthless bastard stood there fucking his god damn brains out?

She had her voice. She had a pitch of voice that would most certainly reach. But with what words? She must use words. They must be very elemental speech to penetrate his stupid daze.

The woman seized him by the ears and bellowed: "Squirt me! Squirt me!"

18: Episode Fourteen Point Two Five: Cute Couple

We cannot explain reality. But we try. For example:

The other plot line in this book – where a busload of souls are reborn at the correct times to reenact this year's march together one thousand six hundred forty-one years later – was accurately predicted, pretty much, by a small coterie of highly intelligent metaphysical philosophers, of a Pythagorean sect you may be sure, most of whom came from considerable distance at considerable expense and quite a lot of trouble, to do that year's march, unlikely as it seems.

Despite all difficulties, they foresaw the other plot line.

Yes! In fact, most of these Pythagoreans had no choice but to put up in a rented hovel in a malodorous suburb ever since arriving in ones and twos in time for the cleansing rite in the temple by the river by the city wall the preceding February. And certainly they viewed it as a once-in-a-lifetime research opportunity and personally quite an exotic excursion. They had organized themselves by letter over many months. Two of them were all the way from Syracuse.

Anyway, these Pythagoreans got the physics data in their grand calculation drastically wrong in several major respects. Most egregiously, they believed the Earth and other planets swing around the Sun in epicyclic orbits whereas in fact, of course, the planetary orbits are parabolas. Not quite so horrible as that, but still a crucial weakness in the theory, they chose to use an Earth diameter that was several thousand meters off. And yet (like Newton's calculation of gravity) their metaphysical calculation gave a good result. I don't know how.

And so, I think that what we really need here is a meta-metaphysical approach to the entire question taken as a whole. But I don't know how to do that. And that right there is just my point.

And furthermore, you needn't take my word for it. No, you can see them for yourself, these Pythagoreans. There they are, that tired but intent half-dozen, standing all together in the moonlight in the last valley where Elfesis Hill rises up to fill the view ahead. There you see them, that tight knit little group, still all of them together, right there amid the great throng, watching while the costumed children from the hill ahead, wailing ghostly plaints, have just emerged from the Sacred Precinct's gate and begun to rush down toward the mob. There, those two of them in particular: The couple from Syracuse.

(They are married, in their thirties. Confidentially, I can tell you that he is the toy flute boy in 1971 and she is his granny.)

The gentleman remarks: "I think this is lovely."

The wife replies: "You would. Scenic, huh? Superstition. Ghosts, nineteen times out of twenty, are hallucinations. You know that. You've said so yourself."

The husband puts an arm around her waist and cuddles up. With no response from her to that, he says, "You used to think I was romantic."

"Sex! Sex! Sex!" the wife replies, "That's all you think about. You used to say that I was smart. You loved my brain. Remember that?"

But he's not surprised and answers, "I remember lots of things. There was a moon just like this several years ago. Do you remember it? That night at the beach. In the summer."

"Oh!" she says. "You got me drunk."

"No such thing at all." he answers. "I remember. You were perfectly sober. And didn't we make some promises?"

She thinks about that. She puts her arm around him. She leans against him. He leans toward her. They lean their heads together.

She says, "I remember that."

They watch the moon.

She says, "Those damn magistrates, why did they stop me from giving those damn lectures in the park? I paid the damn fee for it, for mercy's sake."

"I stood up for you."

"I know darling, thank you. That took courage. But why did they?"

"Not because you're female."

"No?"

"We're Pythagoreans."

"Oh that! Damn narrow minded yokels."

They contemplate the narrow minded yokels for a moment.

But he gets tired of that very soon and changes the subject. He says, "One thousand six hundred forty-one years later, that's your calculation."

"Oh well," she answers, "I did the final bit of it."

"I know," he says, genuinely very impressed, "you did."

They kiss.

And there, you see, that's my point.

19: Episode Fourteen Point Two Six: Ordinary People

There is a kind of thoughtful compassion that adults feel when watching children play. In part, that is what the ghosts' parade was expected to produce. Mostly, however, it was meant to work like the ridiculous comic scenes Shakespeare would insert before the holocaust in some of his most horrible dramas. Not to say it was ridiculous – except in some particular years when the children were inspired to make it so – but rather that it mainly performed the same function for these pilgrims near the climax of their trek that the great playwright would later craft for London theatergoers. It was culturally equivalent. It invited them to release their mounting fear and grief into irrelevant good humor, so they would not just fearfully reject whatever else lay ahead, so they had mental space to think and feel and understand more fully. It was comic relief. But in this year when Phillipus took Athens something more is needed. And of course, as one would expect with the immense flexibility of Greek Paganism, more is provided.

A carved stone mask of Medusa is displayed beside the entryway to many Greek temples. For good reason. True, to most people in this age these conventional emblems mean little more than a straightforward sign that you are crossing a boundary here to a sacred precinct. They simply seem to be an official warning that the laws are different here so you'd best be on your good behavior. After all, they do not purport to show the monstrous primordial gorgon herself, but only a better looking mask of her that can be worn by much more respectable deities. Of course you might experience a little thrill of fear if you give the old Medusa tales a moment's thought; but still, all that antique stuff is so obscure. Even, maybe, superstitious. And so, of course, a carved Medusa mask lies there, deeply modeled in the stone, pale marble with accents in paint, glowering up at you as you pass, howling open mouthed with snakes for hair, there beside the road in the moonlit valley of the ghosts' parade.

But of course a mask of the sacred is a potent thing. It depicts an experience we humans always have when we imagine gazing out beyond our conscious realm to the realm of infinite reality; we see the obviously living beings out there look back at us and we clothe their faces. And of course the division of the gods into monstrous "archaic" and respectable "modern" forms, a cultural coping mechanism, an idea which the Greeks of this period are fond of entertaining, is entirely fictitious because all of them are always with us. So: Masks float at the threshold of mystery, animated from beyond. And the "old" Medusa stories are actually the currently applicable versions. So of course that year on that temple road that image stirs.

Consciousness constantly shapes physical reality in powerful ways. That is a firm conclusion of a very reputable metaphysical science called Quantum Mechanics in the age when this novel has been printed out on paper. There are lots and lots of physics PhDs who say this. Okay so far? Not too big a leap? Then to that highly respectable fact please add this author's less well known conclusion from an actually scientific investigation of many years into the subject of divination. The main conclusion from my lengthy study of divination, a conclusion which I claim can be demonstrated in any reasonable test that accurately reproduces the method I developed, is this: If the work of divination is properly conducted, in search of wisdom, then the right Tarot card or such, the Tarot card or such that will teach you wisdom, actually turns up in your hand every time. Still okay? I hope so. Now, finally, please add to that some basic information on a kind of divination often practiced by the old Greeks: reading omens. They would often walk out in the world with mind strongly focused on a pressing issue of some sort. And naturally the world would respond. Some actual physical incident would happen to give them wisdom about that subject. And of course I am fictionally referring to the animated marble Medusa mask sculpture among that fearful grieving crowd who are going to Eleusis.

Gentle reader, have you gotten this far? Are you still with me? Thanks. Sincerely. But before returning to our story I will trespass on your patience for the length of one more essay paragraph. After all, Melville did insert in Moby Dick a whole big whopping essay on the natural history of whales. I won't do that. I'd only like to discuss the children's costumes. In the ghost parade. This is only to help you more concretely imagine the astonishing incident this year.

When I was very young, for Halloween, parents would often throw an old bed sheet over their child, snip out some holes for eyes and mouth, paint a howling face, and pull it all together very loosely with a bit of rope around the waist. That was a perfectly satisfactory ghost. So please imagine how you'd feel, right now, to see a big swarm of gleefully wailing children participating in some organized activity where it is moonlit night and they all swoop down a hill toward you costumed like that. Lots of them. Got the picture? This is not to say the costumes were actually like that in the countryside of Athens in 330 BCE but it was culturally equivalent. It was something to give you that same feeling. All right? So please feel free to see the children just like that as you read the balance of this Episode. Okay?

Thanks again. Back to the story.

Honestly, she'd never really been particularly religious. An ordinary woman, that's all. But here she sat beside the road, alone among the crowd, absorbed in thought, gazing at the sculpture of Medusa's face which gazed up into the moonlight.

A bit of lark it was when she was young – cheap adventure really – her girlhood chums larking toward Elfesis. But her journey had been interrupted with just the February starting service done when a fella suddenly came courting and the sudden marriage, and the three pregnancies and births and the constant work and scheming to tie up every day's loose ends. What could you expect, the dockside life, wedded with a warehouse porter? But one day she'd walked the long steep street up to the Athens marketplace itself in search of olive oil at better prices and just happened in at the temple by the river by the wall, the big old shoddy market basket just hanging on her arm, and just asked somebody there. And the good Matron came out for a nice chat and answered yes, that old cleansing thing was still good and she might stitch a beggar's shirt from sacking, if it were clean of course, then try to keep to house for the week before and most certainly say her prayers, and seek the Hall of Mysteries this year.

So here she sat, just an ordinary woman resting for a bit, wondering what it was about this enraged stone face that fascinated so. To tell the truth, to be real honest, if it could talk it looked like it might say a thing or two that she might say herself.

Oh, he was a decent fella. Hard worker, not a drunk, not a gambler much, not a thief, nice for the kiddies, and not cruel. True, he had some winning ways. He had whipped her once, with a god damn stick, and that was shameful, but she had got him back fair and square soon enough. And anyway, it was those damn militia buddies of his that put him up to it. And honestly, that was in the months after the second birth when they were hungry and she must admit she had laid in to scolding pretty bad. Even her own elder brother was not sympathetic. "Wise up," her own elder brother said, "this is life." What would you expect, wedded with a warehouse porter? But now this war and somebody killed him. And he had been her chum, and her surest ally in the daily struggle, and the guy she whispered with under the covers, and he was dead, and there was that militia pension, and the family could help, and definitely there was always a few more loads of laundry to be taken in and a few more corners to be cut, but the second child must now be sent to labor sooner than she wanted. That chat with the Matron had been nice. She felt stronger after. And the week of praying was a help even with the waste of time, for the Matron had told some special prayers. And Mother in the throne beside the tree had called her Eldest Daughter. Some things did seem to make sense now maybe.

The surprising bit about this carved face, screaming up into the sky like it was, and the snakes for hair, was this was how she felt herself sometimes. That is to say, now that she studied on it, now that it sort of seemed like turned inside out like she could pick it up and wear it, she realized there were times when she felt her hair was snakes and she was screaming this loud up into the sky and now she could put her finger on exactly when that was. There were times when she honestly felt stronger from the troubles and that was when she felt like she could look in a mirror and look like this. When the troubles were like strong food and she was crazy fierce. All of that no matter right or wrong, no matter law or crime, and stronger for it. How could that make sense? But honestly it did. It just depends how deep you look into the source of life.

She is Demeter wearing Medusa's mask.

And she is fitting on the mask.

She remembers: There was a very sacred moment when she looked between her legs, below the birthing stool, and saw the second baby's head full out, cradled in the midwife's hands. And those two tiny eyes, lidded though they were, looked up in hers. She had told none of this, for all these years, but just the temple Matron, for it was very sacred. The way she looked out to herself, for two, and therefore all, were one.

And too there was a winning way the fella had when you were wanting and he was wanting so you would open and he would slide right in but then he'd stop and you would see him smiling down the same way you were smiling up. And this she'd told to none because there was a way the world would all spin round and stop, but opened out just like there was a way that you might reach your hands to everywhere because everywhere was here.

Therefore, from all of this, it seems natural entirely – and with a bit of thought quite normal too – that all the snakes and even worms of these wide fields – and there are many – have now risen to the surface of the Earth. And they are mightily surprising the big crowd, these serpents great and small that all now make their way slithering, slithering among their feet, among their sitting or reclining human bodies, slithering toward the spot where she is sitting in divine contemplation.

Nor is it strange that squads of children amusingly costumed as ghosts dash through round about among the people, howling as loudly as their little voices can. They are whirling actual real live snakes about their heads in every hand. And they are lovely children.

And it is not peculiar in the least – for actually it is surpassing beautiful – that a tremendous wailing shriek, rising out of the darling kiddies' moans and groans plus the gasping exclamations of the crowd plus some deeper factor summoned from some other place, now begins rending the air that before had been nearly silent, had been merely dimly humming with the lagging conversations of weary worried people. In fact, the new sound is like a choir singing one astounding single ululating note, a single complex quavering harmonizing chord that somehow visibly parts a curtain, as though a blinding fog were suddenly lifting, that has veiled her eyes for all these years.

Now she seems to stand amid huge turning spheres of colored light in a shining clear sky.

Nor could it disturb her in the least, for in truth she does not notice, that within the next third of an hour the great crowd have all gone from the furthest extent of abject horror, leaping up and falling into one another's arms, to dancing all their cares away in laughter and lying down in one another's arms as the great wail fades, relaxed although still weary, content at least for now to wait and see what life will bring.

Indeed, the rushing wind of fear and grief which rises from the bosoms of the people while they dance, and surges toward this place, toward the mouth of this sculptured mask which has opened very wide, this mask which she is wearing so to speak although it stands out there forward, this gale seems to the ordinary woman like nothing else so much as a bracing seaside breeze. She can see it obviously flowing past across this place like a shore where she is standing, through the gaping aperture, out to join the winds of the greater world beyond the veil of ordinary seeing. And her exhaling breath is powering this.

Nor do the serpents of all shapes and sizes surprise her as each arrives, heavy with the feast of darkness it has eaten, and slithers down into the cavern which was opened as the great stone stretched itself and rose.

Then when all of this is finished, the veil and cavern closed, the stone become itself again, the song faded, she has come into herself and rises. Seeing those who lie at ease, the ordinary woman takes a few steps only then lies her own self down, adding all that was beheld to the unspoken treasure of her memories.

20: Episode Fourteen Point Five: Angelus

She was awaking very slowly with a wet rag wiping at her face and Diotoma urging worriedly, "Victory, can you stand up? Can you walk? Dearest dear, sweetheart, please talk to me."

Still more than half asleep, and quite reluctant to wake up, she was trying to mumble that she didn't know yet and anyway couldn't she please be left alone for just a minute more? Why not? Hadn't she earned a little nap?

But a loud slap cracked the air. By the gods! What was that? It sounded like a slap against a face.

And another.

And a coarse slurring growl: "Ee's comin to."

Victory sat up. She was still nude, except that someone – Diotoma – had spread the silver dress over her previously inert body, and now it had slipped down into her lap.

Here was the moonlit glade. Here she was still by the sacred cart. There was Phillipus lying right over there with two extremely burly men in Macedonian army undershirts kneeling over him solicitously.

One of them glanced at her, suddenly whacked the other hard up side the head and pointed her direction. Then he looked at his own pointing finger, decided that was not a good idea, and pulled it back. The second glanced at her and, startled, looked down to the ground. They mumbled urgently to one other. They both rose simultaneously with eyes averted, quite efficiently grabbed their vaguely moving king by armpits and knees and easily hoisted him away among the trees, bowing their way out of her divine presence.

Victory said; "Well, then, that's alright."

"You've got to wash!" Diotoma threw the rag into the bucket, squeezed it full, tossed the silver dress aside, and wrung it out, drenching Victory's crotch.

It was cold. She gasped.

"You've got dirt plastered from your navel to your knees!"

"What! What happened?"

"His slime, you nit! There must have been a gallon."

Victory grinned. She was with child. Twins. But she pulled a pinch of the crusty concoction off of her left knee – mostly old pine needles and suchlike bits of forest stuff – and smelled it, tasted. With only another woman there, she spoke confidentially. "Actually I think there's a lot of me in that. With the way I had him pounding, I think I must have been lubricating pretty good."

But then a voice from up above behind: "A-hem!" A male. Petronus. "Man present! I'm not sure I want to hear about this."

"Then don't listen!" Diotoma snapped. And she had hold of Victory's arm, smaller woman though she was, pulling urgently up.

There was a grinding sound above, up there on the cart, like heavy stone on wood, and the whole structure shivered.

"Petronus!" Victory called, struggling to her feet despite her friend's attempt to help her up. "Good Petronus, what is wrong up there?"

"Oh nothing really." He stuck his head out of the shadows, shrugged. "You didn't snap the axle or anything but the statues kind of kiltered. No damage done. Just the foliage left to fix. Finished in a minute."

"Goddess!" Diotoma swore. "Unbelievable! The ox! Can you walk? Please tell me that you can!"

Leaning on her friend and trying out a few unsteady steps, "Oooo" Victory said in some discomfort, very tender in certain spots, but then getting better. She could walk. Salve might be good. "Must admit it was a little more energetic than the original plan called for. Feel like I just gave birth." Then suddenly terrific joy: "But I'm pregnant!"

"Yes?" her friend asked, rather sourly.

"Yes! Twins! I am great with child!"

"Okay, I'm happy for you. Really. I really am. I really really really am. I know that's what you want. I really understand. But why on earth did you let that donkey do it that way?"

She began an honest explanation: "Oh, well, see, his thing is nice and thick but not really very long."

And then, "A-hem!" from Petronus. There was rustling going on among the decorative shrubberies.

And Diotoma also cut her short. "He was hurting you! It was awful! That screeching! I almost whacked him with the ax."

And little Phaedrus suddenly now appeared, dashing in along the path and skidding to a halt on the soft ground. "News!" he cried.

"What news?" Victory asked.

But there he stood stock still and clearly staring at her breasts.

She held them up to look herself and asked, "My good friend, haven't we seen each other bathe like maybe a hundred times? What are you staring at?"

"No no. I mean. They're different."

He had apparently studied them. But could he know? He said, "It's twins."

But Diotoma fairly shouted at him, "What news, my lad? What about her screeching?"

"Oh that," he answered, "that's all fine. The whole mob jumped up in a fright. Noise like that out of the holy glade of the holy cart at the ghosts' parade; they'll tell their children and grandchildren. It's already famous."

"What news then?" Petronus called. "Spit it out, for mercy's sake!"

"The pulling crew," young Phaedrus shrugged, "they're here. I held them up. What should I say?"

"I fucked the conqueror of Athens," Victory answered with a grin, waving both fists, "I fucked him damn near dead, I did."

"No don't say that!" said Diotoma. "Keep them waiting. Say the Lady's meditating. Say she's at her prayers."

And Phaedrus sped away.

"What screeching?" Victory now demanded. "Diotoma, no. My dear friend, it was beautiful. It was! What a holy insertation! I went to heaven. I rode one of the horses of the Sun. I'll have to do a discourse. Will the Eldress be impressed! I think I shouted something once."

Petronus, now seating himself wearily up there on the platform's edge; "Uh, well, Mistress . . . "

And Diotoma too: "I almost whacked him. I really did."

"Really? When"

"When? I don't know when! You were screeching like the fiend herself. I ran up right behind him with the ax. I would have done it too."

"Well then, why not?"

"You kicked my head."

"I didn't."

"You did. Is that friendship?" Diotoma rubbed her forehead hard. "Wouldn't be surprised if I have a permanent toe print. If I get your job next year, you just watch out."

But Victory was breaking down in laughter.

21: Episode Fourteen Point Six:
The Second Nun's Tale

Diotoma was pondering aesthetics:

If you're going to have sexual intercourse out in the open air because you've found a beautiful spot and you're alone together celebrating Nature through your privately shared passion that transcends the ordinary lives both of you share with other people – despite the unexpected chance a passerby might see – then of course that is most certainly one thing. But if you drag the fellow off behind some rocks just for convenience, because you want it now and there you are – well, if it's honestly the right thing at that point in your relationship, really necessary for the future in the circumstances of the moment – but if you are, at that moment, accompanied by other people who know beyond doubt it's what you're dancing off behind the rocks to do, then should you do it? Well, surely, yes. After all, sexual behavior is so normal and necessary to life. So if anyone is offended then it ought to be that one offended person who is expected to correct their attitude.

Diotoma pondered further:

That is, of course, provided that you have not made a spectacle of yourself. Other people might be jealous, frankly. The way she had danced with him! Someone, even a genuine friend, might be envious of your freedom. Even if your friend wouldn't want that dirty man of yours in a million years.

And that dirty old sailor had laughed so very loudly and crudely to see Victoria lead Phillip away from the circle of firelight with such powerful, graceful and erotic beckonings. It had been extremely beautiful and mythic and dramatic in the highest sense of art and yet that dirty old man had been shouting ingenious encouragements – that she was hauling him off by a rope, meaning his penis – and such as that. The horrible old monkey had even, for a few shocking moments, run to catch up and capered along beside the blindly oblivious Phillip throwing up handfuls of sand and tugging the boy along with the little flute.

And was it really necessary for her to screw Phillip now at this moment? But Diotoma knew: Yes, to tame him. It was completely obvious that Phillip needed to be calmed and, furthermore, subdued immediately if matters were to go ahead. For the sake of everyone concerned. So Diotoma finally decided: Yes, lady, screw him and do it well. It is a power women have and ought to use.

At that exact moment Victoria was doing that very thing, making a small rotary motion with her hips while kneeling astride and grasping tight to a slippery and well satisfied but still quite sensitive male human member which, due to her grip, was scarcely shrinking at all. Her hands were on the fellow's flat hard muscular belly to brace a little up – it's not that the thing was actually turning inside but her clitoris did, you may be sure, get a little carefully selected va-va-voom with each rotation – and his hands were rather idly toying with her titties, as he liked to call them – they being squeezed together now between her arms – and he was doing it in such a tender affectionate way that she was kept warm and somewhat wanting. A sea breeze was tickling at the nape of her neck and his toes. All the flesh in sight was painted tawny glowing colors by the moonlight on the sand. They were in love. I leave their smiles to your imagination.

The sensation of her ministration certainly held, for him, a quite definite sense of coaxing but he only thought she was coaxing for a harder cock until she licked her lips with unfeigned carnality, enjoying the little rough sensation of her own tongue, and then she spoke:

"So we're going to live together, right?" She grinned and added a tiny bump to the rotary rhythm.

"What? Yeah! You bet!"

"West Texas might be nice."

Surprisingly, he was apologetic: "Oh, well, the home place is way out in the country." She tried a little bosom motion to gratify his hands and he immediately added; "But it is a beautiful country. Yeah, most definitely if you don't mind."

"Hmm . . . I've often thought of riding horses."

"You have? Really? No shit! I'll get you a good one. Fast but gentle."

She had to lick her lips again because her mouth was dry. "Do you think I'll be good at riding horses?"

He had to laugh, which tickled. She was having difficulty now, really gaining interest in this peculiar kind of masturbation and losing interest in the talk. But she must keep her mind on business for the future's sake.

Victoria let herself smile really quite mischievously.

Phillip grinned so Vicki pressed on: "And if your people want us to get married legally, then we will, right?"

"Oh, nobody's gonna care. So it's up to you. What-ever you want. Especially for the kids. Sure. You bet."

His hands were kneading more intently now, not exactly comfortable to her, but it made her wiggle. She could not help it. So then she moaned quite miserably, as quietly as possible: "Oh god, I'm horny again." She shook the hair out of her eyes and waited for the wiggle to subside, then firmly asked; We'll both take care of both of the kids, right? You're not going to be, like, absent."

"Gee, yeah. Naturally."

"I mean you won't be absent."

"Gee, yeah, what did I say? I mean I won't be absent. What kind of crud would that be?"

"Do you promise?"

"Yes. You got my word; both of us raising both the kids. Full time. Do you want some more after this?"

"What, more fucking? Yes."

"No, I mean more kids."

She slipped very playfully into a very slipshod Australian Texas movie drawl; "Aw, well; two of 'em do sound like a handful don't it?" She found the accent was a breathless struggle with the way she was riding now, and the cock was reaching further in, but she managed a little more; "Par-tic-ly considerin the breeding stock, eh? What a Maw and Paw for a pair of young 'uns to have, huh?" But then she had to slow the movement back until she found the tiny motion of before, to bespeak the man seriously and tenderly: "Maybe a few more, darling, maybe not. We'll see."

"Do you think it's really twins? A boy and girl?"

"You bet partner! There's absolutely no doubt of that. I can tell. And there won't be any medical difficulties; and they'll both be perfectly strong healthy beautiful children; headstrong though. Stubborn kids. I'm absolutely sure of all that."

"You are?"

"Yes I am." She arched her eyebrows. "I am a witch you know!"

He laughed again. "Yeah? Well, you can cast a spell on me any time at all, yes ma'am!"

"You mean it?"

"Yes."

But she could not stand it any more to be so far from him. She would gladly sacrifice, for now, the chance of another proper rogering in glad exchange for this moment's peace with him. And so she nestled down, body on body, into his safe and warm embrace and finally she lay still at last. It was so good to press her breasts on him so carelessly and to press her face into his cheek and let her hands just find whatever part of him they wished. It was so good to have the freedom of another person's body.

But then of course she must be very careful in the movement of her butt. She had at least waited long enough to be a little dry – of his if not her own now replenished fluid – for she must internally seize the limp little chickadee and then must keep her thighs tight shut till Phillip understood and did his part in what was being demonstrated: the way a gentleman in these prolonged coital situations can part his legs just enough so that the lady lies relaxed between, her thighs held by his and thus her lips pressed firmly, safely and comfortably shut around him.

Victoria wondered when or where she'd learned this technique. Had someone told her? Was it in the Kama Sutra? It just seem obvious and natural.

They simultaneously discovered how that pleasure would be a wonder in the remainder of their lives, how it would comfort their old age, how it would, for them, incline the human heart toward warmest sentiments, and how – if you have the holy luck to fuck the one you truly love – intercourse can feel exactly like really being home.

And thus indeed she did relax. There must be time for this, there must, or else the world in its entirety was wasted. She was thinking that she ought to whisper in his ear and took a moment trying to compose a thought – a tenderness or joke? – and only then discovered with surprise a thing she knew was there. Her lips had ruffled up his hair and found the puckered battle scar.

And so a niggling thought, given up for lost when conversation faded, returned to mind with new importance.

She very lightly kissed the ancient wound, not even half enough for him to know she had, and then, with palms against his manly chest, pressed up from him enough that they were gazing eye to eye.

She said; "But only when you want me to. I mean, me casting spells on you."

He made a study of her countenance. She was too serious for him to really smile. He knew not what to say and only made a tiny shrug.

"I shall wend you with my womanly wiles, I shall, but only when you wish it. That is a promise, friend."

22: Episode Fifteen: Pythoness

Half a stadia to go. Well past midnight now. The shadow shaped Hill its very self was risen on the sparkling sea horizon of its little bay to fill the eyes and hearts of the mass of holy tramps slowly surging up the wide country lane which led through autumn fields of cut and gathered barley to the awesome gate. The Galaxy – the Milky Way – that broad and infinitely deep and infinitely glowing ever circling river of celestial mother's milk, as these people thought and spoke of it, spanned the sky above, casting its weird white suffusing light upon the ramparts of the spiritual fortress. Here came the Queen and King and the hardiest of their invited guests, then the deities trundled by a weary crew, and then the rest. The city folk in all their thousands would soon fall back, to camp out in the valley of the ghosts' parade and then go round to greet the pilgrims exiting the little gate at the far side of the Hill tomorrow afternoon.

The Moon was quickly sinking down, the last sliver of her silver sphere now glowing very wanly on the shoulders of their sacred shirts from the direction they had come. They had the starlight now. Many friendly faces from the temple staff were out to come along among the crowd, to lend a helping hand where it was needed and to light their dragging steps with lamps.

One third of a stadia to go. These were fields that she herself had tended. There was the big gate ahead standing right there in the shadows of the high sculptured wall.

Little Phaedrus made his move, his final chance. He forced his steps to regain ground, dodged and elbowed through among the others with apologetic nods, around the swaying cart, striving to reach the tall woman there in front, the one he loved. Was his guess correct? Did he really know what she was planning? Whatever she would do, he wanted very much to understand it from her lips. He wished to help. He did not wish to spend the whole rest of this life shrugging stupidly when people asked for an explanation.

And he was almost there, beside a man with a lamp, a man from the temple staff whom he vaguely recognized, who nodded to him with a friendly and concerned smile, stepping along patiently a little way behind the Lady. She herself was walking arm in arm with Diotoma and Petronus, all supporting all, all silent in the dancing light that cast a silhouette of the Basket Priestess on the road ahead.

A few long steps and he was there indeed, his gaze filled with the profile of her face with the tall basket's ribbon on her cheek – he panting pretty hard despite the wish to still his breath and speak – and he let his hand find its way up to the shoulder of Matron Diotoma.

The Matron looked around. "My good boy!" she cried. "How are you? Are you keeping strength?"

"Almost home!" little Phaedrus squeaked.

He labored hard to take big breaths several times then spoke again without sounding so much like a dying sheep.

"Good Matron!"

"Yes; please, what is it?"

Petronus and the Lady Love of course too were looking at him, waiting for whatever news this was, but he avoided their eyes and spoke to Diotoma.

"Your pardon, please."

"Yes indeed!"

"It is a matter for the Order of Elfesis, you see."

"I beg your pardon?"

"It is I who beg your pardon ma'am." He shook the damp hair out of his eyes. "But the pressing time. It's a matter of our order. I require a word with Mistress Elfesinia."

"Oh. Well then, of course." The good lady looked to her friend, who nodded, and so then carefully let go of Victory's arm and faded back to walk beside the man with the lamp.

Victory reached to pull him forward and even then linked her arm through his so that he even felt her strong graceful moving body, even felt her rather swaying pregnant mother's breast pressing on his shoulder. But there was Petronus, still with traces of Agamemnon's painted visage round his eyes, craning round to look. Well, how to be rid of him? By ridiculous technicalities Petronus was a member of their order.

"Good sir;" Phaedrus said; "by your leave . . ."

"Yes, my friend?"

"This apprentice has a question for his teacher."

Victory smiled at that, smiled down at him.

Petronus pulled a wry mouth. "Really! Phaedrus, you're a stitch. If you want a private word with her, and if she's steady enough on her feet, just say so for the gods' sakes. The gods know you've earned my courtesy."

Victory finally spoke with quite good humor: "I am steady enough for now, good King Petronus, and I do suspect there is a matter or two this teacher should discuss with her apprentice."

So then they were alone, alone as they could be at the head of a marching throng, and Victory quietly said: "Try to keep your voice down and don't gesture. Naturally they'll be straining for anything."

"My Mistress;" he began with formal words but gazing deep into those beautiful eyes that shone with light like that of all the stars; "Petronus told me something you said . . ." He looked away around the fields, down to his feet, up to the sky, then back at her. "Of course it's hard to know if he's ever got things straight at all . . ."

"Phaedrus." She tugged his arm.

"Yes ma'am?"

"If you don't feel a true respect for Petronus then one must assume that you are laboring under a false opinion of some kind."

"Lady, the man's a dolt."

"Shhh! Keep your voice down. Of course he is. What an obvious thing to say. Is that the sum of your observation?"

"Lady, there's hardly time . . ."

"What other man would you want for a king if not a good humored well intentioned perfectly sane dolt of average intelligence? Do you prefer one like Phillipus?"

Phaedrus sagged at the mention of the man he felt to be a rival, and one with infinitely more success than himself. He tried not to lean too heavily on the Lady's arm, but she was strong. But then he braced himself up, saying to himself that she had actually spoken of his rival in less than glowing terms. And for Heaven's sake there was this thing at hand.

"Lady! You were talking about a sacrifice."

"Yes, a small one, at the Hall of Mysteries; but look here, my worthy companion, you are a very sweet boy and a very strong man."

"Mistress?"

"And besides those virtues of the heart, you have virtues of the mind that bring the highest honor to your teachers and may well earn considerable honor for yourself; because they will let you do considerable good."

"Mistress . . ."

"In all good reason, you must feel as secure and confident as any person can in this surprising world, secure and confident that you will have opportunities to do what you should. And so – speaking as a priestess of the order in which you will be a priest – I ask you to do this: look on your fellow beings in this world with charity."

"Mistress . . ."

"I know you love me. Perhaps some other time, some other place, perhaps; simply not this time and place."

"Mistress!"

"Petronus has constantly done his duty. He's walked among us and stepped forward wherever he had the wit to see what was required. He's taken every suggestion, without exception, in good heart. He's kept our spirits up. He's helped us deal with any other kings who happened by. What more could you ask for from a king? Why else would we have one?"

"Mistress!"

"Do you see? About Petronus?"

"Ah . . . yes. Yes, yes."

"So you'll try to look on people in this world with charity? I would appreciate your promise now that you will always try to keep that principle in mind. With your promise, of course I trust that you will not forget this conversation."

He almost stumbled. He shook his head. Amazing! She was advising for his good. She of the Holy Pregnancy was looking toward his future happiness and peace of mind quite as sincerely as the finest wife would do.

"I promise. Certainly."

"About the other thing."

"Yes!"

"Have you guessed my intentions? At the Hall of Mysteries?"

He whispered; "You're going to resign your office. When you set the basket down on the altar on the porch."

"You have! Oh, you are smart! Good Phaedrus! You are good! The offspring of Phillipus cannot be raised in our community. Whatever good that place would do for the children, I can try to do. They might bring danger from his enemies and he might believe they held the place in pawn for him somehow. And what would they believe about themselves? In truth, I have no notion yet of how to deal with that out on my own but even less inside the temple. And certainly there is the matter of the rite. We do not want this thing of kings and conquerors and all that lot making their own use of the rite to occur again. We must stop that. For Phillipus to have children born into Elfesis, and their children and theirs, would cement it instead. Even though my babies were created by divine intent, and by a divinity whom we worship, still we of the priesthood must stand up for human needs and keep the rite in working order for as long as it is needed. Even though everything was all done by divine intent, we must do what our people need. Even though this day has been, for all of our company here, a great success."

He took a moment to take that last bit in, about their great success, meaning personally that he had proved himself in her eyes, then hesitated, then spoke his heart's desire; "May I come out into the world with you?"

She reached to touch his cheek. "No. You must hold Elfesis Hill in the coming generation."

"Where are you going?"

"Home. For a while at least. But! I am still a priestess of Elfesis! Always! New duties may call me out, to heal or teach or pray among the people, or to lead them, and I will go. I have a sense of a distant journey."

"A journey . . ."

She touched his lips with fingertips for silence. "I have seen another meeting between you and I. A far distant time. Another march to Elfesis. You will come out of the place to guide me. There is some different kind of cart and the walls and gate have changed. And you will have a different lady then. It is possible and very fortunate, you know, to truly love more than one. And she will be a friend to me. I see no betrayal in this."

"Mistress . . . I don't know what to say."

"Then hear me finish speaking. Do not fear for my safety or the safety of my children, whom I will love dearly and rear up strong in secret safety far away. I do not understand this yet, but Phillipus will come when I am alone. He'll come in peace this time for healing of his grievous wounds and our love will heal him. We'll find each other on a journey where there is a cave with firelight and whispering and many vagabonds, then stones that stand up from the Earth like mushroom spawn of Titans in a huge ring where I shall speak to myself of secret things, and there is love and magic. I see a beautiful country where I shall ride fast horses."

Her eyes were glittering in the starlit dark.

23: Episode Sixteen: Nighthawks

The bus was moving. The old sailor – Oodeseoos? – had somehow, in some way that seemed confusing to tell but did involve the flute boy playing while his granny ladies sang, had somehow encouraged Phillip and the other men to start the bus out on the road by hauling at a rope. But they were going now. All three of the saints – they were real life size – stood beside her smiling in the aisle. Her daughter was here, one of the happy smiling statues, but when Vicki gazed into the tall girl's face she only saw herself. Her son – could that be him? – was outside riding one of the racing horses that pulled them dashing along beneath a setting moon. Was this a dream?

She felt the brakes applied and felt the swaying to a stop and thought of waking up but did not do it. She heard the mechanical door open and shut. Someone had gotten on, someone kneeling in the aisle beside her. It seemed to be the very sweet young man she seemed to know. She felt him touch her hand which she then realized was in her lap so this could be an intimate touch but very carefully restrained. That made her start.

"Miss. Miss Victoria."

She rubbed her eyes. It was night and dark of course but in a moment more she knew him. It was the helpful young fellow called Socrates. She felt a new affection for him that she had not felt before.

She mumbled something, really only; "Mmm??

"I have got the key. For the big gate. We are there almost." Still kneeling down as the bus swayed steeply up the hill, he looked forward through the windscreen where the yellow double cone of their headlamps shone on a rising dirt road. "I must squeeze through and open from inside, for it only opens that way you see."

Now they were going very slowly with grinding noises from the rear, bouncing in new or ancient ruts and pot holes.

On one of the bounces she pushed herself up from the snoring person she was leaning on and peered ahead through the windscreen, as best she could, into the bouncing yellow light. She asked Socrates; "We're almost there?"

"Oh yes. This little road is all. That was the outside gate we passed already. The guards are friendly, for they know me when I come to dig. I explained that we are coming for a special educational tour."

"Mmm . . ." Vicki said, really studying the enthusiastic look on his friendly face despite the jouncing shadows; "is this all right?"

"Oh yes! While you were at the cafe I telephoned to Professor Milonas at our university and explained. I did not say that you are hippies, only foreigners on a religious tour, delayed by a bus collision with the Army, you see. She was very sympathetic. I know she sees Elephesis as a real living religious place, as I do."

"You're very helpful. Resourceful. You're very smart."

He shrugged but then nodded in agreement, in a humorous way feigning modesty just long enough to soften his own pride. "Thank you. Thank you very much. Professor Milonas told me to do as well as she does."

Now the hill's rounded top came into view against the infinitely distant sky which their headlamps did not penetrate, and a high fence of woven wire was there. Their nose tipped down and they leveled off. And the fence was larger. There was a high gate of woven wire too. On the wide round summit beyond there lay the low vague shapes of fallen ruins.

They stopped. Their valiant engine quit with a chugging cough.

Staring at the apparition through the forward glass, Vicki tugged the arm of the snoring person by her, thinking it was Phillip for the fleeting time of half a thought it took to realize the arm she shook was Diotoma's.

Where was Phillip? She remembered: when she had seen him last he'd been lying in the wide seat across the back, somewhat stoned, well and truly fucked. Snoring. And she examined in herself the very brief moment of alarm, just then past, when her intoxicated husband – as it seemed okay to say – had apparently wandered off somewhere. She had a husband. That was peculiar but she didn't want to lose him. They're often useful and, anyway, she loved him.

Vicki said; "Diotoma, we're there."

Diotoma roused herself. She stood up with a bit of courteous help from good steady Petronus. She shook out and brushed off her sacred beggar's shirt, as if that made some difference after all the road dust of their walk. She said; "Sorry Mistress. I seem to be a city woman after all. Are we finally ready?"

Victory answered; "Apparently, yes."

Here just before the awesome gate they had been waiting half an hour, for the straggling pilgrims to be all gathered close enough. Every one of them had a very proper right to participate in this, as witnesses of the brief ceremony where the Sacred Precinct opens in their welcome. Of course the new initiates would not know the chant but old timers would carry it well enough. The marshal's men and temple staff were going through among the crowd passing word that things would now resume. Many people were rising from a weary rest. There stood the Sacred Cart with its hardy crew already leaning in the harness. The high gate towering above them looked like it had been sculpted from the dancing light and shadow of their little lamps.

Looking round the crowd, Victory nodded. By now she was forgetting to hold her head up constantly to prevent the holy basket wagging. "Good;" she said to no one in particular; "very good. Very very very good indeed." There was only this bit here where she must start the chant then cry for the gate to open and then – aside from staggering through the entry court and round the corner to the Hall – just that sticky bit of business on the porch. But she had a decent speech prepared for that. Then on into the Hall of Mysteries and pick a seat and watch the show. Then tomorrow or next week or perhaps a month or so, or springtime at the latest, and it's off to home. And then a different life. What a day this had been, and most of it just since noon.

She raised her hands and started in: "We're here, every-body." But the language barrier had slipped her mind again. Some were rising from their seats but more were peering through the windows at the darkness, wondering what to do.

But here was the funny driver by her now, calling in his gruff but happy voice, gesturing for all to rise and disembark; "Parakalo! Parakalo!"

So off the bus they trooped, Vicki first and Phillip last with all the rest between. Then all the pilgrims gathered in a little space before the wire mesh gate, their talk dying down to whispers and then an obviously reverential hush.

The ancient famous chanted hymn wended ragged to its final turn and straggled to an amateurish stop. Victory turned to face the sculptured parapet atop the sculptured wall beside the sculptured gate, her hands now raised again, then cleared her scratchy throat and called to someone who surely must be waiting up there in the dark; "Our Mother and Our Sister and Our Brother, with all their folk . . . are home! In peace!"

Her voice had not faltered.

Yes! A signal light up there was waved.

The heavy gate was slowly trundling inward on its squeaky wheel. There was Socrates switching on a massive flashlight so the ground before their feet exploded into dazzling colors; sun bleached stones and verdant weeds. He switched it down to very dim. With that dim light he waved them in.

Who was this standing there among the others in the torch bright open gate? By some trick of flaring shadow, could it be little Phaedrus with his arms outstretched to greet her? Yes it was. How was that possible? And now at last a dizziness was on her. "Mercy!" Victory cried but Diotoma and Petronus got her arms across their shoulders and bore her up. She found that she could walk.

So then the stumbling walk in through the narrow court, with Victory looking back high up at the Basket Priestess statues who did indeed smile down and speak a wordless reassurance: this day's work was properly concluded, except the pending business that she knew. She looked away ahead but then there came a gentle tapping on her mind and she looked back again. The Priestesses spoke in wordless reassurance for her happy future life. There would, of course, be various difficulties.

And then it seemed that she had simply just forgotten how the water sprinkled on them – as they passed the Grotto Shrine there at the corner – a job for temple girls come back from the ghosts' parade that she had done three times – could be a bracing shock, and the psychic reinforcement from it, those few drops of Hadian cool water from the well inside the cave, tossed from olive twigs onto her face and shoulders, bringing strength back to her soul from the realm where all things are renewed.

So then the four steps of the porch were at her feet. She trod up alone. And here there was the altar, here the Elders smiling, gathering close and arms outstretched to hold her, hands to loose the ribbon ends and finally help her trembling hands set down Our Mother's basket, upright here where it belonged, at home. And here was their embrace.

No words were here required of her. This job was done until, perhaps, next year would set her to this arduous task again. But it would not.

Victory watched the Elders' faces while she spoke. These reverend men and women pressed very close to hear her privately and hold her up. Each and every one in every individual way, had taught and loved her. Their hope and trust had been in her for these past years. Their smiles reduced to sadness as she spoke so she spoke quickly. No faces looked away but hands came up to cheeks and fingertips to lips and some eyes overflowed warm tears.

Almost at the end, she recommended Phaedrus very warmly to their kind attention, then reiterated the advisory of peace between the city and Phillipus, although foreign war. Finally she spoke her confidence of worthy work among the people, their own love constant even at a distance, and happiness in Paradise when that call came. She had, before all other news, told of herself carrying the Macedon's twins in graceful hints which all would guess.

The senior married couple of them blessed her head, then blessed her womb and breasts.

Now Victory was free to go her way, for the mighty Hall of Mysteries – to be precise about the situation of her resignation as she understood the question legally – was optional for her tonight.

But there she stood before the doors where King Petronus beat three times for the last time he would ever do it in that life. Then when the doors swung open, into that awesome place she stepped. And in the other pilgrims followed.

24: Episode Seventeen: Starhawks

In that year when Phillip first begot his twins upon a priestess of Elfesis, Phaedrus – or Socrates as he was named in other lives before and after – was not yet the priest whom he would be in later years. In that year he was yet a child. In that year he was not yet then the reverend Chief Officiant for the great initiation rite.

Indeed, on entering the Hall of Mysteries for that first time – the first time in that life – Phaedrus was not yet firmly settled on the path ahead. He was only hoping in some future day to gain the virtues promised by his teacher, powers which would in fact be raised in him by adulthood's demands and opportunities in full measure, just as his Lady prophesied.

But in our story's other year – nine dozen generations after, where Phillip the Barbarian next begets his twins on that same reverend worthy mother – then Socrates, or Phaedrus as he was named in other lives before and after, quickly found, although with some surprise, that he was very well prepared indeed to give a special educational lecture – for he was indeed officially in that reality a Special Professorial Assistant – to a group of persons Fate or Luck had gathered huddling in the ruins in the starlit dark.

(That number nine dozen is a geometric harmonic average of the generations counted along the various branches of the family tree through which he would become again, by 1971, ancestor to himself.)

It was a quite surprising and very peculiar and pleasurable sensation young Socrates distinctly felt. Oh, he knew he had an aptitude for lectures. He was, in fact, eagerly anticipating a newly created job his university professors were arranging for the next term, wherein he would address advanced introductory classes, primarily for visiting masters of other arts and sciences, on the very subject that he was addressing for these ad hoc pilgrims now, and some related topics in addition.

But he had never studied acting. He knew he had a keen perception and compassion for fellow beings but had not realized how well those powers help an actor tell a story. He was delighted and intrigued, but unfamiliar till that hour, with the curious temporal echoing sensation where you seem to be the puppeteer and puppet both. These seeming living spirits which seemed to manifest out of his sounds and movements, and to perform there before the audience the drama which he was describing, seemed to be conjured from timeless time somehow by his own remarkable psychological or metaphysical configuration. Or from some place. Or all of the above.

What was he doing? He seemed to know. He seemed to know, simply from the fact of being human in uncountable dimensions, the perfect images and metaphors with which to wake this ancient show of shadows. He seemed to know the gestures. He thought the spirits were emitted from the ground.

What made it most peculiar was the way so many things popped into mind. There were things he didn't think he knew before and yet was absolutely sure did fit properly and perfectly into the countless riddles, as though there were a well constructed illustrated script he'd memorized and now was wending through. Thoughts seemed to manifest out of the distant dark overhanging vault of night with its vast arching river of Mother's milk and its pale haunting starlight shadows cast here everywhere on Earth – or from the rocky Earth itself beneath these massive flooring stones on which he walked about to strike the standard poses, on which the people lay or sat embracing one another, watching him with fascinated eyes – or from the big rounded rock behind him there in the open center of the floor which reached out of the Earth like a fingertip or phallus tip to touch the Sky exactly here where Sky lay down to touch the Earth. Or else these answers echoed from the ghostly forest that had once stood here and then had been reborn as the hundred vanished marble pillars in the ancient Hall.

There were so many questions! There were so many answers not yet dug out of the tumbled walls. The ancient folk had kept their secrets very well. But now he seemed to find that everything was simply obvious if you would just shut up with the endless questions and just instead tell what you know while listening to yourself.

He spoke in Greek. And yet that didn't seem to matter to the hippies. They watched him wide eyed like the rest. They gasped and sighed just where a human being ought to, listening to the holy story of the way Our Mother and Our Sister and Our Brother came here to this place and found their home. There seemed to be no language barrier at all. That seemed peculiar too at first, until he realized how sparsely he was using words. He scarcely spoke. Instead, there seemed to be a book of sacred pictures which opened page by page before his inner eye, pictures in which each succeeding turn of life was given into powerful form, form a human body could express.

But then he felt the anti-climax of the tale approaching. Resolution of all fear, fulfillment of every yearning, attainment of the human heart's own dear desire here in this Earthly sphere. How should he do that? Resolution of all fear, fulfillment of every yearning, attainment of the human heart's own dear desire here in this Earthly sphere. What could he possibly do with that? Resolution of all fear, fulfillment . . .

And then he knew. He saw the picture as the page was turned. He saw the very simple pose. He knew exactly what it meant. Our Brother's wondering gaze into his outstretched palm – Our Brother's outstretched palm from which Our Mother's stalk of barley – Our Mother's stalk of barley which is Our Sister – Our Brother's outstretched palm from which Our Sister as a stalk of barley – sprouted up and grew. The Plowman King and all of that. Of course. Family. Oh what an elegant pantomime! But did he have the courage for this consummate bit of work? The ultimate and final culmination sure must follow this immediately and so this gesture of looking at the palm – Our Brother looking at his outstretched palm from which Our Sister as a stalk of barley grew – must wrap the people's fulfilled souls compact enough to fling into the sky. Exactly how to place his feet? Just so. Exactly how to raise the hand? Like that. And now to indicate with staring gaze exactly this and nothing else: a sprouting stalk of grain.

He saw the grassy thing take shape out of his flesh then stand and rise and bloom and seed and ripen into shining gold, glittering in the light of stars, as real and palpable as every other thing here in this earthly realm.

He could not help but murmur; "Oh . . ." He now remembered that he had forgotten how to do this. Musical Electric Force harmonics.

He snuck a peek then at the audience from the corner of his eyes. Yes! That astonished face he wanted was on every one of them, every gaze was riveted to the amazing golden stalk, and then there was the startled tension of alarm at this abnormality. And then realizing they had seen this in dreams. Then realizing all of them had dreamed it. And then finally, the meaning of the pose took hold of them, slowly enough that all the startlements before became nothing but a passing worry, even the shock of the trick's evident reality melting like he wished into the fulfilled ecstasy of revelation for every individual. Life's nourishing and wondrous always ripening fullness is ever in one's hand. The Plowman King and all of that. Family. Home is where the heart is.

So now a few deep breaths were needed; then the grand finale.

He had no means of making thunder, none that came to mind, but there wa

(lacuna)

immediately as the doors were swinging shut, after the lamps had marched out and before the few dim torches on the inner pillars flared, as the doors were closing and the eyes were reaching for a focus through the darkness growing in them like dark water overflowing from the Hadian pool, just with the starlight glowing through the open center of the roof, and the countless half-seen spirits carried in that milky light, you might be one of those who dart a glance about despite your resolution to be brave, in startlement at the sound of some frightened person's short sharp laugh or else some person's pitiful whimpering.

Then you might, as little Phaedrus was, be one of those who recovers from the momentary startlement and wraps a reassuring arm about a huddled stranger by you on the low stone bench.

You might, as Victory was, be one of those who suddenly recalls the grandeur which this timeless time and placeless place has brought into your life in previous years, the endless beauty which these holy mysteries have proven past all doubt.

You might, as Diotoma and Petronus were, be one of those who feel the coming shocks and strive your best, as every year, to open out the self-protective armor round your heart.

You might, as Conqueror Phillipus was, be one of those who count the steps that brought you here and vainly yearn to count the steps ahead.

25: Episode Eighteen: Houdini

At the ruined Hall of Mysteries today, beneath the massive flooring stones where archaeologists have not yet steeled themselves to dig, there is a stone lined conduit as we might say, "the pipe" as it was known when operational, both of its ends concealed by soil and rock ever since the mournful day when a different conqueror came that way and the mourning temple staff were forced to flee. This hidden stone lined covered trench, about thirty inches square in cross section, runs beneath the floor from a spot beside the natural rock outcrop which was the Hall's mystic centerpiece, forty feet approximately straight out back to an apparatus shed that is now empty of its gear and buried by the tumbled walls. Long gone now from the corroded brass suspension hooks, in that damp and dripping subterranean "pipe", is the clever set of pulley ropes that used to run those forty feet to work the famous temple's second-most famous trick. Gone too is the little shrine built around the central rock, its door that opened by remote control, the interacting levers and the willow wood piston machine with leather gaskets that would infallibly swing out its iron nozzle at the great ritual's penultimate moment to squirt a brief but very tall jet of flaming alcohol up through the open center of the roof, visible to all the countryside around and to any ships that might lie in the bay.

Gone now is the big brass gong, and the curtained niche in the Hall's rear wall where it used to hang, and the door through which the operator in the shed would reach with a pair of mallets to conjure soft approaching and then crashing thunder just before the pulley ropes were worked.

Now missing from the empty buried shed is the big piezo-electric crystal generator switch that, powered by the operator's hammer blow upon its wooden lid at the ritual's beginning, would send a jolt through thin copper tubing up the wall, across the roof and to the central pillars where it sparked the gas of the dimly flaring oil fueled carbureted torches which would precisely illuminate the reverend Chief Officiant's dramatic performance of the holy story and the actual physical transmogrification of living flesh (by means now currently unknown) into the semblance of a golden barley stalk sprouting from the reverend's hand at the presentation's close just before the thunder rolled, the transmogrification being, of course, more famous than all other tricks.

Gone now too is the society where folk, with the lives they led, would intelligently understand, appreciate and use such tricks as this in genuine spiritual practice, and keep the secrets. The thing is this: They were not fooled. They were ennobled. A certain small segment of the public there – a few individuals who reliably took an active role out in the world on the temple's behalf and also swore a mighty oath – were admitted to an ancient reverend select committee, bestowed with mythic titles as "Comrades of Heracles" and a holiday on which to meet and a meeting room on temple premises and a delicious dinner and choral hymns too. These "Comrades of Heracles" (in guise of an inspection ceremony) were annually shown the genuinely impressive mighty squirt machine, the pulley ropes, the gong, the switch and all of that. In fact, the piezoelectric crystal switch torch lighting trick was demonstrated for them. The remainder of the public naturally guessed all this or more or less. But they did not tell. It was a tremendous spectacular theatrical performance of a holy story that was good for them, both individually and as a whole society, and it was very beautiful. They kept it operating for many years.

After all, anyone anywhere who goes about spoiling such a thing as that is liable to be hauled into a court for criminal trial or even possibly lynched if public circumstances are extreme. It was a willing suspension of disbelief, enforced by social norms, that was very useful.

But it was more than that. May I state the underlying overriding truth by means of terminology which modern Western scholars of the occult have inherited from Greek antiquity? May I please? Okay? Well then, I'll state it thus: Take the mighty piston squirt machine for an example. Gentle reader, you have most likely noted the erotic metaphor already. (If not, kindly reference our Episode titled after Chaucer "The Nun's Tale".) According to the understanding of existence that we have inherited from Greek philosophers of magic – Trismegistus, Pythagoras and all that lot – reality consists of nothing else than harmonies and dissonances similar to music. Sounds sensible to me. And then, assuming that there is some practicality in this classic principle of metaphysics, one would certainly suppose that a symbolic enactment of Earth and Sky copulating energetically, with orgasm as a sort of musically attuned lightening bolt, repeated frequently, attended by generation after generation of humans in heightened and empowered states of psychic arousal – there being no fundamental barrier between mind and matter since both are simply music – would naturally, indeed, create some kind of standing harmonic field.

Thus equipped with a bit of background information, gentle reader, you are now cordially invited to tune in to our story again.

She had been sent, in these last few hours, to the farthest extremes of both fear and pleasure. And she had walked through that test with head held high, through it to the other side where now she sat, faint with weariness, now again supported by caring friends, on a low stone bench with spirits crowding close. And she was thinking of the countless joys this place had given so fully to so many, joys that in the future must become to her the treasured jewels of memory.

So of course there then arose fully into consciousness the nagging worry Victory had dismissed as best she could. In every moment that had passed since then it had seemed a pointless worry in comparison with every other thing requiring attention. What had Our Sister meant by the one whispered word which had come so very clearly through the sighing branches of the moonlit trees? Amid the visionary scenes of an exile future which had filled her eyes, and that strange journey, there had also come a single whispered word powerful and deep with loving comfort. Our Sister had spoken this: "Home."

She was going home.

But wasn't this her home? If not Elephesis, what else could be meant? She had assumed it meant the poor old lonely shack by the mountain stream, the village yard and that. The tanning of the hides and salting of the fish, hired labor on the valley farms and all, now surely with the added duties of a township priestess. Perhaps, with luck, some husband with a willing hand and affection for her children, not too badly given to the comforts of the flowing bowl, would presently appear. To bring forth and then die on the same narrow bed where she herself was brought to birth, where she had finally lain in the sparse shelter of a slackening embrace of thin wasted arms, sobbing childish guilt and grief, until a last labored breath freed the woman who had borne her; was that to be her fate? If so, then at least would that beloved woman's ghost come by night or day to bring the welcome gift of a long lost voice and face? Would her mother's ghost befriend her? If so then she thought that she could live that life with happiness enough.

So then, because she was preoccupied, it was a considerable surprise to Victory when her thoughts were broken by awareness of a touch on her mind and she looked up and found one of the starlight spirits standing floating in the air before her.

The fellow said, with a disarming shrug, in the kind of echoing silent voice to which Victory was somewhat accustomed from such persons; "Mistress, for mercy's sake, why are you worried?"

But, despite the perfectly comfortable tone of the visitation, Victory found herself rather surprised by the apparition's appearance. No good reason to be surprised, but still. It was a young man wearing a breeze-blown ghostly version of the holy beggar's shirt with the proper royal pattern of embroidery on its sleeves and the proper Agamemnon makeup painted on his ghostly face. She'd never seen this fellow before but this was probably the founding spirit of the Elephesian boy priest king.

She had lost the thread of the conversation and only answered him with this thought: "I beg your pardon?"

Now he crossed his arms on his glowing vaporous chest and shook his head with an air of impatience that she found frankly somewhat amusing. "Mistress, please." he said. "I know you're tired, and the gods know you've earned a bit of rest, but it really would be good at least if you could pay attention through the end of the ritual."

"Oh?" she thought with an open silent laugh. "And why, good sir, is that required?"

The torches that stood high on the inner pillars made their customary pop and for the customary instant flared. The spirit rather jumped and cast a startled glance back over his shoulder at the lighted space. In the light, now dim but growing, he was fading.

"Mistress!" he cried silently in parting. "For Heaven's sake, just please pay attention. Remember: Home!" He gestured with upheld hands for patience. "You'll see. It will be clear as anything in just a few minutes." His voice trailed off into the distance. In the dim but spreading gaslight the spirit vanished.

So as the reverend Chief Officiant struck his first pose (the office Phaedrus would fulfill so well in later years) Victory asked herself; Well, then what? Phillipus was to come someday. Would he rescue her from the village? Then off away to home in the beautiful land with horses? Did that fit all the clues?

Then a startling tap on her shoulder from behind. Victory turned to look and found there was a middle aged woman on the bench behind, leaning toward her, quite ordinary looking, the shirt of common sacking, the thin hair of the matron's bun disheveled from the march of course, the woman's muscular arm now falling slowly to her lap. Victory recognized at once a shallow trance of prophecy, half there, half here. The woman was conscious but utterly absorbed, her creased and weathered face staring off vacantly into space where pictures were evidently being shown, her tongue and lips already some-what moving, mumbling inaudibly before the words took definite shape. Then suddenly the words; "Phillipus is dead by the hand of a friend, not a half hour's walk from his own safe bed, three years from now."

"What!" Victory cried.

"Another spear. Alexander takes the family business. You know his son Alexander?"

"Yes ma'am."

"First thing Alexander does is fook his mother."

"What!"

A vague hint of a shrug. "Something those barbarians do. Then he starts the war with Persia."

"Oh?"

"Incredible success for him, for Alexander. Lots of battles. Don't loose one hardly. Egypt, everything; famous forever. But doan' hope fer a husband. Half the men and boys in Hellas march w' him. Fallow fields. Empty streets. Empty gymnasiums. Empty beds. And doan' hope fer treasure ships neither; Alexander marched 'em way far east and there he'll die. A palace burning by a river."

The woman seemed to sag. The trance was ended. She looked at Victory finally and shook her head. She had no more to tell.

26: Episode Nineteen: Flight

So truly where was home? She pondered, though of course she knew.

While the play of spirits came and posed and gestured how the Holy Family once had found this rock up on this forest hill, or really on this hill in Paradise, and all of that, of course she knew but strove to work the consequences out. Was something left here in this realm and in this age that others could not do and she must do instead, or that she could not do with best results in other time?

She answered that with darting careful thoughts. After all, this seemed to be just fundamentally a case of practical choices.

So when the golden stalk of grain – Our Mother as Our Sister – rose up from Our Brother's open hand, and proved the truth that home is where the heart is, the major question left on her agenda was whether this physical body where she currently lived possessed sufficient courage.

But when the awful thunder rolled and struck no chord of fear here in these bones and sinews, that was also answered.

So when the little house's little door swung open, Victory stood and lightly stepped down to the forest clearing for a proper look, as a final check. Could her eyes confirm what she had been taught, what her heart now fondly wished? Did the path in actual reality – in actual reality – lead on from here?

Then when the gout of flame rose up she saw in fact, to her, this was the real and actual door itself.

She ran and leapt.

Nothing then was left of her there in that realm and age except a swirl of glowing ash like fireflies that rose up through the open temple roof into the sky and gently spread across the land.

27: Episode Twenty: Porridge

It was the gentle tugging at her hair that woke her. The gentle but persistent strokes felt like the easy throbbing of a resting heart. Her conscious soul was pulled a little farther upward every time until she blinked. And she was there.

"Ah, Dearie!" the woman who stood behind her chair spoke and pulled a final pleasant stroke through a handful of Victory's soft long tresses before she paused in the work to speak again; "Yer welcome home."

For a moment Victory caught her breath. But then she could not help but gasp in great relief.

And too, there was a breeze. It was a kind of breeze that could have made a person drunk, so loaded full it was of burly salt and an even more heady scent of fully ripe fruit or green mead or early summer honey. This very pungent sweetness touched her brow and cheeks when she faced into it, and her breasts. She was nude, damp and cool from being washed. The breeze was drifting through a sunny window.

Out there, beyond a verdant kitchen garden, stood an orchard full of gnarly apple trees all full of pink blooms shining in the light among green rustling leaves. The orchard sloped down further on away to a clear fair bay of sparkling waves with distant arms of land curving round to embrace on either side that bit of homeland sea, filling the scene's horizon.

Victory found there was a brightly polished mirror by her hand lying on the table, along with the towel, wet wrung rag and silver basin. She breathed deeply once then picked the mirror up. She looked. Yes, this was her face.

The woman bent so that another rather plump and very kindly face was in the bright mirror too, peeking from behind and smiling. Webs of creases round the eyes and lips told of happy years.

Victory knew her. But the poor old woman had been thin and haggard the other time; ragged, worn and worked.

The woman said; "We shall get ye neat." She nodded. "Then perhaps a spot o' porridge eh? World o' good. Honey. Milk? For sure. Fine fat goats, and o' course it's kiddin' time." She nodded firmly. "But then a spell o' rest. Most surely rest. Ye'll wake all fresh, right here, in fuller strength. But anyway, no need ye lyin' down like a ragamuffin, eh?"

So the old woman stood again and resumed the wonderful sensation with the brush.

Victory had to rouse herself from the pleasure and from the undeniable beckoning weariness that was very full in her too, but she lifted the mirror again to watch and spoke; "Mommie?"

"Yes, me dearest?"

"Did I do well?"

"Oh! Very well indeed, me sweetheart. Think of all ye learned. All ye taught."

"But Mommie . . . the twins?"

"Ah, another time. Love conquers all."

"Really?"

"Aye me darling, love conquers all. Ye'll have them babes. Just wait, ye'll see. Ye'll fook the same benighted sod – worthless he may be or not – and birth em and raise em up strong ye will. Stubborn ones they'll be. Same as ye was." She laughed. "Same as me. And a time will come for horses."

"Really?"

"Aye; yer mommie promises. O' course, that is, if ye settle on going back at all. That's up to you o' course, with all ye've done already." But then she paused again with brush and hair in hand. She looked down in the mirror, stared hard there in Victory's eyes. She spoke very firmly; "Not yet ye shan't in any case."

"Ma'am?"

"Ye shan't be going back awhile yet. A good long while. I won't have it, hark ye?"

"Yes Mommie, I hearken."

"Ye best."

"Mommie, I hearken."

"Ye be me favorite babe, ye see. And I shall have yer company's pleasure this time for a good long while, I shall."

Victory turned. They threw their arms about each other and pressed kisses on each others cheeks. They finally wept.

About The Author

Stone Riley
Photo by Evelina Kremsdorf
Used by permission.

Who Is Stone Riley?
April 2015:
I'm an old artist / activist / fortune teller.
Been doing all of that for 50 years.

   I practice arts – painting, drawing, computer, poetry, memoir, the novel, teaching, conversation, conversation – some of it quite well. After all, I work hard at it, love a challenge, love doing it myself, first hand, in person. Because, of course, the most beautiful of all beautiful art is supposed to be your life and I love life. You study, study, study, practice, practice practice – of course you do – but this is a dance.

   I came up as a working stiff so-called-white boy in a dirty dangerous industrial city in neo-slavery land, the jim crow USA South, came up just in time for the Vietnam War machine to murder a friend of mine in our youth. All that made of me a lifelong pro-peace pro-Earth pro-human pro-democracy agitating activist more or less, at least jumping up into that kind of work when opportunity presents. I am now a Green Party member and I'm optimistic now at last because it seems the tide has turned.

   And fortune telling? What? Why that? Well, if life has ever put you in a circumstance to sit with some weeping woman and help her share a last farewell with a loved one lost beyond the veil - and you've judged the ghost there in the room definitely is somehow real although apparently only you can see it clear enough - if fate has vouchsafed you that piece of work just once, that joy and kindly tender pleasure most sublime, then you won't ask me why I also do that sort of job.

And really it's all one.

The great art philosopher Rabindranath Tagore certainly described how I started out. Tagore described the proper way to start an art career like this: First you look around where you are and see what is most horrible there. Then from that you see what is most beautiful. Then, being who you are, you ask how art work there can aid the beautiful. And so you have begun.

When I started work our nation was a prison nation, our every thought a prisoner's thought. So we did enormous crimes. That was the horror. So the greatest loveliness I saw was freedom of the mind, and the broadest cleanest most courageous freedom our young generation did was this: Rebirth the perennial undying spiritual technologies which are common property of human kind and know we are divine. What was there for me to do in that?

I wished to make myself a proper artist. There were some pictures people raved about, very hard profound pictures somehow stacked up neatly in a deck. And then an initial one-year project in Tarot vastly exceeded all my hopes. Tarot proved itself at once to be the most profound of politics: an instrument of mercy shared among us prisoners. And then I grew into it. It became my guide book in the art of democratic life, for it made a healing teaching priest of me.

So here's my advice:

Don't stop walking when there is no way ahead.
Your walking makes the path.
The place you started from was cleared by others
and others will soon follow you
and pass and step ahead.

Author's Self-Portrait

**New Apuleius:
Self-Portrait While Writing Dark Of Light**

Drawing by Stone Riley
Ink on paper, 6 x 6 inches.